T0012166

A
GREATER
GOAL

DANESHA ADAMS • MICHELLE AKERS • KORBIN ALBERT • HEATHER ALDAMA • AMY ALLMA
YAEL AVERBUCH • SAMANTHA BAGGETT • BETHANY BALCER • NICOLE BARNHART • TRACEY BA
TAMI BATISTA • JUSTI BAUMGARDT • LAKEYSIA BEENE • DEBBIE BELKIN • KEISHA BELL • DE
BENDER • JENNY BENSON • ANGELA BERRY • JACKIE BILLETT • KYLIE BIVENS • DANIELLE BORGM
SHANNON BOXX • DENISE BOYER-MURDOCH • JEN BRANAM • AMBER BROOKS • THORI (STA
BRYAN • TARA BUCKLEY • SHERI BUETER • SUSAN BUSH • LORI BYLIN • JANE CAMPBELL •
CASSELLA • LORI CHALUPNY • BRANDI CHASTAIN • MANDY CLEMENS • SAM COFFEY • DAN
COLAPRICO • LISA COLE • ROBIN CONFER • KERRY CONNORS • KIM CONWAY • ALANA COOK • ANN C
• PAM (BAUGHMAN) CORNELL • STEPHANIE (LOPEZ) COX • ALEISHA CRAMER • AMANDA CROMW
• COLETTE CUNNINGHAM • ABBY DAHLKEMPER • MARIAN DALMY • TIERNA DAVIDSON • CINDY D
• SAVANNAH DEMELO • MICHELLE DEMKO • KRISTI DEVERT • TINA DIMARTINO • IMANI DORS
BETSY DRAMBOUR • TRACY (NOONAN) DUCAR • JOAN DUNLAP-SEIVOLD • CRYSTAL DUNN • DAN
EGAN • TINA (FRIMPONG) ELLERTSON • WHITNEY ENGEN • STACEY ENOS • JULIE (JOHNSTON)
• RONNIE FAIR • LORRIE FAIR • JOY (BIEFELD) FAWCETT • KAREN FERGUSON • JESSICA FISCH
MIA FISHEL • KENDALL FLETCHER • MEREDITH FLORANCE • DANIELLE (GARRETT) FOTOPOUL
JULIE FOUDY • EMILY FOX • ADRIANNA FRANCH • MICHELLE FRENCH • CARIN (JENNINGS) GABA
• LINDA GANCITANO • MORGAN (BRIAN) GAUTRAT • WENDY GEBAUER • GRETCHEN GEGG • NA
GIRMA • LISA GMITTER • CINDY GORDON • SANDI GORDON • JEN GRUBB • SARAH HAGEN • KRIS
HAMILTON • LINDA HAMILTON • MIA HAMM • HALEY HANSON • RUTH HARKER • ASHLYN HARR
MARY HARVEY • ASHLEY HATCH • DEVVYN HAWKINS • TUCKA HEALY • TOBIN HEATH • APRIL HEINR
• HOLLY HELLMUTH • LORI HENRY • SHANNON HIGGINS • JAELENE HINKLE • LAUREN (CHE
HOLIDAY • LINDSEY HORAN • JAELIN HOWELL • ANGELA HUCLES • SOFIA HUERTA • SARAH HUFF
• LINDSEY HUIE • PATTY IRIZARRY • MARCI (MILLER) JOBSON • LAURA JONES • NATASHA K
CHRISTINA KAUFMAN • BETH KELLER • DEBBIE KELLER • SHERRILL KESTER • AUBREY KINGSB
• MEGHAN KLINGENBERG • JENA KLUEGEL • TAYLOR KORNIECK • NANCY KRAMARZ • ANNA KR
• ALI KRIEGER • CASEY (SHORT) KRUEGER • JENNIFER LALOR • ROSE LAVELLE • AMY LEPEI

A GREATER GOAL

THE EPIC BATTLE FOR EQUAL PAY IN WOMEN'S SOCCER—AND BEYOND

ELIZABETH RUSCH

Greenwillow Books
An Imprint of HarperCollins*Publishers*

A Greater Goal: The Epic Battle for Equal Pay in Women's Soccer—and Beyond

 Printed in the United States of America. For information address HarperCollins Children's Books, a division of HarperCollins Publishers, 195 Broadway, New York, NY 10007.

epicreads.com

The text of this book is set in 11-point Arno Pro.

Book design by Paul Zakris

Soccer ball image by Rifat-Ahmmed/Shutterstock.com

Soccer field diagram by sabri deniz kizil/Shutterstock.com

Library of Congress Cataloging-in-Publication Data

Names: Rusch, Elizabeth, author.

Title: A greater goal : the epic battle for equal pay in women's soccer—and beyond / By Elizabeth Rusch.

Description: First edition. | New York, NY : Greenwillow Books, an Imprint of HarperCollins Publishers, [2024] | Includes bibliographical references and index. | Audience: Ages 14 up | Audience: Grades 7-9 |

Summary: "A history of the more than 250 women who have played for the U.S. National Soccer Team and their battle for equal pay"— Provided by publisher.

Identifiers: LCCN 2024004884 (print) | LCCN 2024004885 (ebook) | ISBN 9780063220904 (hardcover) | ISBN 9780063220928 (ebook)

Subjects: LCSH: Soccer—History—Juvenile literature. | Women soccer players—History—Juvenile literature. | Pay equity—Juvenile literature. | Sex discrimination in sports—Juvenile literature.

Classification: LCC GV943.25 .R84 2024 (print) | LCC GV943.25 (ebook) | DDC 796.334—dc23/eng/20240131

LC record available at https://lccn.loc.gov/2024004884

LC ebook record available at https://lccn.loc.gov/2024004885

24 25 26 27 28 LBC 5 4 3 2 1

First Edition

GREENWILLOW BOOKS

For Danielle

CONTENTS

DANESHA ADAMS • MICHELLE AKERS • KORBIN ALBERT • HEATHER ALDAMA • AMY ALLMAN
YAEL AVERBUCH • SAMANTHA BAGGETT • BETHANY BALCER • NICOLE BARNHART • TRACEY BAT
TAMI BATISTA • JUSTI BAUMGARDT • LAKEYSIA BEENE • DEBBIE BELKIN • KEISHA BELL • DE
BENDER • JENNY BENSON • ANGELA BERRY • JACKIE BILLETT • KYLIE BIVENS • DANIELLE BORGM
SHANNON BOXX • DENISE BOYER-MURDOCH • JEN BRANAM • AMBER BROOKS • THORI (STAP
BRYAN • TARA BUCKLEY • SHERI BUETER • SUSAN BUSH • LORI BYLIN • JANE CAMPBELL • E
CASSELLA • LORI CHALUPNY • BRANDI CHASTAIN • MANDY CLEMENS • SAM COFFEY • DANI
COLAPRICO • LISA COLE • ROBIN CONFER • KERRY CONNORS • KIM CONWAY • ALANA COOK • ANN C
• PAM (BAUGHMAN) CORNELL • STEPHANIE (LOPEZ) COX • ALEISHA CRAMER • AMANDA CROMW
• COLETTE CUNNINGHAM • ABBY DAHLKEMPER • MARIAN DALMY • TIERNA DAVIDSON • CINDY D
• SAVANNAH DEMELO • MICHELLE DEMKO • KRISTI DEVERT • TINA DIMARTINO • IMANI DORS
BETSY DRAMBOUR • TRACY (NOONAN) DUCAR • JOAN DUNLAP-SEIVOLD • CRYSTAL DUNN • DANI
EGAN • TINA (FRIMPONG) ELLERTSON • WHITNEY ENGEN • STACEY ENOS • JULIE (JOHNSTON) E
• RONNIE FAIR • LORRIE FAIR • JOY (BIEFELD) FAWCETT • KAREN FERGUSON • JESSICA FISCH
MIA FISHEL • KENDALL FLETCHER • MEREDITH FLORANCE • DANIELLE (GARRETT) FOTOPOUL
JULIE FOUDY • EMILY FOX • ADRIANNA FRANCH • MICHELLE FRENCH • CARIN (JENNINGS) GABA
• LINDA GANCITANO • MORGAN (BRIAN) GAUTRAT • WENDY GEBAUER • GRETCHEN GEGG • NA
GIRMA • LISA GMITTER • CINDY GORDON • SANDI GORDON • JEN GRUBB • SARAH HAGEN • KRIS
HAMILTON • LINDA HAMILTON • MIA HAMM • HALEY HANSON • RUTH HARKER • ASHLYN HARR
MARY HARVEY • ASHLEY HATCH • DEVVYN HAWKINS • TUCKA HEALY • TOBIN HEATH • APRIL HEINR
• HOLLY HELLMUTH • LORI HENRY • SHANNON HIGGINS • JAELENE HINKLE • LAUREN (CHEN
HOLIDAY • LINDSEY HORAN • JAELIN HOWELL • ANGELA HUCLES • SOFIA HUERTA • SARAH HUFF
• LINDSEY HUIE • PATTY IRIZARRY • MARCI (MILLER) JOBSON • LAURA JONES • NATASHA K
CHRISTINA KAUFMAN • BETH KELLER • DEBBIE KELLER • SHERRILL KESTER • AUBREY KINGSB
• MEGHAN KLINGENBERG • JENA KLUEGEL • TAYLOR KORNIECK • NANCY KRAMARZ • ANNA KR
• ALI KRIEGER • CASEY (SHORT) KRUEGER • JENNIFER LALOR • ROSE LAVELLE • AMY LEPEI

Pregame

YDNEY LEROUX • GINA LEWANDOWSKI • KRISTINE LILLY • KELLY LINDSEY • LORI LINDSEY •
RLI LLOYD • JOANNA LOHMAN • ALLIE LONG • JILL LOYDEN • KRISTIN LUCKENBILL • CATARINA
CARIO • HAILIE MACE • SHANNON MACMILLAN • HOLLY MANTHEI • KATE (SOBRERO) MARKGRAF
LLY MARQUAND • ELLA MASAR • JEN (STREIFFER) MASCARO • KIM MASLIN-KAMMERDEINER
MERRITT MATHIAS • STEPHANIE MCCAFFREY • MEGAN MCCARTHY • SAVANNAH MCCASKILL •
RCIA MCDERMOTT • JESSICA MCDONALD • TEGAN MCGRADY • JEN MEAD • KRISTIE MEWIS •
MANTHA MEWIS • TIFFENY MILBRETT • HEATHER MITTS • MARY-FRANCES MONROE • ALEX MORGAN
LIVIA MOULTRIE • SIRI MULLINIX • CASEY MURPHY • ALYSSA NAEHER • CHRISTINE NAIRN • NATALIE
ATON • JENNA NIGHSWONGER • CASE[illegible] [illegible]AKES • KEALIA OHAI • KELLEY O'HARA •
ILY OLEKSIUK • HEATHER O'REILLY • LAUREN ORLANDOS • ANN ORRISON • LESLIE OSBORNE • CARLA
ERDEN) OVERBECK • MEGAN OYSTER • JAIME PAGLIARULO • CINDY PARLOW CONE • TAMMY PEARMAN
EMILY PICKERING • CARSON PICKETT • LOUELLEN POORE • CHRISTEN PRESS • NANDI PRYCE
MIDGE PURCE • CAROLINE PUTZ • SARAH RAFANELLI • CHRISTIE (PEARCE) RAMPONE •
YSSA RAMSEY • SARA RANDOLPH • MEGAN RAPINOE • KERI (SANCHEZ) RAYGOR • SHARON
CMURTRY) REMER • KATHY RIDGEWELL • STEPHANIE RIGAMAT • TIFFANY ROBERTS • LEIGH
N ROBINSON • TRINITY RODMAN • AMY RODRIGUEZ • SHAUNA ROHBOCK • CHRISTY ROWE •
L RUTTEN • ASHLEY SANCHEZ • BECKY SAUERBRUNN • KELLY (WILSON) SCHMEDES • MEGHAN
HNUR • LAURA SCHOTT • LAURIE SCHWOY • BRIANA SCURRY • NIKKI SERLENGA • JAEDYN
AW • DANIELLE SLATON • GAYLE SMITH • SOPHIA SMITH • TAYLOR SMITH • HOPE SOLO •
ILY SONNETT • ZOLA SPRINGER • AMY STEADMAN • JILL STEWART • JENNIFER STRONG •
DI SULLIVAN • MALLORY PUGH SWANSON • JANINE SZPARA • LINDSAY TARPLEY • BRITTANY
YLOR • ALYSSA THOMPSON • CHRIS TOMEK • RITA TOWER • INDIA TROTTER • ERIKA TYMRAK
RACHEL (BUEHLER) VAN HOLLEBEKE • TISHA VENTURINI • M.A. VIGNOLA • ALY WAGNER • KELLY
LBERT • ABBY WAMBACH • MARCIE WARD • MORGAN WEAVER • SASKIA WEBBER • KRISTEN
ISS • CHRISTIE WELSH • SARA WHALEN • KACEY WHITE • CAT (REDDICK) WHITEHILL • LYNN
LLIAMS • STACI WILSON • ANGIE WOZNUK • KIM WYANT • VERONICA ZEPEDA • MCCALL ZERBONI

Nowhere to Go

Once upon a time, not so very long ago, there was a little girl named Danielle Schulz. Growing up in Greenville, South Carolina, her parents signed her up for a coed soccer team. She loved how the ball felt on her foot, how she could dribble up the side of the field and cross the ball into the center or take a shot. She was especially good at passing to a teammate who was making a fast break toward the goal.

When Dani was in eighth grade, her family moved to Guilford, Connecticut. She wanted to play soccer for her high school, but Guilford High didn't have a team for girls. With a passion for soccer and nowhere to go, she practiced with the boys' team during their off-season. And she talked to other girls in town who also dreamed of playing on a high school team.

Dani learned there was a federal law called Title IX that had been passed in 1972, when she was eight years old. The law prohibited sex discrimination in any education program or activity receiving federal money. The high school received funding from the federal government and the boys were allowed to have a soccer team, so why not the girls?

She and other female players wrote letters to the editor, gathered signatures, and petitioned the school board. In 1980, in Dani's sophomore year, for the first time ever, Guilford High School fielded a girls' varsity soccer team.

In 1982, the year she graduated high school, Dani was invited to play on a United States select team in a tournament in Scandinavia. There was no U.S. Women's National Team at the time. There was no women's Olympic soccer team, no Women's World Cup team.

Recruited to play soccer at Princeton University, Dani started every game all four years, earned First Team All-Ivy honors three times, and served as team captain.

But when she graduated, Dani's soccer career was over. There was no way to make a living playing soccer. There were no women's professional soccer teams, and the pay for the new national team was a pittance.

Dani is my sister, and this book is for her.

LIST OF MAJOR CHARACTERS

U.S. WOMEN'S NATIONAL TEAM

More than 250 women have played on the U.S. Women's National Team, and most contributed to the battle for equal pay. For ease of reading, this book focuses on a handful of players.

RETIRED PLAYERS (in order of appearance)

Megan Rapinoe (midfielder), outspoken, pink-haired playmaker, U.S. Equal Employment Opportunity Commission (EEOC) complainant, and federal lawsuit plaintiff

Carli Lloyd (midfielder), Jersey-girl attitude, workout machine, EEOC complainant, lawsuit plaintiff

Mia Hamm (forward), leading scorer and soccer icon

Julie Foudy (midfielder), also known as Loudy Foudy, later an ESPN commentator

Briana Scurry (goalkeeper), suffered career-ending and life-threatening concussion and devastating poverty

Cindy Parlow (forward), suffered career-ending concussion, later became president of U.S. Soccer

Abby Wambach (forward), a very physical player, loved scoring off headers, ESPY Icon Award winner

Hope Solo (goalkeeper), EEOC complainant, lawsuit plaintiff

CURRENT PLAYERS (in order of appearance)

Alex Morgan (forward), graceful, dynamic player and spokesperson, EEOC complainant and lead plaintiff in lawsuit

Rose Lavelle (midfielder), EEOC complainant, lawsuit plaintiff

Becky Sauerbrunn (defender), EEOC complainant, lawsuit plaintiff, union president

Christen Press (forward), lawsuit plaintiff, union leader

Crystal Dunn (defender), lawsuit plaintiff, collective bargaining agreement negotiator

Jessica McDonald (forward), lawsuit plaintiff

Women's Legal, Union, and Public Relations Support

Ellen Zavian, players' attorney

Rich Nichols, union leader and players' attorney

Jeffrey Kessler, co-council for lawsuit

Cardelle Spangler, co-council for lawsuit

Rebecca (Becca) Roux, union leader

Molly Levinson, public relations executive

U.S. Men's National Team

Tim Howard (goalkeeper), retired

Tyler Adams (midfielder)

Walker Zimmerman (defender)

U.S. Soccer Presidents

Sunil Gulati, declined to be interviewed on the record for this project

Carlos Cordeiro, did not respond to multiple requests for interviews

Cindy Parlow Cone

Basic Soccer Positions

Though there are eleven players on the field for each team, players' positions and team formations vary as dictated by the coach. There is always a goalkeeper who can use her hands to catch the ball while in the penalty box. Three or four defenders near the goal focus on stopping the other team from scoring. Midfielders both defend their goal and attack the opponent's goal. Forwards focus on shooting and scoring.

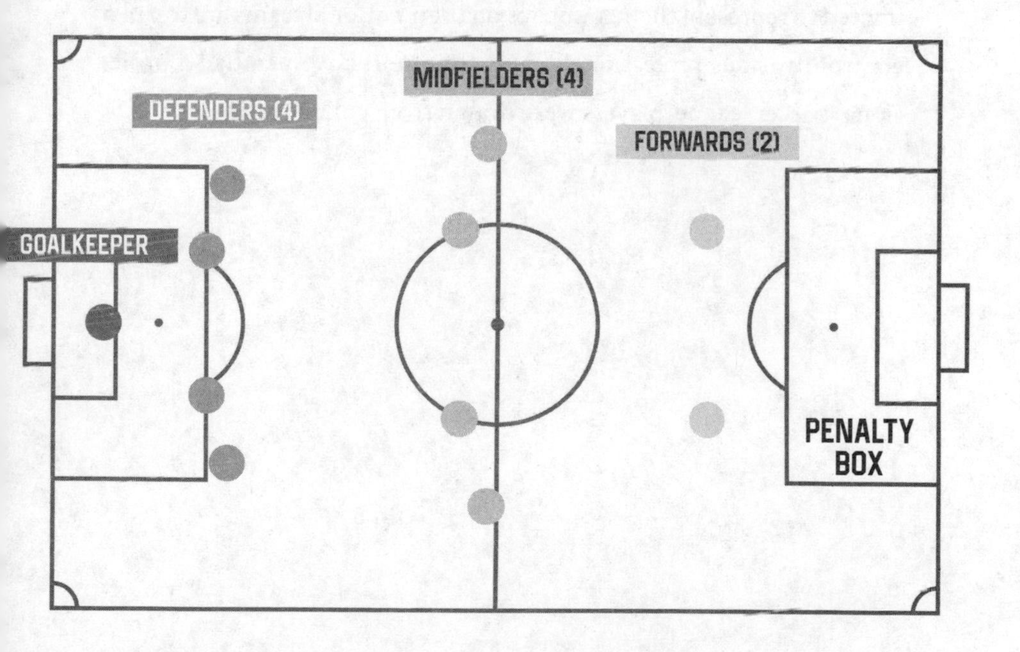

International and Professional Soccer

Professional soccer is different from international play. Professional soccer teams are owned and run privately. For international soccer, each country has a federation. All the federations play under the Fédération Internationale de Football Association (FIFA) rules and guidelines. Federations choose players from their countries to represent them in international non-tournament games, called "friendlies," and in international competitions such as the World Cup and the Olympics.

Federations can choose players however they like, but most players invited to represent their countries on their national teams are top players from various professional teams. Before the women had a professional soccer league, players were drawn from college teams.

INTERNATIONAL SOCCER

(Governed by FIFA)

U.S. SOCCER FEDERATION

(U.S. Soccer/USSF/ the federation)

U.S. Women's National Team USWNT/WNT

U.S. Men's National Team USMNT/MNT

211 OTHER FEDERATIONS

Other countries' teams (women and men)

U.S. DOMESTIC PROFESSIONAL SOCCER LEAGUES

(Each team privately owned)

National Women's Soccer League
NWSL
2013 to present
(currently 14 teams)

Major League Soccer (men)
MLS
1996 to present
(currently 29 teams)

DANESHA ADAMS • MICHELLE AKERS • KORBIN ALBERT • HEATHER ALDAMA • AMY ALLMAN
YAEL AVERBUCH • SAMANTHA BAGGETT • BETHANY BALCER • NICOLE BARNHART • TRACEY BAT
TAMI BATISTA • JUSTI BAUMGARDT • LAKEYSIA BEENE • DEBBIE BELKIN • KEISHA BELL • DEN
BENDER • JENNY BENSON • ANGELA BERRY • JACKIE BILLETT • KYLIE BIVENS • DANIELLE BORGMA
SHANNON BOXX • DENISE BOYER-MURDOCH • JEN BRANAM • AMBER BROOKS • THORI (STAP
BRYAN • TARA BUCKLEY • SHERI BUETER • SUSAN BUSH • LORI BYLIN • JANE CAMPBELL • G
CASSELLA • LORI CHALUPNY • BRANDI CHASTAIN • MANDY CLEMENS • SAM COFFEY • DANIE
COLAPRICO • LISA COLE • ROBIN CONFER • KERRY CONNORS • KIM CONWAY • ALANA COOK • ANN C
• PAM (BAUGHMAN) CORNELL • STEPHANIE (LOPEZ) COX • ALEISHA CRAMER • AMANDA CROMW
• COLETTE CUNNINGHAM • ABBY DAHLKEMPER • MARIAN DALMY • TIERNA DAVIDSON • CINDY DA
• SAVANNAH DEMELO • MICHELLE DEMKO • KRISTI DEVERT • TINA DIMARTINO • IMANI DORSE
BETSY DRAMBOUR • TRACY (NOONAN) DUCAR • JOAN DUNLAP-SEIVOLD • CRYSTAL DUNN • DANIE
EGAN • TINA (FRIMPONG) ELLERTSON • WHITNEY ENGEN • STACEY ENOS • JULIE (JOHNSTON) E
• RONNIE FAIR • LORRIE FAIR • JOY (BIEFELD) FAWCETT • KAREN FERGUSON • JESSICA FISCHE
MIA FISHEL • KENDALL FLETCHER • MEREDITH FLORANCE • DANIELLE (GARRETT) FOTOPOULO
JULIE FOUDY • EMILY FOX • ADRIANNA FRANCH • MICHELLE FRENCH • CARIN (JENNINGS) GABA
• LINDA GANCITANO • MORGAN (BRIAN) GAUTRAT • WENDY GEBAUER • GRETCHEN GEGG • NA
GIRMA • LISA GMITTER • CINDY GORDON • SANDI GORDON • JEN GRUBB • SARAH HAGEN • KRIS
HAMILTON • LINDA HAMILTON • MIA HAMM • HALEY HANSON • RUTH HARKER • ASHLYN HARR
MARY HARVEY • ASHLEY HATCH • DEVVYN HAWKINS • TUCKA HEALY • TOBIN HEATH • APRIL HEINRI
• HOLLY HELLMUTH • LORI HENRY • SHANNON HIGGINS • JAELENE HINKLE • LAUREN (CHEN
HOLIDAY • LINDSEY HORAN • JAELIN HOWELL • ANGELA HUCLES • SOFIA HUERTA • SARAH HUFF
• LINDSEY HUIE • PATTY IRIZARRY • MARCI (MILLER) JOBSON • LAURA JONES • NATASHA K
CHRISTINA KAUFMAN • BETH KELLER • DEBBIE KELLER • SHERRILL KESTER • AUBREY KINGSB
• MEGHAN KLINGENBERG • JENA KLUEGEL • TAYLOR KORNIECK • NANCY KRAMARZ • ANNA KR
• ALI KRIEGER • CASEY (SHORT) KRUEGER • JENNIFER LALOR • ROSE LAVELLE • AMY LEPEIL

PART I
The First Half

No country can ever truly flourish
if it stifles the potential of its women
and deprives itself of the contributions
of half of its citizens.

—Michelle Obama, former First Lady

YDNEY LEROUX • GINA LEWANDOWSKI • KRISTINE LILLY • KELLY LINDSEY • LORI LINDSEY •
LI LLOYD • JOANNA LOHMAN • ALLIE LONG • JILL LOYDEN • KRISTIN LUCKENBILL • CATARINA
CARIO • HAILIE MACE • SHANNON MACMILLAN • HOLLY MANTHEI • KATE (SOBRERO) MARKGRAF
LLY MARQUAND • ELLA MASAR • JEN (STREIFFER) MASCARO • KIM MASLIN-KAMMERDEINER
ERRITT MATHIAS • STEPHANIE MCCAFFREY • MEGAN MCCARTHY • SAVANNAH MCCASKILL •
RCIA MCDERMOTT • JESSICA MCDONALD • TEGAN MCGRADY • JEN MEAD • KRISTIE MEWIS •
ANTHA MEWIS • TIFFENY MILBRETT • [illegible] • MARY-FRANCES MONROE • ALEX MORGAN
IVIA MOULTRIE • SIRI MULLINIX • CASEY MURPHY • ALYSSA NAEHER • CHRISTINE NAIRN • NATALIE
TON • JENNA NIGHSWONGER • [illegible] • KEALIA OHAI • KELLEY O'HARA •
LY OLEKSIUK • HEATHER O'REILLY • LAUREN ORLANDOS • ANN ORRISON • LESLIE OSBORNE • CARLA
RDEN) OVERBECK • MEGAN OYSTER • JAIME PAGLIARULO • CINDY PARLOW CONE • TAMMY PEARMAN
MILY PICKERING • CARSON PICKETT • LOUELLEN POORE • CHRISTEN PRESS • NANDI PRYCE
IDGE PURCE • CAROLINE PUTZ • SARAH RAFANELLI • CHRISTIE (PEARCE) RAMPONE •
SSA RAMSEY • SARA RANDOLPH • MEGAN RAPINOE • KERI (SANCHEZ) RAYGOR • SHARON
MURTRY) REMER • KATHY RIDGEWELL • STEPHANIE RIGAMAT • TIFFANY ROBERTS • LEIGH
ROBINSON • TRINITY ROOMAN • AMY RODRIGUEZ • SHAUNA ROHBOCK • CHRISTY ROWE •
RUTTEN • ASHLEY SANCHEZ • BECKY SAUERBRUNN • KELLY (WILSON) SCHMEDES • MEGHAN
NUR • LAURA SCHOTT • LAURIE SCHWOY • BRIANA SCURRY • NIKKI SERLENGA • JAEDYN
W • DANIELLE SLATON • GAYLE SMITH • SOPHIA SMITH • TAYLOR SMITH • HOPE SOLO •
LY SONNETT • ZOLA SPRINGER • AMY STEADMAN • JILL STEWART • JENNIFER STRONG •
I SULLIVAN • MALLORY PUGH SWANSON • JANINE SZPARA • LINDSAY TARPLEY • BRITTANY
LOR • ALYSSA THOMPSON • CHRIS TOMEK • RITA TOWER • INDIA TROTTER • ERIKA TYMRAK
ACHEL (BUEHLER) VAN HOLLEBEKE • TISHA VENTURINI • M. A. VIGNOLA • ALY WAGNER • KELLY
BERT • ABBY WAMBACH • MARCIE WARD • MORGAN WEAVER • SASKIA WEBBER • KRISTEN
SS • CHRISTIE WELSH • SARA WHALEN • KACEY WHITE • CAT (REDDICK) WHITEHILL • LYNN
IAMS • STACI WILSON • ANGIE WOZNUK • KIM WYANT • VERONICA ZEPEDA • MCCALL ZERBONI

Kickoff: The Chant

World Cup, 2019

It's a scorching July day in 2019, and the soccer stadium in Lyon, France, is packed with 60,000 screaming fans, faces painted red, white, and blue. They are the colors of both teams facing off in this World Cup final, the U.S. Women's National Team versus the Netherlands.

Though the Americans are the defending champs—with household names such as Alex Morgan, Megan Rapinoe, and Carli Lloyd on the team—the players battle exhaustion after tough games against home-turf favorites France and powerhouse England.

The U.S. players feel added pressure to perform. Just months before the tournament, the team launched a major battle off the field. All twenty-eight members of the U.S. Women's National Team filed a lawsuit against their employer, the U.S. Soccer Federation. The lawsuit accused the women's employer of wage discrimination based on gender. The women demanded equal pay with the men's national team.

The World Cup was a perfect example of the inequity. The year before, in 2018, the U.S. Men's National Team had failed to qualify for their World Cup. If they had simply qualified, U.S. Soccer would have paid the team $8 million—$38 million if they won. In 2019, the U.S. women's team had qualified, won all three group-stage games, and won all three games in the elimination round so far. Even if they won the whole tournament, taking home the World Cup trophy, U.S. Soccer would only pay the team $4 million.

"Everyone is ready for this conversation to move to the next step," said star forward Megan Rapinoe. "We're done with 'Are we worth it? Should we have equal pay? [Are] the markets the same?' Everyone's done with that. Let's get to the point of, 'What's next?'"

Even with the lawsuit hanging over their heads, the players need to focus on the fight before them. The Dutch opponents are notoriously wily, tending to lock down the defense until they see an opportunity to counterattack. "I don't think a lot of the U.S. media realize how good [the Dutch] team is," U.S. coach Jill Ellis tells a reporter.

When the whistle blows to start the game, the women's worst fears become reality. Accustomed to scoring early in the game, the U.S. players storm toward the Dutch goal again and again but can't get the ball past the defense or goalkeeper.

The first half ends scoreless.

In the second half, the U.S. women keep pressing. Ten minutes tick by. Fifteen minutes. Then a Dutch defender guarding her goal kicks her leg high into the air, whacking U.S. forward Alex Morgan on the chest and arm. The referee waves off the high kick, but U.S. fans in the stands scream, "FOUL!"

The ref strolls up to a screen to review the play on video. If she sees a clear and obvious foul, she has to call it. Players and the audience watch, awaiting her ruling.

She returns to the field and blows her whistle: dangerous kick, a foul in the box. The U.S. has a penalty kick. It's a great scoring opportunity.

Megan Rapinoe, the firecracker forward with pink-dyed hair, grabs the ball and places it carefully on the penalty kick spot twelve yards (eleven meters) from the goal. It's just her and the goalkeeper. The players on both teams line up behind her, ready to rush in if the ball rebounds. Megan takes a deep breath, walks back, and lines up to take the kick. The stadium falls silent.

A quick three steps to the ball, and Megan rockets it low and to her right. The goalkeeper leaps left. The ball hits the back of the net. GOAL!

The crowd goes wild. Megan, grinning proudly, spreads her arms out wide, reaching toward the field and the fans in her iconic pose. Teammates dash toward her and leap on her like puppies.

But the 1–0 lead feels precarious.

A few minutes later, young American Rose Lavelle gets the ball. She starts dribbling fast toward the Dutch goal. The defenders stay compact. Expecting someone to step forward to challenge her, Rose searches the field for tall, pony-tailed attacker Alex Morgan, hoping to slip the ball off to the more seasoned player. But the Dutch players hunker down in front of their goal.

As Rose continues her aggressive dribble up field, the space in front of her remains open. She cuts in toward the goal. Another glance around. No one else has a clearer shot. It's up to her.

A quick dodge of a defender, and Rose aims for the goal and shoots. SCORE! 2–0!

When the final whistle blows, the U.S. players sprint toward one another and leap into each other's arms.

A chant rises up in the stadium. At first it sounds like "U.S.A! U.S.A!"

The chant grows louder and louder, with more and more voices joining, and the message becomes clearer: "Equal pay! Equal pay!"

Surprise registers on Megan Rapinoe's face, a wide smile spreading across it. Teammates lock eyes and hug even harder. It seems the whole world is with them.

Would their fourth World Cup victory and the upswelling of support finally convince the U.S. Soccer Federation to pay its female players at least as well as the men?

The Begining: Pay to Play

1985-1990

The U.S. Soccer Federation—also known as U.S. Soccer, USSF, and the federation—is the nonprofit organization that runs soccer in the United States. In addition to governing youth soccer, training coaches, and licensing referees, the federation runs several national teams. In 1985, fifty-five years after creating the U.S. National Team, for men, U.S. Soccer created the U.S. Women's National Team to represent the country in international competitions.

For three teenagers—Mia Hamm, Julie Foudy, and Kristine Lilly—it all began in a hotel room in Blaine, Minnesota, where they had gathered for training with other players on a youth under-nineteen (U-19) team.

The coach of the senior national team stepped into the room.

"I would like you guys to join the U.S. Women's National Team," he said.

The players were dumbfounded.

Powerful midfielder Julie Foudy had been away all summer and didn't know there was a senior national team. The sixteen-year-old with shoulder-length brown hair and a wide smile blurted out, "Oh my gosh, I want to go home."

"Do you know what I'm asking you?" the coach said. "I'm asking you to represent your country on the U.S. Women's National Team!"

"That sounds pretty important," Julie admitted. "I guess I should do it."

Mia Hamm, who was only fifteen, nodded. The daughter of an Air Force pilot and a ballet dancer, Mia had been born with a clubfoot and wore corrective shoes as a toddler to fix it. Now she darted around the pitch, ponytail swaying, with the explosiveness of a jet and the grace of a dancer.

Kristine Lilly, sixteen, said she'd ask her parents.

These new young U.S. Women's National Team players were often referred to as "the Title IX babies." Title IX was a thirty-seven-word section of a federal education bill that stated "No person in the United States shall, on the basis of sex, be excluded from participation in, be denied the benefits of, or be subjected to discrimination under any education program or activity receiving federal financial assistance."

Though the words were simple, their creators knew they could be powerful. When the bill was being considered in Congress, Representative Edith Green of Oregon asked other representatives who supported the bill to be hush-hush about it. "I don't want you to lobby, because if you lobby, people will ask questions about the bill, and they will find out what it would really do."

Because what Title IX did, after its passage on June 23, 1973, was revolutionary. The law made it illegal for schools, colleges, and universities to offer unequal education to boys and girls, young men and women. That meant no more publicly funded law schools and medical schools that admitted only men. No more tracking girls into home economics and boys into science, shop, and math classes. And it meant that schools could no longer offer abundant sports teams—football, baseball, basketball, wrestling, track, tennis, and soccer—to boys, with little for girls other than cheering on the sidelines.

Soccer, known as football internationally, had been a wildly popular men's sport across the globe since the 1850s. American boys had begun jumping into the game after the country's first successful men's professional league launched in 1968.

At that time, women had no professional soccer leagues, and some countries even barred females from playing the sport. But in the wake of Title IX, American girls began flocking to the soccer pitch. High schools and colleges expanded their girls' and women's sports programs. Some began offering tuition scholarships for female athletes. The quality of play skyrocketed.

But after graduating from college, these new world-class athletes had nowhere to play. That is, until 1985, when U.S. Soccer decided to field a women's national team. Invited players had two weeks to prepare for the national team's first tournament in Italy.

U.S. Soccer picked up travel expenses, and the young women were offered $10 a day for team duty. If they traveled, trained, and competed for ten days, they earned $100. The young women didn't mind the miniscule pay so much when they were still in high school. But when they were in college and beyond, midfielder Julie Foudy and her teammates realized that playing for the USWNT was a big-time commitment and a financial strain. "[When] you get into the real world and have to make a living," said Julie, "you realize, 'This isn't working! I have to pay rent!'" Players moved back home with their parents, depended on support from their partners, or took low-paying but flexible jobs like waiting tables.

Holding down a job in addition to national team service was tough. For instance, Julie tried working at a pizza joint. When she had a national team training camp or tournament, she told her boss, "I'm sorry, I have another trip for the next three weeks." After this happened a few times, she lost the job.

While struggling to survive, the young women began to hear

rumblings that the men's national team was making a decent living. "That just doesn't seem right," Julie thought.

The players asked for pay to cover their costs of living. U.S. Soccer told them not to be greedy. "Come on, sweetie, you should be happy you get to wear a USA jersey," Julie remembers them saying.

U.S. Soccer outfitted the women in uniforms that appeared to be hand-me-downs from the men's teams. The shorts flapped around the women's knees and the sleeves around their forearms.

The players and their trainers hemmed the pants as best they could. And they begged for uniforms of their own, sized to fit their bodies. The mindset then, according to Julie, was, "You should just be grateful, darlin', that you have a place to play. . . . Stop asking for more."

And they *were* grateful. The women were thrilled to be traveling the globe, playing for their country. But other inequities were equally glaring and exhausting.

U.S. Soccer bought their plane tickets, but at the airport, waiting to be assigned seats, the players got used to asking, "Who's in the middle?" Invariably, everyone raised their hands. The team, wearing matching red U.S. Soccer sweatshirts, formed a clear red stripe down the middle of the plane. "What the hell?" Julie thought. She took a photo and sent it to U.S. Soccer, begging them to at least get the athletes preassigned seats. Meanwhile the women heard that members of the men's team were flying first class or on charter flights.

Once, the women gathered in France for a "friendly" match, an international match not linked to a tournament. A male U.S. youth team, the under-twenty-three-year-olds, or U-23s, were playing nearby at the same time. The women were put up at a bed-and-breakfast where they all bunked together in one giant room. The young men were spread out in a hotel.

The women were carted around in a small shuttle bus. While out for a training run one day, the senior players saw the youths' transport: a luxury bus. One of the women called out, "Hey, can we put our luggage on your bus?"

"It was just one thing after another," Julie said. "So the little things become big things and you get angry."

Julie and her teammates began to wonder. "Why are the men getting more?"

And was there anything they could do to change things?

Gender Bias and the Pay Gap

1900–1990s

The women faced more than opposition from U.S. Soccer in their campaign for equal treatment. Conscious and unconscious gender bias about what females can and can't do has limited girls' and women's choices, opportunities, and success for centuries. In the United States, until 1900, women were not considered capable of handling their own wages or owning property. Until 1920, they were not considered smart, educated, or savvy enough to vote.

In the 1980s, biases continued to affect the roles that girls and women were expected to play at home, school, and in the work force. Culture has painted a clear picture of who cooks and who mows the lawn; who's responsible for caring for the family and who works outside the home; and who is expected to earn more money.

At that time, women in the United States made on average about sixty to sixty-five cents for every dollar men earned. Data suggested that the pay gap was even worse for women of color. There were probably also wage gaps for transgender, nonbinary, gender queer, and gender fluid employees as well, but at the time, there was little research on the pay gap for these workers. "If you don't have the data, you won't see the problems," said M.V. Lee Badgett, professor of economics at the University of Massachusetts Amherst.

Widespread gender bias extended to sports as well. It affected people's perceptions about which kids were expected to be strong, skilled, physically dynamic, and dominant; which deserved coaching and training; and which athletes were fun and impressive to watch. Girls in this realm were often dismissed as "tomboys" or outliers.

The bias extended to women at the top of their game. In 1966, Roberta Louise Gibb was the first woman to finish the Boston Marathon. She ran despite being barred from the race by organizers who claimed that women were "not physiologically able to run a marathon." In the 1970s, female tennis players were offered a fraction of what male tennis players won at international tournaments. In 1988, only 26 percent of athletes at the Olympics were female—and that was an all-time record. And soccer was even further behind.

The M&M's World Cup

1991

In 1991, for the first time ever, the young women of the U.S. national team would get to show their mettle in the first Women's World Cup tournament in China. But FIFA, the international governing body of soccer, thought the women's tournament didn't deserve the "World Cup" title. The candy company Mars, which made M&Ms, sponsored the event, so they called it, awkwardly, the FIFA World Championship for Women's Football for the M&M's Cup. Though the women athletes were accustomed to playing regulation ninety-minute games on their club teams and varsity high school and college teams, FIFA scaled back game time in the tournament to eighty minutes to "make things easier on the ladies."

Team captain April Heinrichs quipped, "They were afraid our ovaries were going to fall out if we played ninety."

No one knew how the U.S. women would perform in international qualifying games. Women's soccer was in its infancy worldwide, with mostly informal teams and just a few sporadic continental and international tournaments. "When you're a little fish swimming around in little ponds, you have no idea how you are on the global stage," April said. The Americans played five preliminary matches in Haiti, staying in a hotel with spotty electricity and water. They bathed in the swimming pool and played cards by candlelight in the evenings. Despite the adverse conditions, they won all five games.

When the men's team qualified for the 1990 World Cup, every player got a $10,000 bonus. When the women's team qualified for theirs, they were rewarded with T-shirts with a Budweiser logo.

Still, the U.S. women were flying high, thrilled to be part of the momentous occasion as they boarded the plane for the long trip to China. But they didn't head straight there. To save money, the plane picked up the Swedish, Norwegian, German, and Danish women's teams, adding more than a dozen hours to the long flight.

The tournament proved to be a wondrous spectacle, with flags from the twelve competing nations flapping behind motorcyclists zooming across the field, Chinese pop songs blaring from the loudspeakers, and showers of fireworks. The Chinese government declared the tournament a national holiday and filled the stadiums with gray-clad factory workers, ordering one section to root for one side and another section to root for their opponents.

The U.S. team was not considered the favorite. But they trounced every team they played, outscoring opponents twenty-five to five goals over six games. FIFA had instructed the women on how to conduct themselves during the tournament, how to stand and walk, and even told them not to rush onto the field at the end of a game. But when the final whistle blew for the final game in the tournament, announcing the United States as the winner of the first women's World Cup, "We broke every rule they had," said April. "We were out on the field being maniacs."

The women embraced the experience but couldn't help but notice the stark contrast between the way U.S. Soccer treated them and the way they treated the U.S. men's national team.

The men had a $25 per diem for expenses while traveling. The women had just $10. The female players survived on peanut butter and jelly, oatmeal, and Pop-Tarts they brought in their luggage, and Snickers bars available in bulk from the tournament sponsor.

Though the men's World Cup got lots of hype, U.S. Soccer did little to promote the women's tournament. The women were also disappointed that none of their games were televised. Most Americans didn't even know the World Cup was happening. *Sports Illustrated* sent a reporter with no experience covering soccer to the tournament.

When their return plane touched down in the U.S., after dropping off the other teams, the women proudly donned their gold medals. But only two people met them at the airport—their bus driver and a U.S. Soccer staffer.

When Julie Foudy returned to Stanford University for classes, everyone asked her, "Where the hell have you been?"

"We came home to nothing, no one knows, no one cares," she said.

A few weeks later, players received cards in the mail from U.S. Soccer. Caitlin Murray, in her book *The National Team,* recounts that the note basically said, Congratulations on your success. We're so incredibly proud of what you and your teammates have achieved. You're changing women's soccer forever. Enclosed is a $500 bonus for winning the World Cup.

At the time, prize money for men's World Cup was roughly $50 million for the winning team.

Another book written about this time by sports journalist Clemente Lisi noted that "After the U.S. victory in China in 1991, the team was essentially disbanded. . . . The federation did little to promote the team (even though it was the world champion) and poured all its money and efforts into trying to make the men's team a success."

Shannon Higgins, a powerful midfielder who assisted in two key goals in the run for the World Cup, retired right after the tournament.

She wasn't injured and she wasn't likely to get cut. But she was barely getting by financially and couldn't afford to play on the national team anymore. "I gotta go get a job," she told the team.

Midfielder Julie Foudy, known fondly by teammates as Loudy Foudy, was dismayed. "That's not right," she said. "It doesn't seem fair that a player is forced to retire well before her sell-by date." Male players were making lots of money, in the millions, playing for their professional teams, especially internationally, and they were also making more for playing for the national team, she pointed out to her teammates. Women didn't have a professional league nor livable wages from the national team. Soccer as a career was a dead end.

"Why do we have to make the decision to retire so early, and men don't?" Julie asked.

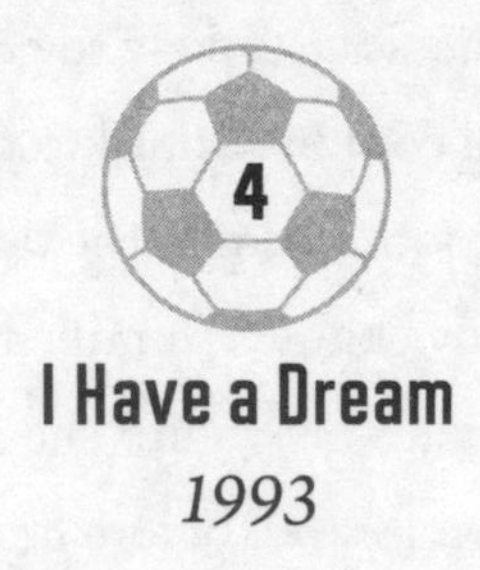

I Have a Dream

1993

In 1993, Briana Scurry was a star goalkeeper at the University of Massachusetts. In the fall semester of her senior year, a few days after her team barely lost the championship game, her coach called her to his office.

As she recounted in her memoir, *My Greatest Save,* Briana worried there was a problem. Maybe she hadn't turned in her whole uniform or practice gear.

"Guess what?" he said.

"What?"

"You've been invited to a U.S. National Team camp."

Growing up in the small town of Dayton, Minnesota, Briana had buzzed around dirt trails on a motorbike at fifty miles per hour and played American football with boys. Worried about the danger Briana faced against burly boys in this high-contact sport, her mom had made her quit football at age twelve.

Briana wanted to try soccer, but there were no girls' soccer teams in town. That was the reality of being born in 1971, nine months before the passage of Title IX, the federal law that was just beginning to open up a world of sports to girls.

So Briana tried out for a boys' soccer team. She was the only Black athlete and the only girl on the field. On the first day, since Briana had no experience or foot skills, the coach said, "Why don't you go over there and get in the goal?"

Though Briana also played some basketball and softball and competed in track, the act of leaping to stop balls rocketing toward the soccer goal eventually became her life.

At age fourteen, inspired by the words of Martin Luther King, Jr., Briana hung a handwritten poster on her bedroom wall, proclaiming her ambition:

OLYMPICS
1996
I HAVE
A DREAM

As Briana grew in stature and into the game, her reach was astounding. Sometimes as balls flew toward the net, she jumped so high that she hit her head on the crossbar eight feet above the ground. Briana found life as a goalkeeper to be more than a physical challenge. "It demands hyper-alertness from the first moment to the last," Briana said. "I would come off the field feeling like I'd played twelve hours of chess."

In the 1990s, the U.S. Women's National Team was still in its infancy. But U.S. Soccer had a development program that recruited boys and girls in their early to mid-teens to play on the under-sixteen, or U-16, youth national team. Players often moved up to U-17 and U-18 teams before winning a spot on the senior national team.

When Briana was invited to join the national team, she had "never been U-anything except maybe 'Who Are U'?"

She was flabbergasted and stoked to be invited. She flew to the U.S. Women's National Team training camp at the Cocoa Expo in Florida. "The place itself was drab and droopy, with weeds sprouting through cracks in the outdoor hallways, lizards popping out of overgrown vegetation, and the whole complex in bad need of a paint job," she noticed. But even the rundown hotel where the players stayed next door couldn't dampen her excitement.

Briana learned and loved the mentality of the U.S. Women's National Team from the get-go: "We are coming for you, and we are going to beat you."

Lockout

1995

In the spring of 1994, Briana Scurry had twelve credits left to graduate from the University of Massachusetts, and she planned to finish them that semester. But she was called to another national team camp as the number one goalkeeper. "How can I pass on this opportunity?" she asked her mom. "There's an Olympics coming up in a couple years. How long have I been talking about being an Olympian in 1996? Remember that sign in my room? This is my best chance."

Figuring she could finish her credits and graduate later, Briana took the semester off to play with the USWNT. To support herself, she juggled jobs on the side, training young kids at a goalkeeper camp and working at the camp store selling USWNT gear and other items.

Briana and her teammates were pumped to represent the United States in the 1996 Olympics, the first time the international competition would include women's soccer. But then their contracts from U.S. Soccer came in the mail. The federation offered about $1,000 for a month of intense training in the gym, exhausting drills, and competitive scrimmages to prepare for the tournament. And the contract only rewarded the women's team with a bonus if they won gold. The men's Olympic team, also employed by U.S. Soccer, got bonuses for bronze and silver too. Briana didn't understand why there should be a double standard.

The female players cried foul. But U.S. Soccer wouldn't budge.

Captains Michelle Ackers and Julie Foudy set up a conference call with their teammates to discuss the situation.

Julie had recently been at a small conference of female athletes where tennis star Billie Jean King shared the story of her fight for equal pay for women in tennis. When Billie Jean won her first Wimbledon in 1966, her prize money was less than half of what was paid to the male champion. She threatened to boycott the U.S. Open and pressured the tournament to pay men and women equal prize money. And she won.

Inspired, Julie called Billie Jean after the conference for advice.

"We're facing the same problems," Julie told her.

"What are you guys doing about it?" Billie Jean asked.

"We're asking for more money, more support."

Billie Jean had tried asking nicely too. That didn't work. "You have to stop asking," she said. "You have to find your power, find your leverage, and get it done yourself."

"Our power?"

Billie Jean was blunt. "You don't play," she said. "That's the only leverage you have."

To Julie, the idea of striking was terrifying. And she said so.

Do it for female soccer players of the future, Billie Jean suggested. "It's not what you're building for you," she said. "It's what you are building for the next generation. So, think about what you want it to be for them."

Julie, Mia Hamm, and other team leaders decided to dig deeper into the problem with U.S. Soccer. They asked to see the nonprofit's budget. Numbers were skewed by gender across the board. For example, why, the players wondered, were 80 percent of the federation's development funds going to twelve-year-old boys and only 20 percent to twelve-year-old girls?

At team dinners, Julie talked about Title IX and how that law had made their careers possible. How each generation had to fight for the next generation. On conference calls with the players, the captains pointed out that the contract that U.S. Soccer had offered them did nothing to improve their traveling conditions and promised nothing close to what their employer paid the men. The women deserved more, and so did the players who would come up behind them.

As the team unified, they began strategizing about how they could stick together and demand more. The team brought in Ellen Zavian, the first female attorney to represent National (American) Football League (NFL) players, to help with contract negotiations. She advised the women to mark up their contracts to reflect their demands and send them back, unsigned.

Nine players out of the usual eleven starting lineup stepped up to do it, including Julie Foudy, Mia Hamm, and Briana Scurry.

U.S. Soccer was outraged. "How dare you?" U.S. Soccer leadership told Julie.

"We were asking for so little," Julie recalled, "and they were still not moving on any of it."

U.S. Soccer disinvited all nine—Julie Foudy, Mia Hamm, Briana Scurry, Michelle Akers, Joy Fawcett, Kristine Lilly, Carla Overbeck, Carin Jennings, and Tisha Venturini—from the next training camp, scheduled to take place in Chula Vista, California.

When the press caught wind of the women demanding to be paid bonuses for silver and bronze, the head of U.S. Soccer, Hank Steinbrecher, told reporters, "We cannot reward mediocrity. . . . Bonuses are paid for superior performance. Our expectation should be playing for gold and winning it."

Since when are silver and bronze medals mediocre? the players wondered. And why were they only "mediocre" for women, not for men? It made no sense.

The federation stuck to its position that the women should be grateful to be going at all.

"I was extremely thankful to be on the field," Briana said. "But I also knew when I was being screwed."

Locked out of camp, some players hinted to the press that they might boycott the 1996 Olympics, which were to be held in Atlanta. Star forward Michelle Akers called a strike a "definite reality." But really, no one wanted to boycott. They had worked incredibly hard to make the national team. The athletes yearned to play in their first-ever Olympics and were doubly excited to compete on home soil. They didn't want to jeopardize their lifelong dream. "The Olympics stole my heart when I was eight years old and never let it go," Briana said.

Julie found the prospect of losing this opportunity "super scary" too. But she urged her teammates to hang tough. "If we stick together and stay united, they can't cut the whole team," she told them. "Our unity is our strength."

U.S. Soccer retaliated by replacing the nine protesting players for an upcoming tournament. The nine locked-out players were shocked and tried to prop each other up during conference calls.

Kristine Lilly said, "Jules, I don't know. I'm really scared that I won't play in the Olympics."

"Well, I am too," Julie replied. "But this is gonna make a difference." She reminded her teammates, "If they start pulling us apart, then we're done."

U.S. Soccer's tactics put the replacements in a difficult position. The coach invited Brandi Chastain—who had been cut from the roster earlier—to the tournament. "Oh crap," Brandi thought. Her heart was with the locked-out women but the competitor in her was eager to go.

She called Julie Foudy. "I'm standing by you, Julie, but I've been invited to camp, and this might be my only chance to get back on the national team." Julie got a similar call from Shannon MacMillan. Julie was torn. She knew that eventually the team would need these young players as teammates.

"We're good," Julie replied. "You go in and we'll get it done from our side." But, she added, "There may come a point when we all need to hold out together. We'll let you know. For now, go in and crush it."

The solidarity of the locked-out players and the reluctance of the replacement players must have unnerved U.S. Soccer. One day at six a.m., lawyer Ellen Zavian answered her phone.

It was the president of U.S. Soccer.

He started screaming at her about the defiance of the players.

Shaken, she called a friend to get his advice.

"When they're screaming, they're going down," he told her. "So just hold out."

So the women did the only thing they could do. They stood their ground, and they waited.

Playing for Olympic Gold

Atlanta, 1996

The waiting paid off, somewhat. U.S. Soccer added a small bonus if the U.S. women won silver. Still, the pay was paltry. Experienced players earned $3,000 a month. Newcomers got only $2,000.

Cindy Parlow was one of the new ones.

Born in Memphis, Tennessee, Cindy was painfully quiet and known for her Southern politeness when she did speak. But on the soccer field, she was a beast. She had grown up constantly competing and wrestling with her two brothers. On the soccer field, as a towering powerhouse forward with a whipping-straight blond ponytail, she was fearless leaping into the air to head the ball.

At age sixteen, Cindy left high school a year early to play for the University of North Carolina. Why? She thought she had a shot at making the first U.S. women's soccer team to go to the Olympics.

Indeed, she soon got the call to travel with the U.S. Women's National Team to Brazil for some games. "She was a quiet little skinny kid," said co-captain Carla Overbeck. Cindy was so quiet that Carla questioned whether or not she could talk.

Cindy was more than just quiet. She had an intense fear of failure. She felt like she had to be the best at everything, in sports and academics. In fact, she would avoid doing things unless she could be the best. And she usually was—in school, on the basketball court, and on the soccer field. That is, until she stepped on the field with the U.S.

Women's National Team. "Holy shit," she thought, "these women are good." It was eye-opening and deeply uncomfortable. "Why would they want me?" she wondered.

Like a growing number of people, Cindy was a huge fan of the national team. She had a poster of dynamic scoring fiend Mia Hamm on her bedroom wall. In Brazil, Cindy shared a room with Mia. Seventeen-year-old Cindy worried about how to behave. Should she let Mia brush her teeth first, or do it quickly and get out of her way? When Mia got a phone call, should she leave the room? For how long?

Mia, Carla, and the other players tried to put Cindy at ease. They sat at the end of her bed, chatting, even if she was too terrified to say a word. Cindy thought, "Why are they in my room and talking to me?" She was just a kid, vying for a position on the team, maybe even one of *their* positions.

As she continued to train and play with the powerful, inspiring women, Cindy had to face that she was not the best on the field. She had to figure out, "What do I bring to this team? What can I contribute? How can I make an impact?"

Cindy got into her first national game in Brazil and smashed the ball into the back of the net in a match against Russia. She made the Olympic roster too. She didn't expect to play much, so she decided she would focus on doing anything she could to help the team be successful.

Briana had higher expectations. While the U.S. team had been the dark horse for their first World Cup win, they were the favorites to win Olympic gold.

The whole team practiced hard, often with rock music booming from loudspeakers. The coaches wanted to get the women used to playing in packed stadiums where a boisterous crowd could overwhelm players' calls to each other. The team worked to find other ways to communicate on the field.

On the day of the first match of the 1996 Olympics in Atlanta, Briana focused on visualizing the game, what plays might happen, what she needed to do, how it would feel. She thought about her feet "being strong and solid beneath me, my attention on the ball unwavering." She pictured herself standing in goal, "not feeling any nerves or pressure, just resolving to not let a soccer ball get inside."

All that calm went out the window when the team arrived at the stadium. Briana thought she might be hallucinating. The stands were packed with more than 25,000 screaming, cheering fans. Mia Hamm found the atmosphere to be "electric." It gave teammate Carla Overbeck goose bumps.

In an exhausting three games in five days, the USWNT took down Denmark in 102-degree heat, then Sweden, with Mia being carried off on a stretcher from a twisted ankle. Then they eked out a scoreless tie with China. The U.S. came back from behind to beat Norway in overtime in the semifinals. That put them in the finals for the first-ever gold medal competition for women's soccer in the Olympics. They would play China, who they had only managed to tie in the preliminaries.

More than 75,000 fans filled the stadium for the gold medal match, more than had ever attended a women's sporting event worldwide.

The U.S. women came out strong. Twenty minutes in, Mia rocketed a ball toward the goal. The Chinese goalkeeper got her fingertips on it, and it ricocheted off the post to the feet of Mia's teammate Shannon MacMillan. Shannon tapped the ball in, and the Americans took the lead.

But they seemed to tire while the Chinese players seemed to wake up. China took control of the ball, and forward Sun Wen charged toward the goal. Briana moved off her line to meet her. Sun Wen lofted the ball over Briana's head and into the goal. The score was tied.

The second half opened with China still in control. Fifteen minutes in, a Chinese player came charging down the center of the field and hit a solid shot on goal. Briana dove and blocked it.

Then the U.S. players came to life again, pounding the Chinese goal once, twice, three times. Each shot was blocked, but the team threaded pass after pass, until finally Tiffeny Milbrett smashed it in. The score was 2–1. The Chinese team never gave up, stepping up to every ball and pressing hard on goal. Players on both teams were bruised and battered. Near the end of the game, the balletic Mia Hamm, who was the spark behind both goals, was taken off the field on a stretcher, again with an ankle injury.

Finally the whistle blew.

The stadium erupted in applause. Briana sprinted out of her goal and into the arms of her teammates. They were no longer individuals with a dream. They had learned to work together, fight together, and win together. Mia jog-limped around the field, waving to the crowd. Curly-haired Michelle Akers ran up the sidelines waving a huge American flag.

Julie was swept up by the frenzy of the fans. "They want to take your shoes, they want to take your shin guards," she said. "You can literally throw these smelly, ripe socks right into the stands, and they're like 'YES!'"

The domination of America's female athletes was *the* story of the Atlanta Olympics, according to the British newspaper the *Guardian*. The U.S. women's basketball, gymnastics, softball, and swim teams all gave stunning performances, raking in gold medals. But coverage of the women's soccer game was thin, with NBC only airing a few minutes of highlights.

When it was time for their awards ceremony, the soccer players changed out of their sweat-drenched and grass-stained clothes and into pristine medal presentation uniforms. They had never participated in an Olympic medal ceremony, so when Team USA was announced for gold, the players looked at one another. "What do we do?"

They grabbed each other's hands and stepped up to the top of the podium to the roar of the crowd.

As Briana bent down to receive her medal, thinking of her poster, her dream, and the amazing women by her side, she couldn't believe how substantial the medal felt around her neck.

Finding Fans

1999

U.S. participation in soccer was blossoming. Since the founding of the national team, the number of girls playing high school soccer and women playing college soccer had tripled. And excitement was building for the 1999 women's World Cup, scheduled to be played on home soil, in the United States. But USWNT players were surprised and disappointed to learn that FIFA had reserved mostly high school stadiums for the matches. The women pointed to the growing popularity of the sport and their recent history of filling large venues with tens of thousands of spectators. They begged for the chance to play bigger.

The women's national team had to convince those in power in the soccer world—predominantly men and fans of men's soccer—that they could excite, captivate, and impress sports fans, if only they were given the chance.

The women lobbied hard, and the organizations relented and booked larger stadiums. But to market the event, U.S. Soccer only allocated one-tenth of the amount they had spent promoting the men's World Cup held in the United States five years earlier. That meant that to create a successful World Cup, the woman could not just focus on training. They had to fill the stadiums.

"It was all hands on deck," Julie said. "We were willing to do anything it took to get butts in seats." While on the road for training camps or international non-tournament friendly games, and sometimes on their own dime, players visited cities where World Cup matches would be held, showing up at local kids' tournaments, handing out fliers, offering clinics, playing games, talking with media, and signing autographs.

The women were dismayed that often when they traveled for exhibition games, locals would have no idea the team was coming to town. Julie Foudy and her teammates continued to press U.S. Soccer for more support. "What are you doing to market us?" Julie asked the federation.

They didn't seem to know what she meant, so she explained: marketing brings in fans and fans bring in dollars that could help support the team. "Nothing is posted about [our visits] and no one knows anything," she said. "How are people supposed to come to see us play if they never know we're playing?"

Briana Scurry, who knew what it was like to be the only Black kid on her soccer teams growing up, worked to reach beyond the white suburbs where soccer was already popular, to neighborhoods where families like hers were less familiar with the sport.

While doing this second, unpaid job of promoting the upcoming World Cup, the women still had to train, drill, and play matches. From 1997 till the World Cup started in June 1999, the team played sixty-three games, winning fifty-five, losing four, and tying four. "It wasn't easy to do both," Briana said. "Imagine if an NFL or NBA team had to devote time and energy to traveling the country to promote their sport in the runup to the Super Bowl or the NBA Finals."

It was emotionally draining too. On the one hand, Brandi Chastain thought, "Oh heck yeah, we got this. We're going to fill all the stadiums, and it's going to be awesome!"

At the same time, she worried, "Oh shit, is this going to happen? How can we be saying this is going to happen?"

• • •

The opening game of the 1999 women's World Cup was scheduled to be played in Giants Stadium in New Jersey. At eleven a.m., a few hours before kickoff, the players piled onto a bus at their hotel. As they neared the stadium, traffic came to a standstill on the New Jersey Turnpike. Briana Scurry wondered, "Why would they schedule something else on the day of our first World Cup game?" Cars lined the highway heading toward the stadium for as far as the players could see.

"What the heck?" Brandi Chastain thought.

"What's going on?" Loudy Foudy asked. "Why is it so crazy?"

The players became concerned that they might be late for their own game. Then they noticed that many of the cars were flying U.S. Soccer flags or had windows painted with GO USA! or WE LOVE YOU, MIA!

"Oh my god!" Julie shouted. "We created this traffic jam. This crowd is for US!"

Children hanging out of car windows had their faces painted red, white, and blue. They cheered at the bus, blowing kisses, their eyes wide and full of excitement.

Inside the bus, the team's press officer announced, "We sold out the stadium!" That was more than 75,000 seats. The players cheered and screamed and danced. To Julie, it was a moment of euphoria and pure joy.

Finally a police escort led the bus off the road and onto the shoulder to get the players to the game on time. The parking lot was a lively scene with families tailgating and kicking soccer balls around. The families waved and took pictures of the players. The players waved and took pictures of them.

Before the game, the starting eleven and the substitutes lined up in the dark, cavelike tunnel that led to the field. Fans chattering among themselves made a joyful hum above. As the players walked toward brilliant daylight, the women could see the bright green grass and the colorfully decked-out cheering sections. When they stepped onto the field, cameras flashed and the chattering hum grew to a roar. Players said it "sucked the breath out" of them. Some laughed uncontrollably or burst into tears. To Briana, the sound in the stadium was the "sweetest, most high-pitched cheer I've ever heard in my life. It sounded as if the average age of the 78,000-plus fans was about ten."

The women were amazed, pumped, and a tad nervous. "The funny thing about selling it so well was now we had to go out there and win the damn thing," Briana said.

The Whole World Watching

1999

Sixty-three nations competed in more than 140 games to qualify for the 1999 World Cup. The sixteen teams that qualified were divvied into four groups of four teams each. The teams in each group would play each other, with the top two graduating to the knockout stage. When the opening whistle blew, Denmark, Nigeria, and South Korea stood between the United States and the eight-team quarterfinal.

The group stage started out well. The U.S. shut out Denmark in the opening game, 3–0. All three goals—by Mia Hamm, Kristine Lilly, and Julie Foudy—were scored with their left feet. When the stadium rocked with applause, Julie thought, "NO WAY THIS IS REAL." When the final whistle blew, Julie, who had been standing midfield, did a 360-degree circle, clapping to the fans.

In front of a sellout crowd of more than 65,000 people at Soldier Field in Chicago, they trounced Nigeria 7–1. In Foxboro Stadium in Massachusetts, the USWNT kept South Korea scoreless at 3–0. "It was like a big snowball that just kept getting bigger and bigger," Julie said. "Every place we went there was more media, more attention."

A tight win of 3–2 against Germany earned the team a spot in the semifinals against Brazil. In an effort to attract more fans, the semifinal game would be followed by a men's professional game. Indeed, more than 73,000 fans packed the stadium at Stanford University. "The fans were in a frenzy," Julie said. "The girls, the boys, the teenagers, the moms, the dads." Julie was struck by how the kids seemed to see themselves in the players, how relatable the team was. "You have to see it to be it," she thought.

Just five minutes into the game, the quiet powerhouse Cindy Parlow blasted a header into the goal. The U.S. won a penalty kick toward the end of the game, shutting out Brazil 2–0. That was it. The U.S. Women's National Team had made it once again to the finals.

After the whistle, before the men's game started, 60,000 people left the stadium. They had already seen the game they came to see.

For the 1999 World Cup final, the U.S. women faced China. The Chinese team had beaten the Americans in two out of three of their most recent games and had just crushed Norway 5–0. "If China plays the way it did today," predicted Norwegian player Hege Riise, "with all their speed and the way they attack, they will beat the U.S. team."

Record-breaking crowds, more than 90,000, packed the Rose Bowl in Pasadena, California, to watch the match. Forty million Americans tuned in on television. "Girls have always had to watch guys doing great feats on the field, in front of huge crowds," Julie thought. "Now they can watch women doing great feats on the field in front of great crowds."

The starting whistle blew to a nation captivated.

Usually an agile, attacking team, the Chinese took a different tactic and locked down their defense. American Michelle Akers shot from forty yards out and was blocked by the Chinese keeper. Cindy Parlow went head-to-head with a defender and was tackled in the box before she could shoot. Mia Hamm took off toward the goal on a through ball, but China intercepted.

The day was hot and getting hotter, reaching into the nineties. The players all had tricks to keep themselves focused. Brandi Chastain tightened her blond ponytail. Julie snapped a band on her wrist. Mia pulled up her socks. They focused, and they fought. But neither team could get a goal.

In the final twenty minutes of the game, with both teams still scoreless, pressure grew. Briana Scurry realized "it was going to come down to a moment of brilliance, or a mistake, or the slightest lapse in concentration."

As the clock ticked down, China earned a corner kick. The ball arced high and dropped in front of the American's goal. Briana followed the ball like a laser as players from both teams shoved each other for position. Briana wanted it out of there. So she lunged forward and punched the ball out.

But she also smashed into their curly-haired star forward Michelle Akers, who went down. Michelle argued to stay in the game, but she was dizzy and had to be taken off the field.

Regulation time ended with the score at 0–0. The players huddled on the sideline, sipping water, mopping their heads with cool towels, and stretching cramping legs.

The teams would play two more fifteen-minute halves. But as soon as one team scored, the game would be over. This "golden goal" format, not used in the men's World Cup, put a ton of pressure on the goalkeepers.

The teams battled through most of the half hour with no goals.

Then China earned a corner kick. The ball soared in front of the goal. A Chinese player popped up and headed the ball toward the net. Briana stretched but missed it. The crowd gasped.

But "Title IX baby" Kristine Lilly was standing on the goal line. She headed the ball back out. "Saved off the line!" screamed the commentator. Brandi bicycle-kicked the ball away. It was a close call.

Time ticked down. The overtime whistle blew.

The winner of the 1999 World Cup would come down to penalty kicks. Five players from each team would take turns shooting at the goal from twelve yards (nearly eleven meters) out. Penalty kicks are incredibly hard for goalkeepers to stop. The shooter gets to take aim at a stationary ball from a stable position right in front of the goal, with no defenders in the way. But penalties also put enormous pressure on the shooters. One missed kick could hand the advantage to the opponent.

Players from both teams huddled together, drenched in sweat from battling it out on the hot field for more than two hours. Bright sunlight blazed over the field and the stands.

As the crowd shuffled nervously and chatted excitedly, the teams strategized with their coaches, figuring out which five players would shoot.

American goalie Briana Scurry moved off to the side, "gearing up to go into the goal feeling like the most intensely coiled spring ever, ready to unlock and unleash when the kick came."

The first two players, one Chinese, one American, struck and scored. U.S. 1, China 1.

Two more shots went in: U.S. 2, China 2.

Then the Chinese player Liu Ying lined up to take a shot.

Briana prepped the way she always did, legs apart, slightly crouched, feet solid beneath her. Arms and hands loose yet ready. She checked Liu's stance: were her hips open or shifted to one side? How was she setting up to approach the kick?

Liu was straight on when she strode toward the ball, hips open to the goal. Briana predicted that she was going to side-foot to her right. Briana dove in that direction, her body horizontal to the ground, stretching and stretching, reaching, reaching for the ball.

She tipped it, and the ball bounced away.

The fans erupted jumping and shouting. Briana leapt to her feet, screaming and boxing her fists in the air.

The score remained U.S. 2, China 2. But China had only two more shots; the U.S. had three. If they could nail all three, they would win the World Cup.

Each side took another penalty kick. Each buried the ball in the net.

U.S. 3, China 3.

Two more players, including the leading scorer Mia Hamm, made their shots.

It was U.S. 4, China 4.

China was out of chances, and the United States had just one more kick left. If Brandi Chastain could put the ball in the net, the U.S. would win 5–4 and take home gold.

But Brandi had missed a penalty kick against China in a recent tournament—and the U.S. had lost that game. Brandi would face the same goalie, a psychological challenge Brandi would have to overcome. Hoping to catch the Chinese goalkeeper off guard, the coach asked Brandi to take the shot with her left foot. It was not her dominant foot, but she thought she could do it.

Brandi hustled to the spot and placed the ball on the ground, adjusting it slightly. She took a few steps back, turned to face the goal, and brushed some wisps of light-colored hair out of her eyes. Brandi wouldn't look at the goalkeeper; instead, she tried to quell the pressure pulsing through her body.

The stadium fell eerily quiet.

Brandi peered seriously at the ball for a moment. She shuffled her feet a few times, like a nervous colt. Her brow furrowed. Never taking her eyes off the ball, she took a quick run and then *smack!* She drove the ball toward the goal with her left foot.

It felt so good, so right, but to Brandi it seemed to move in slow motion.

The goalie dove, but the ball was too hard and too high, and it soared past her into the back of the net.

Fans sprang to their feet screaming. Brandi spun around to an explosion of color and light and noise. She whipped off her shirt, swung it in the air, and fell to her knees. In her sports bra, with her arm and abdominal muscles rippling, she threw back her head in relief and ecstasy.

Teammates sprinted across the field to her. They leapt into each other's arms, cheering and laughing and crying. They had won the World Cup. They could hardly believe what they had accomplished, and they basked in the glory.

But the reality of their situation remained sobering. For all they accomplished, for all their work bringing in audiences, for hours and days and weeks of training, for hard-fought battles on the field, the women made about $15,000, what *Washington Post* reporter Sally Jenkins called "waitress pay."

Winning the 1999 World Cup would change everything, Julie Foudy thought. Surely their employer, U.S. Soccer, would recognize their worth, support them, promote them, and pay them more.

Soccer Is Sexy

1999

The 1999 World Cup was a stunning athletic achievement, but some of the media coverage missed that story. The *Los Angeles Times* declared, "Success of the '99 Women's World Cup Is . . . Good Looking." A *Chicago Sun-Times* headline read, "Soccer Has Sex Appeal." The Scripps News Service purported to explain "The Babe Factor in Soccer Team's Success."

Sports Illustrated, Time magazine, and newspapers and television segments featured shots of the muscular, joyful Brandi Chastain in a black Nike sports bra reveling in victory. It was a memorable and controversial photo—men ripped off their shirts in celebration all the time, but some people found the same gesture by a female athlete startling.

Still, the win and the widespread coverage seemed to signal the start of something great.

Robin Roberts, anchor of ABC's *Good Morning America,* described the tournament this way: "I've always believed the most iconic sports events transcend the actual competition and become something much more, a sociocultural marker of sorts." She was referring to the astounding turnout at the World Cup matches and the growing popularity of women's soccer in the country.

Sports Illustrated named the team "Sportswomen of the Year." But U.S. Soccer did not treat them that way. Their contract, signed three years earlier, had expired. And though the women had brought home the gold and the glory, the federation wanted to keep paying them $3,150 per month for January and February to travel across the globe to Australia to play in a tournament. While U.S. Soccer covered travel expenses, the players' income was not guaranteed before or after those two months. To properly train, practice, travel, and play, the women could not hold other jobs. Struggling to pay their rent, health insurance, and other expenses, the players asked for $5,000 a month plus $2,000 per game.

They awaited U.S. Soccer's reply.

Players in the Making

1999

In the small town of Redding, California, a fourteen-year-old girl named Megan Rapinoe and her twin, Rachael Rapinoe, watched their heroes—Brandi Chastain, Mia Hamm, and Julie Foudy—win the 1999 World Cup in spectacular fashion. They recorded the games and played them over and over again, until they had each play as well as the commentary memorized.

Born into an athletic family, Megan and Rachael took to soccer so easily that their older siblings found it freakish. The twins dribbled around the oak tree in their yard, and around cones their older brother Brian set up. At his games, the twins ran along the sidelines, trying to copy all the cool moves they saw on the field. There was no local team for girls. At age six, they were invited to join an under-eight (U-8) boys' team. Eventually their dad set up a girls' team.

It was the 1999 women's World Cup final at the Rose Bowl that showed the sisters what a soccer career might look like. Megan was mesmerized by the massive crowds that flocked to watch the USWNT. She wished it could be her on the field.

But how could she ever get there? She thought she was too small and not fast enough to achieve that level. But she hung a poster of the U.S. Women's National Team on her wall and hoped to win a soccer scholarship to college. She would take it one step at a time.

The B Team

Sydney Olympics, 2000

Shortly after the 1999 World Cup, U.S. Soccer raked in a $120 million sponsorship deal with Nike. The Nike logo would adorn all U.S. Soccer uniforms and other gear, and the nonprofit could use the money as they saw fit.

Meanwhile, the players, struggling to pay expenses and juggling multiple jobs, heard that the federation refused their request for a raise.

So the women decided to create a labor union. Labor unions are organizations of people working for the same employer who coordinate efforts to improve wages and working conditions.

The U.S. Women's National Team Players Association began meeting. The women compiled a list of the differences between the way U.S. Soccer treated their men's and women's teams. After the overwhelming turnout to games in the 1999 women's World Cup, there was really no reason for U.S. Soccer to treat the teams differently, they believed.

Some of the differences were small but insidious. The women had their own uniforms by now, but they had to launder them, while the men didn't. And after tournaments the men got to keep their jerseys, but the women had to turn them in.

The women had to cart around all their equipment—bags of balls, cones, corner flags, goals, and other workout gear—while the men's team had equipment managers who handled everything.

Also, the federation didn't secure reliable ground transport for the women's team. Often, the men traveled in deluxe buses while the women traveled in vans. For one match, the only transportation the team had was a Holiday Inn Express shuttle.

The female players were even fed differently. The men had catered meals during training camps. When the women heard from a nutritionist that they should eat an hour after their first training and an hour before their next session, players ran out to buy bagels and fruit to share so they would have energy. The women also had a smaller coaching and support staff who were not as well paid as the men's support team.

Mia Hamm thought they should shoot for equal pay, equal treatment. "We had just won a World Cup and they couldn't say people won't come watch us play," she said. But that seemed like a huge step, so they decided to start smaller.

The women proposed a two-month contract for the Sydney Olympics for $18,000 per player.

"You signed a $120 million contract with Nike, and we think we had a little to do with it," the women said in a negotiating session.

Their employer seemed unconvinced and said no.

Julie, Mia, and other leaders communicated to their younger teammates about U.S. Soccer's continuing resistance. Once-shy Cindy Parlow, who "quite literally grew up on the women's national team" felt sheltered, protected, and challenged by these veteran players. They demonstrated loyalty and integrity and what it meant to be a true leader and a true champion of others. That was why when the leaders rallied the players to strike, Cindy and her teammates were all on board. They all refused to travel to the warm-up tournament.

"They're currently unemployed," a U.S. Soccer official told reporters. U.S. Soccer announced that they would send their B team, players previously cut from the national team and several players from the youth teams, instead. Some of the replacement players were concerned about being called out as scabs who "crossed the picket line," but the veterans told them to go ahead and play. And the B team won the warm-up tournament.

The national team realized that U.S. Soccer was trying to pit the rising players against the current team. And things would only get better for everyone if they all stuck together. So the top players called every possible replacement player. Brandi Chastain, now a regular on the national team, made a call to one of the replacement players. "Look, they're going to ask you to go to the next tournament and we need you to say no."

Every player agreed.

Players from the senior team also called members of the youth teams, inviting them and their parents to join a conference call about the strike. They asked the young players to stand with them.

"We're doing this for you," Julie told them. "We're trying to build the future for you."

The young players and their families agreed to support the senior players in their efforts.

So the women's national team continued to push U.S. Soccer for a new, better contract.

The federation threatened to bring in the U-20 team.

"You can't," the women responded. "They're with us."

U.S. Soccer threatened to bring in the U-18 team.

But they were united with the national team too. So were the U-16s.

With that unity, and that leverage, and with the 2000 Olympics on the horizon, U.S. Soccer finally had to negotiate. The players won a new contract that offered some stability. For the first time, U.S. Soccer would guarantee some reliable pay—$3,500 to $6,500 per month—for contracted players at least eight months of the year.

Julie and Mia walked out of that meeting laughing. “Who’s driving the bus? We’re driving the bus!” they sang. “We’re driving the bus!”

The women didn’t know how this pay compared to pay for the men’s team—and they suspected they were still paid less—but it still felt like a win.

But did that pay really compensate the women for all they put on the line?

Saving Her Brain

Cindy Parlow, 2001–2004

Forward Cindy Parlow, the quiet workhorse of the team, contributed to every 1999 World Cup game and scored the winning goal in the semifinal against Brazil. Julie Foudy admired how Cindy handled the emotional roller coaster of starting in one game, then sitting out some games or getting just a few minutes of play here or there. "She never ever complained, was never visibly upset, never bitched about the coach or sulked on the bench," Julie noticed. Instead, Cindy's vibe was "I'm all in. I'm behind this team. It's all about the collective, and I'm here to do what's good for the group."

But Cindy could be tough too. For instance, her childhood idol, Mia Hamm, could be intimidating on and off the field, rattling people with her "death stare." But she couldn't stare down Cindy. If Mia said something Cindy doubted, she would counter, "Really? Do you really feel that way? Have you thought hard about that?"

Cindy carried that toughness out onto the field. In 2001, Cindy and a teammate were battling with an opponent for a ball in the air. They all leapt up. Cindy and her teammate collided, hard, their heads like two rocks smashing together. Cindy blacked out.

When she came to, she brushed herself off and resumed playing. Then when another ball soared through the air toward her, she lurched up and headed it again. After, her hands felt odd, her fingers tingling.

At halftime, her trainer diagnosed a concussion and pulled her from the game. But it was only the start of her troubles. "I was just a typical athlete," Cindy said. "I had an injury. We know injuries are part of the game. Just tell me how long I need to sit out and what rehab I need to do before I can get back on the field."

In 2003, the U.S. was playing for third place against Canada in the World Cup. Cindy went up for another air ball. She had another collision. She blacked out again. It was another concussion.

Cindy had been struggling with headaches and fatigue, but it got much worse. She felt off-balance and disoriented. Then one sunny morning in January 2004, Cindy bent down to lace her cleats. Her fingers wouldn't cooperate. She pitched forward, blacking out.

Next thing she knew, she was lying in the smooth cavity of an MRI machine. In her mid-twenties, in peak physical condition, Cindy had suffered a mini stroke.

She loved the game so much. She loved her teammates. But with her health compromised, she had to retire.

Without the game in her life, she didn't know who she was, or what she would do.

Blood and Guts on the Field

2000s

Meanwhile, the national team had a new, strong scoring machine in forward Abby Wambach. Raised on a twenty-two-acre family farm in upstate New York with six older siblings, short-haired Abby loved to mix it up with kids as much as ten years older. She had a strong "head" game—with a keen ability to see plays unfolding before her and a knack for rocketing the ball off her head and into the goal.

With the growing opportunities because of Title IX, Abby won a full scholarship to play on the University of Florida's new women's soccer team. But while still in college, Abby was drafted to play in the second season of a new professional women's soccer league, with a salary of around $30,000. She dropped out of college to go pro.

Many pro players—male and female—also played for the national team. Abby was called up for national service in the early 2000s and pounded out four goals in the 2003 World Cup. In the 2004 Olympics, she banged out three goals and an assist to help her team to the final against Brazil. "Abby Wambach would run through a wall, then a house, then a truck for you and the team," Julie noticed. "Then she'd get up bloody and ask if she could do it again . . . with a smile on her face."

On the raucous bus ride to the final of the 2004 Athens games, Abby's voice boomed above the rest as she sang, danced, and rattled on about anything and everything. Julie, always a jokester and prankster, gifted Abby a T-shirt that said HELP! I'M TALKING AND I CAN'T SHUT UP!

Briana Scurry also loved having Abby on the field, her towering presence, her "You want a piece of me?" mentality. "She['s] so strong she could shed tacklers as if she were swatting away a mosquito," Briana noticed.

In the final match of the 2004 Olympics, U.S. and Brazil battled fiercely for ninety minutes and ended up tied 1–1 at the end of regulation time. As they went into overtime, Abby recounted in her memoir *Forward*, she felt like "a cocked gun, a sharpened knife, a grenade with its pin half pulled."

She craved a goal like a fish craves water. The U.S. won a corner kick, and Abby jostled for position as the ball soared through the air. She leapt as high as she could, stretching her body toward the ball. Forehead met ball and she snapped her head toward the net. GOAL!

The U.S. Women's National Team had won gold again.

For the next few years, Abby continued to give it her all. In the first game of the 2007 World Cup, Abby's big toe was swollen and numb and her ankle wrapped from a "friendly" she had played earlier. During the game, she rammed her head against another player. Her head split open, and blood trickled down her back. She went into the locker room for stitches and charged onto the field again.

In another game, Abby's face collided with a goalkeeper's elbow. Her nose bone cracked, and cartilage was blasted toward her left cheek. The deformity was so grotesque, her teammates looked away as she was taken off the field.

A few games later, Abby collided with a defender in front of the goal, breaking her leg in two places. That meant months of rehab.

In training, friendly games, and tournament play, all the players absorbed crashes, smashes, bruises, and wrenching twists. They pulled muscles and broke bones. They tore ligaments and tendons. They bled. But it was just part of the job.

Life-Altering Injury

2004–2011

By 2008, Briana Scurry had played in a record 173 games for the United States, with 133 wins, twelve ties, and just fourteen losses. Seventy-one of the games were shutouts, which means she hadn't let in any goals. She had won two Olympic gold medals and a World Cup championship.

She was thirty-eight years old, had played soccer for the U.S. national team for fourteen years, but she was still living paycheck to paycheck. She needed a job, so she signed up to play for one of the struggling women's pro teams, the Washington Freedom. "My goal was simply to have a strong positive season or two and figure out the future afterward," she said.

On April 25, 2010, she started the game in goal. Just over a half hour into the match, an opponent took a shot. A 165-pound forward sped toward the goal, hoping to pop it in. Briana leapt after the ball, low to the ground, and scooped it up, just as the forward smashed into her, her rock-hard knee cracking into Briana's temple.

Briana collapsed to the ground woozy but held tight to the ball. But when she got up, she felt dizzy.

"C'mon, keep. Play," the ref said.

Briana passed the ball to her defender, but her balance felt odd, like she was leaning left. And her vision was blurry.

When the halftime whistle blew, Briana began staggering off the field.

The trainer ran out to her.

"Bri, are you okay?"

"No."

The trainer asked what day it was. Briana couldn't remember. The trainer told Briana three words and, a few minutes later, asked what they were. Briana couldn't remember. Lights blared bright, sounds pummeled her, and her head seemed to be splitting. She felt like throwing up.

Briana was out of goal for the rest of the game and put on a two-week injury list. The pounding headaches and terrifying memory loss were crippling. She rested in the dark, exhausted but unable to sleep. She moved to the one-month injury list, then the out-for-the-season list. She failed cognitive tests and felt detached from the world.

Her bosses at Washington Freedom offered to make her general manager of the team, and she tried that for a while. But her head hurt, and she couldn't think straight. She landed a job offering commentary on ESPN for the women's World Cup. But she forgot the players' names and couldn't remember key facts. Unemployment checks kept her afloat for four months. Then she tried to make money training young players. But her head continued to pound, day and night.

And when her pro team folded a year later, she lost all medical support.

The former star was tough and had faced pain her whole career, but the pounding in her head was agony. She couldn't afford rent, let alone find the brain power to figure out what to do next.

When Briana filed for workers' compensation, the insurance company fought it, arguing at first that she was faking it. She wanted to scream.

Once the insurance company admitted that Briana had a brain

injury, they blamed it on all the other hits she had taken, many while on the job with the national team. Even after a judge awarded Briana $1,347 a month (about $16,000 a year), the insurance company fought it and only sent checks sporadically.

Briana handed over the title to her Jeep Cherokee for roughly $4,000 in cash. She pawned the Rolex she had been awarded when she'd played a hundred games for the national team. She got $1,000. She paid rent and covered utilities, but she owed her chiropractor, needed medicine, and had no health insurance. With only $55 to her name and empty cupboards, she missed minimum payments on her watch, and it was sold.

Briana Scurry gave her country everything she had in 173 games, brought home two Olympic gold medals and a World Cup. And now she had nothing, not even her health.

She didn't know what she would do.

A Losing Battle for Gold

World Cup, 2011, Germany

Meanwhile, Megan Rapinoe—the girl who had memorized the 1999 World Cup commentary with her twin sister—had grown into a quick, risk-taking, creative winger who was equally strong with both feet. She had a knack for the unexpected pass, the long pass that was a reach but just might create an opportunity for a goal.

As she recalled in her memoir, *One Life*, Megan signed her first contract with the national team in 2009 for a salary of $50,000 a year. "I had nothing to compare my salary with," she wrote. "And I didn't think to question it."

Megan's first World Cup was two years later, and she was inspired by the team's winning mentality. They believed they were going to win, no matter where the game was played, who the opponent was, and what had gone down earlier in the match. "We train to win, we play to win, and every second of play we're relentless," Megan observed.

Another particularly relentless player who rose through the ranks to the national team was midfielder Carli Lloyd. Teammates dubbed young Carli PITA, as in "pain in the ass," and likened her to a gnat on the field "flitting here and there, finding fresh ways to annoy people." She played with what she called in her memoir, *When Nobody Was Watching*, "Jersey girl attitude," tracking down the ball "like a kid who has had her lunch money stolen and is hell-bent on getting it back."

Once told by a trainer, "You need to be the hardest-working person out there, every time, no exceptions," Carli followed a brutal training program, heading out on ninety-minute runs, 800-meter intervals by the dozens, hill sprints, endless pushups, crunches, and squats. And that was on top of the regular national team training.

In the semifinals of the 2011 World Cup in Germany, the U.S. team was tied 1–1 against Brazil at the end of ninety minutes. The U.S. was down a player, who had been thrown out after a red-card foul. Two minutes into overtime, Brazilian superstar Marta Vieira da Silva, known simply as Marta, scored.

When a team scores in overtime, they usually win.

In the 122nd minute of the game, Megan thought, "We're fucked."

The U.S. women pushed on, hustling, sprinting, struggling, exhausted, their legs like lead, their chests tight. Abby Wambach wanted to "detach my leg or head or both and hurl them at the ball—anything to push it closer to the goal."

The whistle ending the game could blow any second.

ESPN commentator Ian Darke began to ruminate. "It will go down as the USA's worst performance ever in the women's World Cup."

A Brazilian player tried to wind down the clock, keeping the ball in the far corner. But the U.S. stole the ball.

"Now the USA has it," Ian Darke said. "They have got to get everyone forward."

Carli, the Jersey girl, received a pass and began dribbling toward midfield.

"Lloyd's gotta get this pass off," Ian said.

Carli wrangled free of a Brazilian player and touched the ball to Megan on the wing.

Megan was still so far from the goal.

"Everyone's got to run forward now," Ian said, his voice rising a bit in excitement.

Megan crossed the ball far up the pitch, arching it toward the box. She didn't even look up. She thought, "Bitch, you'd better be there. *Somebody* has to be there."

"Rapinoe gets a cross in . . . it's toward Wambach," Ian sputtered.

Abby leapt, slanting her body up and toward the ball. Her forehead kissed the ball, angling it to the goal.

Though Abby kept her eyes open and focused on the net, once her head had directed the ball, she wasn't sure where it went. It was only the cheers from her teammates and the crowd, the weight of teammates jumping on her back and leaping into her arms, that told her she had done it again.

The ball had rocketed into the back of the net.

"OH, CAN YOU BELIEVE THIS?" Ian screamed. "ABBY WAMBACH HAS SAVED THE USA'S LIFE IN THIS WORLD CUP!"

Abby slid on her knees across the grass toward the fans. She found Megan. "Oh my god! Oh my god! Best cross of your life!" Abby hollered as players on the field and off the bench swarmed toward her.

"I know!" Megan screamed back, soon lost in the throng.

It was the latest goal ever scored in a World Cup, and it sent the game to penalty kicks, where the U.S. won 5–3.

The video clip of the cross and header covered by ESPN was picked up and played over and over on news and talk shows across the country. U.S. viewership of the 2011 World Cup skyrocketed, increasing by almost 200 percent over the last World Cup to more than 13 million per game. Sixty-two million watched the final worldwide.

But the U.S. Women's National Team lost that final 3–1 on penalties to Japan, which had recently been devastated by an earthquake and a tsunami. "The Japanese earthquake had just happened, so in that sense it was a tournament that gave everyone courage," Japan's coach, Futoshi Ikeda, later told the BBC.

On the long international flight home from Germany, Megan was in the middle seat in the first row of economy. Sore, bruised, and bummed out, she didn't even have a table to flip down for her water or food.

But when the team arrived back in the United States, they were greeted by something unexpected. Fans thronged around them at the airport and in Times Square in New York, heralding them as world champions, as heroes.

The women shook their head and thought, "But we didn't win!"

The team had become something greater than any one win or loss. They had captured the world's attention. Ultimately, they would use it to inspire change.

Playing for More Than Gold

2012 Olympics, Great Britain

In January 2012, the women's national team qualified for that year's Olympics, blowing away Guatemala 13–0, the Dominican Republic 14–0, Canada 4–0, and Denmark 5–0. But the wins had what Megan Rapinoe called "a sour edge."

"With each passing game, our world dominance intensified, and we could no longer ignore how badly we were paid," she said. U.S. Soccer salaries and contracts were private but public tax documents showed that the top three men's national team players made more than $330,000 from their national team service in 2011, about three times what the women earned.

Veteran players continued to lead team discussions about the fight for equality, what they were fighting for, why it mattered, and what they were willing to give up. "Even if the younger players weren't saying much in these meetings, they were listening, they were understanding the process and what we stood for," said Julie Foudy. That way, when veteran players retired, younger players such as Abby Wambach, Megan Rapinoe, and Alex Morgan were ready to step up and lead, Julie said, "to take the baton and keep running."

The players' association agreement with U.S. Soccer, negotiated every six years, was due to expire at the end of the year. But a lot had happened in those six years. The U.S. Women's National Team was now ranked number one in the world, had been finalists in the recent World

Cup, and had taken home Olympic gold. The team was boosting the national and international audience and participation level for soccer and bringing in lots of revenue for the federation. But the women's compensation continued to lag behind the men's.

The women and men negotiated their contracts with U.S. Soccer separately, and over time, the women's contracts had evolved. During the early years, players only earned $10 a day. They fought for and won monthly payments (in the low thousands) during training camps and tournament periods. Eventually the women negotiated for stable salaries for a set number of players. In their most recent contract, experienced women had a base salary of $70,000. By winning twenty non-tournament friendly games, they could earn $29,000 more, for a total of around $99,000 a year.

The men's contract was structured differently. The men did not have a base salary; their pay accumulated by playing in and winning games. The winning bonuses varied by the ranking of their opponent. But winning twenty non-tournament friendly games could easily net male players $100,000 more than the women.

Players on both the men's and women's teams also got bonuses for qualifying and winning various stages of major tournaments. But these bonuses, especially World Cup bonuses, were even more out of whack.

Still the women dominated in the 2012 London Olympics. They ended the group stage on top and shut out New Zealand in the quarterfinal 2–0. NBC called the semifinal with Canada, where the U.S. squeaked out a 4–3 win, "an instant classic," and the *New York Times* reporter declared it was "one of the best games, involving men or women, in memory."

For the gold medal final against Japan, the U.S. coach urged them to "apply pressure, tackle hard, win fifty-fifty balls, be strong in the air . . ."

They did all that and more, scoring in the eighth and fifty-fifth minutes. Japan answered with a goal but couldn't come back from behind. The U.S. women won Olympic gold, again.

It was a win they were glad to have as they headed into negotiations for a new contract with U.S. Soccer.

Locked In to Low Wages

2013

The 2013 contract negotiations were a disaster. The players, Megan Rapinoe said, were "browbeaten into submission." The new contract had no real raise in salaries for the national team, and the bonus structure remained unequal. U.S. Soccer simply made slight upward adjustments to the terms in the team's expired contract.

The team suffered from the same disadvantage that women everywhere faced in salary negotiations—a history of low pay. Consider a woman who comes to a new job from an undervalued, traditionally female field, or who has skills, education, and experience that were undervalued in her past job, or who was compensated less than equivalent men because her employers assumed that she was not a breadwinner and thus did not need to earn as much.

Women in situations like these can get trapped in a cycle of chronic undercompensation. Potential employers often ask candidates for their salary history. Then they base salary negotiations on that history, generally offering just a bit more than the previous salary. So if a woman had lower pay in her previous job, the negotiation for the new job would use that lower pay as the starting point.

In that way, a woman's lower pay can get locked in, following her throughout her career, with the gap between her wages and a man's wages for similar positions widening over time. "These are things that don't just affect one job; [they] keep women's wages down over their entire lifetime," said Massachusetts state senator Patricia Jehlen, who was working on legislation to close the wage gap in the state.

The accumulation of year after year and job after job with unequal pay made it harder for women to "save the money necessary to provide a cushion for emergencies, for the down payment on a house or security deposit for a rental unit, and for higher education," according to the National Women's Law Center. It also made it harder to "afford quality childcare or to be able to take time off when you are sick or need to care for a loved one," the center found. It could even mean "the difference between going to the doctor and doing without health care."

Pawning Gold

2013

Briana Scurry knew better than many the dire results of long-term suppressed wages as she continued to suffer in private. Nearly three years since her head injury on the field, a doctor diagnosed her as "temporarily totally disabled." A top world-class male athlete in her situation would have a cushion of years of extremely high pay to support him through the tough time. Briana had not earned enough to save anything.

Broken and broke, Briana struggled to leave her studio apartment. When she drove anywhere, she had to jot a note to herself about where she had left the car. Headaches worsened as each day went on, from throbbing, to pounding, to excruciating, like "a butcher's knife to the back of my head." Afraid of getting addicted to painkillers, she waited until ten p.m. to take a Vicodin.

A doctor thought he could ease the pain, suggesting surgery to release the pressure on her occipital nerve. But the surgery would cost $15,000, and Briana had no income, no savings, and no health insurance, and she was too embarrassed to tell her former teammates, friends, or family members how much she was struggling.

Alone one raw February morning, she left her apartment, crossed a parking lot, and took a staircase to a high platform overlooking Little Falls in New Jersey. The white water roared, and mist dampened her face. She inched up to the edge, staring down the deep chasm to the rocks far below, and thought, "I could get rid of my pain forever."

But then she pictured her mother, and how the suicide would crush her.

And Briana backed away.

Still, with the workers' compensation insurance company refusing to pay for surgery, Briana's depression plunged ever deeper and ever darker. Her financial situation was dire.

She remembered an infomercial she had seen on TV. A company called Borro offered quick loans on luxury items. Briana had only two things left in her life worth anything: her two Olympic gold medals.

Borrowing money from her sister to pay for the plane fare, Briana flew to visit her mother, who kept the medals safe in a cedar chest in her bedroom. At the end of the visit, Briana asked to take the gold medals for some upcoming appearances.

"You take them if you need them," her mother said. "You won them, after all."

Briana made an appointment to bring one of the medals to Borro. But she found herself without enough money to buy gas for the trip, and she canceled.

Then, in March of 2013, she dragged herself out of bed, grabbed the small wooden box that held her 1996 Olympic gold medal, and drove toward Manhattan.

It took all of her willpower not to turn back.

In Borro's offices, she explained that 1996 was the first year the Olympics had awarded medals for women's soccer. And her team had won gold.

Borro had never been offered an Olympic gold medal before.

"Wow, it's heavy," the rep said as he palmed the medal.

Briana remembered the weight of the medal around her neck as she stood on the podium sweaty and exhausted but elated, cheering with her teammates.

It took an hour for Borro to authenticate and appraise the medal. (Yes, Briana Scurry was on the U.S. Women's National Team. Yes, they had won gold. Yes, this was that medal.)

They offered her a loan for $5,000 in exchange for the medal. Briana would have to pay off the loan at the rate of $199 a month. To retrieve the medal, she would have to repay the $5,000 plus interest and some fees.

When the meeting was over, Briana couldn't remember where she had parked the car.

She checked the stub.

Once she found her car, she climbed in, grabbed the steering wheel, and sobbed.

The money was nowhere near enough to pay for the surgery, and Briana soon spent the $5,000 on rent and other basics. She returned to Borro and pawned her 2004 gold medal as well.

And she still couldn't afford the surgery that might give her life back.

Turf Battle

2014

Meanwhile, the U.S. Women's National Team continued to dominate and continued to be slighted. When Abby Wambach heard that FIFA and Canada, the host country for the upcoming 2015 women's World Cup, had scheduled the games to be played on artificial turf, she was furious.

No men's World Cup match had ever been played on anything other than real grass—for good reason. For one thing, the ball behaved differently on turf, moving faster and bouncing higher. It was easy to overkick a pass too, which disturbed the flow of the play.

Worse, most athletes playing highly competitive, brutally physical matches find turf to be dangerous. It's harder on their backs, legs, and ankles. Falling or tackling on it, Megan Rapinoe had learned, "takes the skin off your arms and legs like a cheese grater." The concussion danger was also higher with turf, as it didn't offer the same cushioning as grass.

Abby, the queen of sending the ball into the back of the net off her head, knew the turf would constrain her game. "I'm not going for a diving header," she told the *New York Times*. "No way."

Turf even tempers the lively celebrations that players perform after a goal. There would be no dramatic double-knee slides in victory.

"Forget our mounting success and our increased popularity," Abby said. "Forget the fact that artificial turf negatively impacts our play, changing the way the ball bounces and rolls. Forget that it also increases the risk of injury, jostling our joints and sloughing off a layer of skin each time we slide against it. Forget that taking a diving header on turf is akin to taking a plunge on concrete. It's just one more indication that women's soccer is inferior, that women themselves are inferior."

Abby's agent once joked that Abby could sell a ketchup Popsicle to a person wearing white gloves. Though nearing retirement, the star forward decided to carry on the ethos she had learned from the pioneers on the national team and use her celebrity and her natural charisma to speak out about the unequal treatment. She couldn't do much about the unequal pay suffered by every women's soccer team at the hands of their federations across the globe. But players everywhere could work together to improve the playing field for this tournament.

Abby, joined by Alex Morgan and dozens of other top national team players from twelve countries, circulated a petition to FIFA and the Canadian soccer federation requesting grass fields for their World Cup. Thousands signed on.

Abby told the media, "We have to make sure FIFA knows this is not okay. And they know it's not okay. If you were to ask all of them, they know that they would never do this for the men."

The petition got them nowhere.

So they stepped up the pressure. In October, forty international players filed a lawsuit against FIFA. They also sued the Canadian Soccer Association under the Ontario Human Rights Code. "Every person has a right to equal treatment with respect to services, goods, and facilities without discrimination," the code stated.

Star forward Alex Morgan joined the suit for health reasons. When she played on grass, she got sore, but after a game on turf, her body ached, her legs pulsing. After a grass game, she recovered in a day. After playing on turf, she needed three to five days to recover. Tournaments like the World Cup rarely offered that many rest days between matches.

FIFA and the association claimed that grass fields could not hold up to repeated games after long Canadian winters. But Germany and Sweden, which also have severe winters, hosted tournaments on grass. Plus, the World Cup was scheduled to start in June, which allowed plenty of time for the snow to melt and the ground to dry.

With time ticking down toward the World Cup, the players tried negotiating a solution. The women pointed out an easy fix: install temporary grass over the turf. This had been done twice for men's World Cup games, in 1994 and 2013.

FIFA and the Canadian federation wouldn't budge.

The players tried requesting an expedited hearing from the courts, but the defendants opposed it.

In a press conference, a FIFA official got heated and called the whole thing "nonsense."

The players worried that even if they won in court, the organizers might not comply. Instead, FIFA and the federation could just cancel the whole tournament. And if the teams were going to play on turf, and play successfully, the players had to train on the surface.

Should they stand their ground or let the whole thing, painfully, slide?

Watching and Hoping

2013–2015

In January 2015, Abby Wambach and the other players could tell the turf lawsuit would not be resolved before the tournament. They dropped the suit.

The USWNT players turned their laser focus to winning, which would "make it even harder for the federation to deny us equal pay with men," Megan Rapinoe hoped.

As teams from around the globe gathered in Canada, there was one former player in the stands ready to support the U.S. team as they continued their battles on and off the field. Briana Scurry was able to travel with her partner, Chryssa Zizos, to Vancouver, Canada, to attend the 2015 women's World Cup.

It was Chryssa who had turned everything around for Briana. A friend had connected Briana with Chryssa, who was a top public relations executive. Captivated and moved by Briana's story, Chryssa landed articles about Briana's contributions to the national team and her plight in the *Washington Post* and *USA Today* and also won invitations for Briana to tell her story on TV.

When the workers' compensation insurance company got wind of the publicity blitz, they relented. They agreed to pay for Briana's surgery.

In October 2013, Briana was wheeled into the operating room. The surgeon cut open her scalp and removed clumps of tissue surrounding her occipital nerve.

An hour later, in the recovery room, she woke up.

The pain was gone.

Chryssa also helped Briana get her Olympic medals back—and now they were together in the stands, remembering the battles Briana had fought and rooting for the national team's success, on and off the pitch.

The World Watches

World Cup, 2015

The 2015 World Cup games were played, as scheduled, on turf at five out of six of the venues. The female athletes had to contend with unnaturally high bounces, painful dives, and trouble dribbling on the fast, hard surface. *Sports Illustrated* commentator Laurent Dubois wrote, "The artificial turf is a metaphor, a very visible and inescapable reminder of the many ways in which institutional forces continue to hold back the development of the women's game, quite literally impacting its most brilliant and inspiring players." The U.S. women dominated the tournament, which had expanded to twenty-four teams, knocking out China and Germany to reach the final against Japan.

Midfielder Carli Lloyd didn't let her concerns about the turf stop her from giving the game her all. The night before the final, she woke up repeatedly thinking about the upcoming match. In the morning, her heart was racing, and she could barely contain herself until the five p.m. kickoff. She stretched and visualized distributing passes, tackling, and charging toward the goal.

Finally it was game time. She tied her wavy brown hair into a short ponytail, donned a black headband and the captain's armband, and took to the field with her teammates, surrounded by 50,000 cheering fans. The air hung gray and heavy with wildfire smoke and anticipation.

At the whistle, the Americans grabbed possession of the ball and attacked. They won an early corner kick. Megan Rapinoe walked to the corner of the field and placed the ball down carefully. Players jostled for position in the box in front of the goal. Carli stayed out of the fray, about thirty yards away. As Megan was about to strike the ball from the corner, Carli charged toward the net. She met the ball in front of the goal and smashed it in. It was 1–0 just three minutes into the game.

In the fifth minute, Carli dashed in for another cross, beat two defenders, and touched it into the goal, putting the Americans up 2–0.

U.S. midfielder Lauren Holiday scored, making it 3–0.

In the fifteenth minute, Carli intercepted the ball at half field. She tapped the ball past a Japanese player and looked up. The goalie had come out of the box and was moving toward Carli.

Carli had been practicing shooting from the midfield for years. The goal was far away, but wide open behind the goalie. She had nailed kicks like this during training again and again. But it was a long shot.

She nudged the ball ahead and then ran up to it at full speed. She pounded it with as much power and precision as she could. It arched skyward and toward the space behind the goalkeeper. The goalie tried to backpedal to meet it, reaching her right hand skyward and tapping the ball as she stumbled backward and fell. The ball hit the left post and dropped into the net.

The crowd and the players went wild.

Carli had scored an almost impossible goal. It was her third goal of the game—a hat trick, all scored in the first sixteen minutes of play. It was the first hat trick ever scored in a World Cup game by anyone, male or female.

American goalkeeper Hope Solo grabbed Carli in a bear hug. "Are you even human?" she yelled.

Teammate Ali Krieger joked that Carli's success was the most tiring part of the game. "We had to chase Carli after she scored all her goals," she said. "I was like, 'Can she not run around the entire field?'"

In the seventy-fifth minute, Abby Wambach subbed in for the final World Cup game of her career. Carli slid the captain's band off her arm and gave it to Abby.

And they both fought like bulls for every ball for the rest of the match.

The final whistle blew. Carli fell to her knees and was surprised to find she was crying. Players and coaches poured onto the field and embraced and laughed and shed tears.

A record-breaking 43 million Americans watched all or part of the stunning final game—more than any U.S. men's soccer match, more than any NBA final, more than the average television audience for the most recent Olympics. Twitter, now called X, logged more than nine billion tweets about the tournament.

But still, when the women won the cup, they made seventeen times less than the German team that had won the men's World Cup just a year earlier. And the $2 million that the U.S. women brought home for winning the tournament was also dwarfed by the $9 million that the U.S. men's team made for its eleventh-place finish.

Briana was elated by the team's decisive triumph, but she also realized how far they still needed to go to reach pay equity. "When I'm eighty, I'm assuming that we still will be fighting for it," she said. "These are journeys that take a very long time."

Victory?

July 2015

Swept up in the excitement of the moment, the mayor of New York City decided to throw a ticker-tape parade for the women's national team.

Thousands of people lined Broadway from the lower tip of Manhattan to City Hall. Fans of all ages and all genders—but especially teenage girls—crowded the street known as the Canyon of Heroes dressed in red, white, and blue as the team rolled by on floats. Sixteen-year-old Addie Severs and her friend MaKenna Huhnke, twelve, road-tripped eight hours to attend. MaKenna held a sign high that read ONE SMALL STEP FOR WOMAN. ONE GIANT LEAP FOR WOMANKIND.

Erin Schaefer, a local, took a day off work to join the celebration. She was aware of the lack of parity between the prizes awarded to the men's and women's World Cup winners. The women deserved the same $35 million awarded to Germany, she told a reporter.

After the parade, without being able to go home first, the players embarked on a ten-city victory tour, playing celebratory games all across the country.

During the victory tour, Abby Wambach would play her last game on the national team. She began to contemplate life in retirement. She had won Olympic gold medals, twice. She'd won the World Cup. She had also been named FIFA Player of the Year. She scored 184 international goals, an astounding seventy-seven of the goals from her head. But like many women in America and around the world, Abby's retirement looked bleak.

Low wages during a women's career add up to lower income at retirement, according to a 2016 report by the U.S. Congress. In fact, the median annual income for women in the United States sixty-five years and older was $14,000 less than for men of the same age. Abby and her wife were in a precarious financial situation, as well. She wondered, "How will I support myself and Sarah, and our family? What can an aging athlete with an unfinished degree in leisure management do?"

As the tour neared the end, the women found themselves in Honolulu, Hawaii, preparing for a game. When the women walked onto the field in Aloha Stadium to practice, they could not believe their eyes. The field was old, shabby artificial turf that had not been replaced in years. There were gaps in the seams with pieces buckling. Tiny sharp-edged rocks stuck up. U.S. Soccer, which vetted every field before the men's national team played on it, hadn't checked this one.

In fact, in 2015, the women's national team had played fifteen games on artificial turf. The men's team had played none. Even when both teams played at the same turf stadiums, the women played on the artificial surface, while the fields were covered with grass for the men.

Once again, the women found themselves in the "absurd position of being the best in the world while being treated like amateurs," Megan Rapinoe said. They were done with bringing in the crowds, wowing the media and sponsors, and winning, time and time again, with working conditions and compensation never improving.

Soccer blogger Ryan Rosenblatt called the disparity between how U.S. Soccer handled field choice for men and women clear as day. "Argue all you want about turf or grass, even temporary grass," he wrote. "That discussion is not this discussion. This discussion is about sexism, and it's blatant. U.S. Soccer treats their men's team one way and the women another."

The women left the field in Honolulu after just thirty minutes of practice. Outraged, they told reporters that the field was subpar and dangerous and that they wouldn't play on it. In an open letter, signed by every member of the team, they wrote, "We have become so accustomed to playing on whatever surface is put in front of us. But we need to realize that our protection—our safety—is priority number one."

Coach Jill Ellis backed the decision, players tweeted pictures, and this time U.S. Soccer could not ignore them. Just twenty-four hours before kickoff, the federation canceled the game and refunded the tickets, disappointing 15,000 fans.

Still, the victory tour was a resounding success. More than 44,000 fans gathered in Pittsburgh, Pennsylvania, to see the women play. They sold out the stadium in Chattanooga, Tennessee. A crowd of 36,000 packed the stadium in Birmingham, Alabama. Abby's last game was played in front of a record crowd of 32,950 in New Orleans, Louisiana.

At the various venues, commemorative hats, shirts, warmups, zipper jackets, and scarves flew off the shelves, with the money lining U.S. Soccer's pockets.

The women's team was bringing in more and more revenue, and yet the players could not get U.S. Soccer to budge on pay or working conditions. They needed a powerful new advocate to help them.

A More Perfect Union

2015

"Everybody seems to be making money off our victory but us," the USWNT told thirty-one-year-old consultant Rebecca (Becca) Roux when she first met with them. Becca had been a fan of the team since 1999 when, at age fourteen, she attended the World Cup semifinal against Brazil in person. More recently, she had been in the stadium for the exciting 2015 World Cup final, watching in awe as the team scored four goals in the first sixteen minutes. When Becca's bosses at McKinsey consulting asked if anyone was willing to work with the team as a pro bono, or free, project, Becca volunteered. "These women are my heroes," Becca thought. "I want to help them."

Becca reviewed the history of the battle. She noted that in the early years of the U.S. Women's National Team, each player had a separate contract with their employer, U.S. Soccer. Coming off their big win in the 1999 World Cup, the team thought they could do much better facing the federation as a united group. In 2000, the players created a union called the U.S. Women's National Team Players Association so they could negotiate together for one contract, called a collective bargaining agreement, or CBA. But the union didn't seem to be having much impact. And after the big World Cup win in 2015, the women were still desperate to improve their financial situation.

Becca dug into the dynamics of compensation in sports. She realized that sports that paid athletes well had a balance of power between owners and players. In this situation, that balance was skewed. Even though U.S. Soccer was a nonprofit with a mission to support the growth of soccer in the United States, it had complete power over the women's and men's national teams.

Behind the scenes, Becca vowed to find a way to change that.

Stepping Up Their Game

Early 2016

Riding high after winning the World Cup in Canada—and feeling low after their treatment during the victory tour—the women worked with Becca Roux on a new approach. They would try to better harness their own power for this off-field fight.

At union meetings, the players decided that rather than just relying on their lawyers, the team would have their shrewdest women—defenders Becky Sauerbrunn and Meghan Klingenberg and forward Christen Press—act as players' reps in the room during any contract negotiations. Alex Morgan and Megan Rapinoe were already media darlings. They would be more proactive and tell the world about their unequal pay and working conditions. They encouraged young players to get involved too, taking up the mic if they felt comfortable.

The media blitz began, and Megan made the argument that investing in the women's team was simply good business sense. "The women's game can make money," she pointed out in an interview. "It's proven. It's not a handout."

They brought in Jeffrey Kessler, an attorney with a long history of representing players' unions, to join their current union lawyer, Rich Nichols, to help with the collective bargaining negotiations. On January 4, 2016, the negotiating team, lawyers, and players together presented U.S. Soccer with a proposal that was essentially equal pay for equal work. The proposal stated that "the various bonus payments to be paid to the WNT players shall EQUAL the bonuses to be paid the USMNT," among other things.

U.S. Soccer said equal pay was off the table and called the women "irrational," a label tagged on women for years as a way of undermining them.

Jeffrey Kessler, who is broad-shouldered with pale round cheeks and a wide smile, told Matt Lauer of *Today*, "Now that might be a good answer in 1816. It's not an acceptable answer in 2016."

U.S. Soccer put the negotiating team through what Jeffrey called "the poverty presentation." They reviewed their financials—describing the costs they faced running coaches' trainings and youth teams—and concluded with, "Well, we don't have any money" and "You're not really generating the revenue to deserve equal pay."

While it was true that revenue from the men's team had been historically higher, it was also true that the men's team had been around a lot longer and that U.S. Soccer put more marketing dollars behind them. Also, the women and their lawyers pointed out that things were shifting. The women's 2015 World Cup final drew the largest U.S. television audience ever for a soccer match—men's or women's. And U.S. Soccer was a nonprofit, not a for-profit company. With a mission to expand soccer, shouldn't they be riding the wave of excitement around the women's team and pushing toward equality instead of waiting for revenues to get there first?

The arguments fell on deaf ears.

Observers surmised that the men who ran U.S. Soccer, who grew up playing and watching men's soccer, couldn't imagine a world where men's and women's soccer were treated equally. They considered the women's team a nice thing to do, not a serious endeavor. To them, the women's success and popularity was probably just a blip.

The team realized that the cycle of asking and being told no again and again was getting them nowhere. They wanted to get tougher. "You can't go into a campaign worrying about whether people will like you," Megan said. "This is a problem for women. We're socialized to fear being disliked. In any encounter, the burden of social ease often falls on us. We're not supposed to make trouble, and it stops us from getting—or even asking for—what we want."

So the legal team made some trouble. The players' contract had expired years before, in 2012. Instead of a new contract, the women had been working under a memorandum of understanding that updated some terms of the contract. Lawyer Rich Nichols pointed out to U.S. Soccer that the memorandum of understanding could be terminated at any time. Thus, the no-strike clause in the expired contract would not bind the players anymore.

U.S. Soccer, worried about the upcoming Olympics, asked the players' union to agree in writing not to strike in 2016. The union refused.

Then U.S. Soccer dropped a legal bombshell.

U.S. Soccer Sues

2016

On February 3, 2016, the federation filed a lawsuit against the women's team, maintaining that the women were bound by the no-strike clause of the original contract. Rich Nichols told the *New York Times* that "there were no threats about strikes." The players just wanted things equalized before the SheBelieves Cup in March, and they weren't about to sign away their rights.

The women, who were gathering in Texas for some Olympic qualifying games, found this escalation—taking them to court—to be galling. Did U.S. Soccer even realize that they had filed suit against the women's team on National Girls and Women in Sports Day? Did they realize that the women were fighting for equality in pay and working conditions not just for themselves, but for girls coming up the ranks behind them?

The next day, their outrage exploded. U.S. Soccer had included in their court documents the personal home addresses of twenty-eight players and the personal email addresses of stars such as Carli Lloyd, Alex Morgan, Hope Solo, Megan Rapinoe, and Becky Sauerbrunn. "The players are very, very upset," Megan told the press. "We feel disrespected. We feel that our personal information, our privacy, and our safety was handled frivolously and with real negligence."

U.S. Soccer apologized, said it was a clerical error, and redacted the personal information and refiled the complaint. But U.S. Soccer's behavior was galvanizing the players.

An Audacious Idea

February 2016

A few days later, journalist Jonathan Tannenwald of the *Philadelphia Inquirer* published an article picking apart an annual report quietly released by U.S. Soccer. It showed that U.S. Soccer had expected a $420,000 loss for 2016, but revised their numbers to show an $18 million profit, mostly from the women's World Cup victory tour. The report also showed that U.S. Soccer projected the women's team to earn more than $5 million in 2017, while the men's team was expected to lose $1 million.

When Rich Nichols read the story, he "couldn't believe" his eyes.

All along he'd suspected that no matter how much the U.S. touted the men's team, it was no longer as valuable as the women's team. The report was just what the women needed.

In the next negotiating session, Rich brought up the report.

U.S. Soccer called the women's profitability an aberration.

"An aberration?" Rich probed. "Aberrations don't occur multiple years in a row. Aberrations aren't projected. You guys have projected profitability. You projected that the women would bring in more than the men."

U.S. Soccer countered that in the previous four-year World Cup cycle—when the women went to the finals against Japan in 2011 and the men made the round of sixteen in 2014—the men brought in more revenue.

But that was purely due to FIFA paying unequal prize money.

The women and their lawyers argued that two wrongs don't make a right. FIFA winnings went to U.S. Soccer, and U.S. Soccer decided how to spend the money. The federation could distribute windfalls any way it wanted, including equally or unequally among the teams. Further, the contract negotiations were not for the past; they were for the future, when U.S. Soccer itself projected increasing revenues on the women's side.

Would nothing convince U.S. Soccer to change their thinking on equal pay?

Rich Nichols and Jeffrey Kessler had an idea. The national team was gathered in Orlando, Florida, for a training camp. The lawyers invited the five players on the collective bargaining committee to join them in a conference call.

Jeffrey described a radical new approach. What if the women filed a complaint with the federal agency that enforced anti-discrimination laws at work? The Equal Employment Opportunity Commission (EEOC) could tell U.S. Soccer that the unequal pay was against that law. That could change everything.

Only one player needed to file the complaint, he explained. Did the women think it was a good idea, and was anyone willing to stick her neck out?

The five women—co-captains Carli Lloyd and Becky Sauerbrunn, star forward Alex Morgan, star midfielder Megan Rapinoe, and star goalie Hope Solo—pelted the lawyers with questions. Becky had never really had a contentious relationship with anyone before and found the prospect "nerve-racking." Alex worried about being distracted from the game and about what repercussions they might suffer.

It was a scary step to take, and it could affect the whole team. The women decided they only wanted to move forward if a majority of players were on board.

The Players Meet

Early 2016

At a training camp in Texas, the leaders called an all-player team meeting.

The leaders presented the EEOC complaint strategy. The reaction was varied. Some applauded the idea. Others asked, What if the federation just digs its heels in deeper? What if it finds a way to retaliate against the players it thinks are the leaders?

What if U.S. Soccer shut down the team? There was only one women's national team. It wasn't as if the women could just find a job like this elsewhere if things got nasty.

The discussions went round and round.

Finally the team took a straw poll. Every player backed the idea.

The leaders told their lawyers that all five players on the negotiating committee wanted to do it.

"You're kidding me," Rich Nichols said.

They were most certainly not kidding.

The Five

March 2016

On March 31, 2016, Alex Morgan, Becky Sauerbrunn, Carli Lloyd, Hope Solo, and Megan Rapinoe each filed a formal complaint with the federal Equal Employment Opportunity Commission(EEOC). Each complaint was a simple one-page form with CHARGE OF DISCRIMINATION on the top. After some contact information, the form said DISCRIMINATION BASED ON and the women checked SEX and noted "Equal pay."

Each player attached a three-page description of their particulars: how long they had been an employee of U.S. Soccer, the accomplishments of the team, and the viewership and revenue the team brought in. To win a charge of discrimination, the players had to establish that the men's and women's work was substantially similar, so they detailed the work expected of players on both the women's and the men's teams, noting that they both had to:

- maintain their conditioning and overall health such as by undergoing rigorous training routines (endurance running, weight training, etc.) and adhering to certain nutrition, physica therapy, and other regimens.
- maintain their skills by, for example, attending training camps and frequent practices, participating in skills drills, and playing scrimmages and other practice events.

- travel nationally and internationally as necessary for competitive games, which are the same in length, physical and mental demand, and playing environment and conditions.
- promote a positive image for soccer through media and other appearances.

But the women noted a big difference. "The success of the WNT [women's national team], however, has meant and continues to mean that we spend more time in training camp, play far more games, travel more, and participate in more media sessions, among other things, than MNT [men's national team] players," the complaint said. And rather than being compensated more, the women were paid less.

The players included damning statistics.

Winning a non-tournament "friendly" match meant payment of $1,350 for a woman and $9,375 to $17,625 for a man.

Making a World Cup roster meant $15,000 for a woman and $68,750 for a man.

Winning a World Cup brought each women a $75,000 bonus. If the men had won, the bonus would have been $390,000.

Women got $3,000 for a sponsor appearance, while the men earned $3,750.

For international travel, women were allocated $60 per day for expenses, while men got $75.

The women's team accumulated $1.20 for each ticket sold at a U.S. Soccer-organized match; the men's team earned $1.50 per ticket.

The five signed and dated and submitted the forms. That was it.

Jeffrey called it "the strongest case for pay discrimination that I have ever seen."

But would it work?

EEOC COMPLAINT PAY COMPARISON

Sponsor appearance

WNT: $3,000

MNT: $3,750

Per diem

WNT: $60

MNT: $75

Payment per ticket sold

WNT: $1.20 to team

MNT: $1.50 to team

Losing Twenty Friendly Games

WNT: $72,000

MNT: $100,000

Winning Twenty Friendly Games

WNT: $99,000

MNT: $263,320

World Cup Roster

WNT: $15,000

MNT: $68,750

Winning World Cup Gold Bonus

WNT: $75,000

MNT: $390,000

DANESHA ADAMS • MICHELLE AKERS • KORBIN ALBERT • HEATHER ALDAMA • AMY ALLMAN
YAEL AVERBUCH • SAMANTHA BAGGETT • BETHANY BALCER • NICOLE BARNHART • TRACEY BAT
TAMI BATISTA • JUSTI BAUMGARDT • LAKEYSIA BEENE • DEBBIE BELKIN • KEISHA BELL • DE
BENDER • JENNY BENSON • ANGELA BERRY • JACKIE BILLETT • KYLIE BIVENS • DANIELLE BORGM
SHANNON BOXX • DENISE BOYER-MURDOCH • JEN BRANAM • AMBER BROOKS • THORI (STAF
BRYAN • TARA BUCKLEY • SHERI BUETER • SUSAN BUSH • LORI BYLIN • JANE CAMPBELL •
CASSELLA • LORI CHALUPNY • BRANDI CHASTAIN • MANDY CLEMENS • SAM COFFEY • DAN
COLAPRICO • LISA COLE • ROBIN CONFER • KERRY CONNORS • KIM CONWAY • ALANA COOK • ANN C
• PAM (BAUGHMAN) CORNELL • STEPHANIE (LOPEZ) COX • ALEISHA CRAMER • AMANDA CROMW
• COLETTE CUNNINGHAM • ABBY DAHLKEMPER • MARIAN DALMY • TIERNA DAVIDSON • CINDY D
• SAVANNAH DEMELO • MICHELLE DEMKO • KRISTI DEVERT • TINA DIMARTINO • IMANI DORS
BETSY DRAMBOUR • TRACY (NOONAN) DUCAR • JOAN DUNLAP-SEIVOLD • CRYSTAL DUNN • DAN
EGAN • TINA (FRIMPONG) ELLERTSON • WHITNEY ENGEN • STACEY ENOS • JULIE (JOHNSTON)
• RONNIE FAIR • LORRIE FAIR • JOY (BIEFELD) FAWCETT • KAREN FERGUSON • JESSICA FISCH
MIA FISHEL • KENDALL FLETCHER • MEREDITH FLORANCE • DANIELLE (GARRETT) FOTOPOUL
JULIE FOUDY • EMILY FOX • ADRIANNA FRANCH • MICHELLE FRENCH • CARIN (JENNINGS) GABA
• LINDA GANCITANO • MORGAN (BRIAN) GAUTRAT • WENDY GEBAUER • GRETCHEN GEGG • NA
GIRMA • LISA GMITTER • CINDY GORDON • SANDI GORDON • JEN GRUBB • SARAH HAGEN • KRIS
HAMILTON • LINDA HAMILTON • MIA HAMM • HALEY HANSON • RUTH HARKER • ASHLYN HARR
MARY HARVEY • ASHLEY HATCH • DEVVYN HAWKINS • TUCKA HEALY • TOBIN HEATH • APRIL HEINR
• HOLLY HELLMUTH • LORI HENRY • SHANNON HIGGINS • JAELENE HINKLE • LAUREN (CHE
HOLIDAY • LINDSEY HORAN • JAELIN HOWELL • ANGELA HUCLES • SOFIA HUERTA • SARAH HUFF
• LINDSEY HUIE • PATTY IRIZARRY • MARCI (MILLER) JOBSON • LAURA JONES • NATASHA K
CHRISTINA KAUFMAN • BETH KELLER • DEBBIE KELLER • SHERRILL KESTER • AUBREY KINGSB
• MEGHAN KLINGENBERG • JENA KLUEGEL • TAYLOR KORNIECK • NANCY KRAMARZ • ANNA KR
• ALI KRIEGER • CASEY (SHORT) KRUEGER • JENNIFER LALOR • ROSE LAVELLE • AMY LEPEI

PART II
The Second Half

If they don't give you a seat at the table,
bring a folding chair.

—Former U.S. Congresswoman Shirley Chisholm

YDNEY LEROUX • GINA LEWANDOWSKI • KRISTINE LILLY • KELLY LINDSEY • LORI LINDSEY •
LI LLOYD • JOANNA LOHMAN • ALLIE LONG • JILL LOYDEN • KRISTIN LUCKENBILL • CATARINA
CARIO • HAILIE MACE • SHANNON MACMILLAN • HOLLY MANTHEI • KATE (SOBRERO) MARKGRAF
LY MARQUAND • ELLA MASAR • JEN (STREIFFER) MASCARO • KIM MASLIN-KAMMERDEINER
ERRITT MATHIAS • STEPHANIE MCCAFFREY • MEGAN MCCARTHY • SAVANNAH MCCASKILL •
CIA MCDERMOTT • JESSICA MCDONALD • TEGAN MCGRADY • JEN MEAD • KRISTIE MEWIS •
ANTHA MEWIS • TIFFENY MILBRETT • [illegible] • MARY-FRANCES MONROE • ALEX MORGAN
IVIA MOULTRIE • SIRI MULLINIX • CASEY MURPHY • ALYSSA NAEHER • CHRISTINE NAIRN • NATALIE
TON • JENNA NIGHSWONGER • [illegible] EALIA OHAI • KELLEY O'HARA •
LY OLEKSIUK • HEATHER O'REILLY • LAUREN ORLANDOS • ANN ORRISON • LESLIE OSBORNE • CARLA
RDEN) OVERBECK • MEGAN OYSTER • JAIME PAGLIARULO • CINDY PARLOW CONE • TAMMY PEARMAN
MILY PICKERING • CARSON PICKETT • LOUELLEN POORE • CHRISTEN PRESS • NANDI PRYCE
MIDGE PURCE • CAROLINE PUTZ • SARAH RAFANELLI • CHRISTIE (PEARCE) RAMPONE •
SSA RAMSEY • SARA RANDOLPH • MEGAN RAPINOE • KERI (SANCHEZ) RAYGOR • SHARON
MURTRY) REMER • KATHY RIDGEWELL • STEPHANIE RIGAMAT • TIFFANY ROBERTS • LEIGH
ROBINSON • TRINITY RODMAN • AMY RODRIGUEZ • SHAUNA ROHBOCK • CHRISTY ROWE •
RUTTEN • ASHLEY SANCHEZ • BECKY SAUERBRUNN • KELLY (WILSON) SCHMEDES • MEGHAN
NUR • LAURA SCHOTT • LAURIE SCHWOY • BRIANA SCURRY • NIKKI SERLENGA • JAEDYN
W • DANIELLE SLATON • GAYLE SMITH • SOPHIA SMITH • TAYLOR SMITH • HOPE SOLO •
LY SONNETT • ZOLA SPRINGER • AMY STEADMAN • JILL STEWART • JENNIFER STRONG •
I SULLIVAN • MALLORY PUGH SWANSON • JANINE SZPARA • LINDSAY TARPLEY • BRITTANY
LOR • ALYSSA THOMPSON • CHRIS TOMEK • RITA TOWER • INDIA TROTTER • ERIKA TYMRAK
ACHEL (BUEHLER) VAN HOLLEBEKE • TISHA VENTURINI • M.A. VIGNOLA • ALY WAGNER • KELLY
LBERT • ABBY WAMBACH • MARCIE WARD • MORGAN WEAVER • SASKIA WEBBER • KRISTEN
SS • CHRISTIE WELSH • SARA WHALEN • KACEY WHITE • CAT (REDDICK) WHITEHILL • LYNN
LIAMS • STACI WILSON • ANGIE WOZNUK • KIM WYANT • VERONICA ZEPEDA • MCCALL ZERBONI

The Media Reacts

March 2016

Filing a complaint with the Equal Employment Opportunity Commission is like asking detectives to look into a crime. In the case of the five U.S. national team players, it kicked off an investigation into whether U.S. Soccer had violated civil rights laws against employment discrimination. The women hoped the EEOC would find a violation and require U.S. Soccer to equalize compensation.

They also wanted the world to pay more attention to the vast disparities they and other women faced. In a press release about the complaint, the players explained that they had been waiting patiently for years for fair compensation, that it was clear to them that U.S. Soccer had no intention of offering equal pay, and that they felt they had no choice but to take their fight to the federal government.

Alex Morgan pointed out that the problem was deeper than pay. "We want to play in top-notch, grass-only facilities like the U.S. Men's National Team. We want to have equitable and comfortable travel accommodations, and we simply want equal treatment.

"Every single day, we sacrifice just as much as the men," she said. "We work just as much. We endure just as much physically and emotionally."

The EEOC office was flooded with inquiries about the complaint from press all across the globe. *Sports Illustrated* called the move "a bombshell." *Washington Post* columnist Sally Jenkins described the filing as "a turning point."

"A topic can sit in plain sight for years and no one works up much outrage about it, but then the right story comes along, and it hits a throbbing national nerve," she wrote. "What this team's chronic struggle for decent pay shows is that gender bias is so baked into our culture that the discrepancy can't be corrected by slow evolution, or friendly negotiation. They've tried that. A shock to the system—the legal system—was required."

The columnist pointed to how widespread the problem was, how it was "one of the most stubborn facts in American life." She made it personal too, sharing that female journalists earned eighty-three cents for every dollar male reporters earned. For the U.S. workforce on average, women made eighty cents for every dollar men earned. That figure dropped to sixty-five cents for Black women, and just fifty-eight cents for Hispanic women.

Christine Brennan of *USA Today* wrote that of the thirty-five sports that pay prize money for major tournaments, twenty-five pay men and women equally, while ten have a pay gap. In soccer, though, she called it a "chasm, not a gap.

"One might be able to understand these kinds of differences if it were the U.S. men who won Olympic and World Cup titles, who drew the off-the-charts TV ratings, who played the long victory tours in front of tens of thousands of adoring young fans," she wrote. "But it's not the U.S. men who do that. It's the U.S. women."

She also reminded readers that U.S. Soccer was not a corporation with a profit-making motive. It was a nonprofit. "It's also a matter of the mission of a national governing body like U.S. Soccer to promote and grow its game," she pointed out.

Kevin Baxter of the *Los Angeles Times* recognized the selfless quality of the women's effort. After all, four of the five players leading the complaint were at least thirty years old, nearing the end of their soccer careers. "Whatever victories the team wins . . . will provide only limited benefits [for them]," he pointed out.

Still, the broader impacts could be huge. "The world's most popular women's team has again taken us to a place that transcends sports and becomes part of our national dialogue," Christine Brennan of *USA Today* noted.

Male Players React

March 2016

"None of us saw it coming," USMNT goalkeeper Tim Howard admitted to the *New York Times* when asked about the women's complaint.

Like many of the women, Tim had had a long and winding journey to his place on the national team. As a kid, Tim hated school. He had trouble sitting still and focusing. The long hours in the classroom, he wrote, "were what I had to do until I could burst into the open air and get to do things that really mattered: sports." He suffered from Tourette's syndrome and obsessive-compulsive disorder, and his mind barraged him with commands to pick up rocks, do things in an exact order, or touch a person before speaking to them.

Being on the soccer field in the goal was different. When the ball was far away, his mind still bossed him around. "Touch the ground," it said, "twitch, snap the Velcro on the goalie glove, cough, touch the goalpost, blink." But everything changed when the ball approached the goal. All the tics and orders disappeared. It was just him and the ball. Tim's conditions also gave him a compulsion to practice, a strong ability to focus, and keen perception.

All this made him a stand-out goalie, who started for the men's national team in the 2010 and 2014 World Cups. In a game against Belgium, Tim stopped a whopping fifteen goals and became a phenom. Memes of what Tim Howard could block—asteroids, hurricanes, and shark attacks—swept the internet.

Though previously unaware of the female athletes' situation, he immediately got behind their complaint. "Any time, no matter the gender or the race, if someone feels they are underpaid, it is a problem, and I feel they should fight for their rights, no matter what," he told the press.

The reporter wondered if the comparisons of the women's pay, and their success, to the men's pay, and their shortcomings, made him uncomfortable. "As we all know, there are lots of factors that go into labor negotiations," Tim said. "When it comes to arguing those points, every factor and reason and excuse is going to be unearthed." Also, Tim had an eight-year-old daughter who played soccer. He loved how feisty Alivia was, and when he imagined her grown up and in labor negotiations, he hoped her spiritedness and strength would show up there too.

Tim also told the press to take seriously the women's concerns about off-the-pitch factors like per diems and travel conditions. "I'm not sure if those outside sport would recognize . . . there's a lot of factors that go into helping a team win." To prepare for a big game, athletes need to be well rested, well fed, with bodies and minds loose, relaxed, and ready.

Tim aired his support on social media as well, tweeting, "We understand and appreciate USWNT's fight."

Landon Donovan, captain of the U.S. men's national team, wrote on Twitter that USWNT "deserves to be treated fairly in all ways."

Other members of the men's team were not so vocal. An *NBC Sports* commentator noted that the women's complaint put the men's team in "an awkward position." Some of the men were close friends with the women's team players and probably privately supported their fight. But U.S. Soccer also controlled the men's team, so players "may find it difficult to come out and publicly support the U.S. women's team."

Indeed, when the website *Deadspin* later asked members of the men's team to comment on the women's battle for equal pay, they all declined to respond or said, "No comment."

U.S. Soccer, though, had to respond to the EEOC complaint, whether it wanted to or not.

Best Paid in the World

March 2016

U.S. Soccer's first public statement on the EEOC complaint sounded like a parent scolding a child. It said the organization was "disappointed" in the team. "We think very highly of the women's national team, and we want to compensate them fairly, and we'll sit down and work through that with them when all of this settles down," U.S. Soccer's president Sunil Gulati told reporters.

U.S. Soccer soon filed its twenty-page legal defense with the EEOC. The U.S. Women's National Team, it said, were among the best-compensated female players in the world. Their compensation was comparable to or better than the men's compensation. "Any differences in compensation paid to MNT and WNT players are driven by factors other than gender," they argued. They asked for the charges to be dismissed.

The women's team had no idea whether or not the EEOC complaint would come to anything. If the agency dismissed the complaint, the women could go no further. Or the EEOC could rule in their favor and force U.S. Soccer to pay the women equally. Or it could refuse to rule but allow the women to file a lawsuit in federal court.

While the EEOC did its work reviewing documents and interviewing players and U.S. Soccer officials, the women had to train for the upcoming Olympics in Brazil—or make the difficult decision not to go in protest.

To Strike or Not to Strike?

Spring 2016

As the women contemplated striking, they had a lot to consider, for the short term and in the long run. If they did strike, they would miss the chance to be the first team ever to win a World Cup and an Olympic gold consecutively. Sitting out the Olympics might also jeopardize their growing fan base and future corporate sponsorships.

"This is not something I take lightly—I want to play in the Olympics—but I stand with my team, and what my team decides to do is what I'll decide," Alex Morgan told the press. "What we're fighting for is bigger than us and women's sports; it's about women receiving dollar for dollar, not seventy-nine cents to the dollar."

In early May 2016, U.S. Soccer presented the women's team with a new proposal. It was a pay-to-play approach, where the women would be paid the same amount as the men's team for being called into a training camp, the same per diem fee, the same fees for appearing in friendly matches, and the same slice of ticket revenues. But the bonuses for winning or tying friendly matches and for World Cup matches were lower than what the men's team had in their contract.

Though an improvement, the offer was far from equal and did not resolve the conflict. The women and their lawyers were both surprised and not surprised at U.S. Soccer's intransigence. After all, U.S. Soccer could offer whatever they wanted as long as they had all the power.

Female soccer players who aspired to playing for a national team had nowhere else to go.

On June 1, the women made a proposal that would give them some security. While the men's team made hefty base salaries playing on their professional teams, the women's professional league was still in its infancy, and salaries were miniscule. The women asked U.S. Soccer for a minimum compensation of $5,000 per national team game, like members of the men's team earned. But if a minimum of twenty games were not scheduled, a set number of women would still be paid a minimum annual guaranteed compensation of $100,000. The minimum payment would continue in the event of injury. The women players also asked for a year of health insurance after their guaranteed position was offered to a different player. The rest of the compensation, including bonuses, should be the same as the men's team.

U.S. Soccer called the proposal "not acceptable."

The women were incredibly frustrated that they were getting nowhere. Then on June 3, 2016, they suffered another blow. The judge ruled on U.S. Soccer's lawsuit, determining that the athletes were bound by the no-strike clause from the 2013 agreement. No matter how unhappy they were, the women could not strike until their memorandum of understanding expired at the end of the year. But come January 1, 2017, they would be free to walk out.

An Angry Icon

Summer 2016

On July 16, 2016, ABC and ESPN honored Abby Wambach with the prestigious Excellence in Sports Performance Yearly (ESPY) Icon Award.

Like the Academy Awards for movies, the ESPY Icon ceremony was a glamourous event, featuring a huge stage with sparkling lights, larger-than-life images of the athletes, and an audience decked out in gowns and tuxedos.

Abby had scored more professional goals—184—than anyone of any gender in the history of professional soccer. One of the best soccer players of all time, Abby stood between Peyton Manning, considered one of the best quarterbacks of all time, and Kobe Bryant, one of the greatest basketball players of all time. All three received sleek silver statues, gave short speeches, and walked off the stage together to thunderous applause.

The experience should have felt amazing. But it didn't.

"Why do I feel so pissed off?" Abby wondered. "Why do I feel so angry right now?"

She considered her situation in relation to the other honorees. "We made the same sacrifices. We shed the same amount of blood, sweat, and tears. We'd left it all on the field for decades, with the same ferocity, talent, and commitment. But our retirements wouldn't be the same at all."

Unlike Kobe, who made $330 million for playing for the L.A. Lakers, and Peyton, who made close to $250 million playing for the NFL, Abby hadn't made enough money in her career to be able to support herself for the rest of her life.

Abby knew that the NBA and NFL were big business with superstar salaries. American soccer had not yet won the kind of fan base that those sports garnered. Still, she was on stage being celebrated as a top "iconic" athlete in an incredibly popular sport. More than 40 million Americans played soccer, and millions more watched. Soccer had risen to become the fourth most popular sport in the country. Yet her career pay gave her no cushion for retirement. The contrast was stark and painful. "My biggest concern was how I was going to freaking find a new job to pay my mortgage," she realized.

Meanwhile, as the current USWNT ramped up training for the Brazil Olympics, they continued to push for equality. The players made T-shirts and temporary tattoos declaring EQUAL PLAY EQUAL PAY and wore them at media events. They blasted #equalplayequalpay messages on their social media platforms.

In July, players' attorney Rich Nichols nudged the federation again, writing in an email, "We want the SAME PAY PER GAME compensation as the MNT. This is a legal requirement, and we should not even have to bargain for the USSF to comply with the law."

"We would prefer to not have to deal with this," Megan Rapinoe told the *New York Times*. "But we're not going to shy away from it either." Just before the Olympics, Megan read a letter she had written to herself at age thirteen. "If you are feeling uncomfortable about speaking out about something, instead of doing it for yourself, do it for someone else," she had written. "Do it for the people, or the cause, that you are standing up for. Sometimes it's just bigger than you."

Brazil Olympics

August 5–12, 2016

Team USA arrived in Rio de Janeiro, Brazil, heavily favored to take home their fourth straight Olympic gold medal. The team easily sailed through the group stage to the quarterfinals against Sweden.

When the opening whistle blew, the U.S. came on confident, skilled, and strong. Alex Morgan took a shot just past the first minute, but it was kicked away. At minute two, she deflected a pass and missed the goal by inches. The U.S. blasted another shot in the third minute; the Swedish goalkeeper tapped it over the post. The rest of the half, the Americans controlled the ball, pressing to goal relentlessly. But Sweden had locked down their defense, and the half ended scoreless. It felt like bumping up against a brick wall, again and again, not unlike their negotiations with U.S. Soccer.

In the second half, the U.S. again hammered toward the goal. Sweden got physical, fouling attackers once, twice, three, then four times, with clips, trips, and pushes from behind. The ref awarded free kicks, but the U.S. couldn't penetrate to score.

Then, in the sixth minute of the second half, something unexpected happened. The U.S. had been on the attack again, with the defenders pushed up high, when Sweden grabbed the ball. A long, solid kick split the last two defenders. Sweden's Stina Blackstenius met the ball at sprint pace, touched it toward the goal, and scored.

Desperate to tie it up, Kelley O'Hara took a shot that soared over the goal. Eighteen-year-old Mallory Pugh Swanson shot, and it flew high and wide. Mallory crossed the ball in front of the goal and failed to connect. Carli Lloyd missed a header.

In the seventy-sixth minute, a long ball from far in the back lofted in front of the goal. Crystal Dunn leapt for a header. It deflected off her into the face of the defender, where it deflected again, into the path of Alex Morgan. She slid it in for the equalizer.

Regulation time ended 1–1. The teams had been battling for more than ninety minutes, with little to show for it but exhaustion and bruises.

Still, in overtime, the U.S. continued to press aggressively, and Sweden continued to lock them out. With just minutes remaining, the powerful and wily Crystal Dunn crossed a ball to Carli Lloyd. Carli met it perfectly in the air and knocked it into the back of the net. Falling back to the ground, she took a Swedish defender with her. Just as Carli popped up to celebrate the goal, the referee blew the whistle. FOUL! No goal!

Moments later, the Swedes also had a goal called back by the ref. The game went to penalty kicks.

Alex Morgan was first in the lineup. After a few quick steps, she took a shot, but Swedish keeper Hedvig Lindahal anticipated correctly and blocked the ball. Starting a round of penalty kicks with a disadvantage like this was brutal.

The next four kicks were goals, as expected. The score was 2–2.

U.S. goalkeeper Hope Solo took a strong dive high toward the upper corner of the goal and blocked the next Swedish attempt. The teams were still tied .

Two more kicks went in as expected. The score was tied 3–3, and each team had one more kick left.

Forward Christen Press stepped up for the U.S. She took a long run up and blasted the shot. But it soared over the top of the goal.

If Sweden scored on their next attempt, it would all be over. Swedish player Lisa Dahlkvist picked up the ball and walked to the penalty spot. She kissed the ball and placed it carefully on the grass. She stepped back to line up for the kick.

Suddenly U.S. keeper Hope Solo called for a time-out. Her glove was torn, she said, and she needed to replace it. The Americans would use every tool at their disposal to win this, including an equipment delay. Lisa grinned confidently as Hope slowly stripped off the gloves while a trainer ran onto the field with replacements. Hope slid them on, wiggled them into place, and took her stance on the goal line. The ref blew the whistle.

The Swedish player calmly shot, targeting the ball low and to the right. Hope misjudged and leapt in the other direction. Sweden won 4–3 in penalty kicks.

The U.S. athletes were stunned. It was the first time the U.S. women's soccer team would not take home any medal from the Olympics. Some collapsed in defeat. As former champion Julie Foudy said on ESPN2, a loss like this "just burns and burns for years and years and never goes away."

After the Olympics, the team attempted to resolve the pay dispute once again. But discussions did not go well. In October, U.S. Soccer president Sunil Gulati claimed that the women's request for equal pay, especially the World Cup bonuses that were so high for the men's tournament, would "break" the organization.

They seemed at an impasse. "The only settlement was going to be equal pay," Jeffrey Kessler said. "Three-quarters is not equal, 80 percent is not equal, only equal is equal."

Contract negotiations ground to a halt. In December 2016, the players and the federation canceled five negotiating sessions. They couldn't even speak to each other.

Waking to the Problem

2016

Meanwhile, state legislatures began taking the gender pay gap problem in the country seriously. Some states held hearings on the issue to learn more. In spring of 2016, Michelle Ngwafon, a Black undergraduate at Howard University, testified in front of the Maryland State General Assembly about how the pay gap affected her and her future. She shared her dismay at learning that she'd likely make forty cents less for every dollar earned by the average man, no matter the field. "This translates into less money to pay off my student loans," she said. "Over the course of my career, I stand to lose $877,480 because of the wage gap.

"I was once told women should simply be more assertive, we should work harder and be better. And it's so hard not to just scream—women have worked hard forever. Women have been bettering themselves since the beginning of time," she said. "Equal pay isn't about women needing to do better; it's about society acknowledging it needs to do better."

That summer, Maryland, Delaware, and Massachusetts passed bills giving workers the right to discuss wages and salaries without punishment from employers. Transparency would help women negotiate and demand equal pay—because you can't address a gender pay gap if you can't see it.

Delaware, Massachusetts, and Oregon also passed provisions that barred employers from asking applicants for salary history. That would ensure that employers paid workers based on the value of a job, not on what an applicant earned in the past. These measures would prevent women from being locked into low salaries.

Around this time, some sleeping giants in the corporate world were awakening to the pay gap issue. In the spring of 2016, more than two dozen companies, including Gap, Pepsi, and American Airlines, took the Equal Pay Pledge, committing to review their pay by gender. By December, more than a hundred employers had signed the pledge, including AT&T, Mastercard, and Yahoo.

Companies were surprised at what they found when they looked at their books. Some discovered that pay gaps emerged because they had hired more men earlier in the history of their company, or because men were more successful in salary negotiations. The software company Salesforce ended up spending $3 million to equalize pay for their female employees. Jet.com created a ten-level compensation structure that would apply to everyone.

But all of this corporate work was purely voluntary. The vast majority of companies in the United States continued to operate as they always had, with women being paid less than men for the same work.

Worldwide Protests

January to March 2017

"Women's rights are HUMAN rights! Women's rights are HUMAN rights!"

On January 21, 2017, millions of people of all genders flooded into streets across the country to participate in the Women's March. Many carried brightly colored signs. One read WHY I MARCH: FOR MY MOTHER. FOR MY DAUGHTER. FOR MY SISTERS. FOR LOVE. Another said OUT OF THE MINIVAN AND INTO THE STREETS. Marchers in Los Angeles stretched for more than a quarter of a mile. In Phoenix, the diverse crowd yelled, "Tell me what America looks like! This is what America looks like."

Some thought the Women's March was a protest against the inauguration of President Donald J. Trump, who had been caught on camera saying "Grab 'em by the pussy." It was that and much more.

The platform for the Women's March, called "Guiding Vision and Definition of Principles," included statements on reproductive rights; LGBTQ, disability, and immigrant rights; and environmental justice. It also declared, "We believe in equal pay for equal work and the right of all women to be paid equitably. We must end the pay and hiring discrimination that women, particularly mothers, women of color, Indigenous women, lesbian, queer, and trans women still face each day in our nation."

On March 8, 2017, which was International Women's Day, another protest broke out. The international "A Day Without Women" protest posed the question, What would the world be like if women just refused to show up for work?

Women who were able took the day off. With many women out, schools closed. Restaurants that wanted to dramatize the importance of half of the workforce served only half of their menus. Ai-jen Poo, director of the National Domestic Workers Alliance, called the action an opportunity for women everywhere to say, "Women power this economy," and to "think together about how we might shape the future with that power."

Fighting for a Fair Contract

January to March 2017

Meanwhile, with negotiations still going nowhere, the U.S. women called a team meeting during a training camp in southern California. Becca Roux, who had become even more passionate about the plight of the USWNT, left her job at McKinsey consulting and took a substantial pay cut to lead the players' union.

Over her pro bono year, Becca had worked hard to establish the players' trust. She had texted the women individually, asking them to share their concerns. Many worried about the quality of their training and medical staff. Recovery from injury and brutal training was slowed by lack of access to massages and other therapy. The athletes also needed regular access to high-quality nutrition to fuel their bodies. But too often, the food was low quality. Sometimes the schedule for training and eating didn't mesh, so food would sit out for two hours before the players were available to eat it. Subpar transportation had them showing up to training camps and games exhausted. And yes, there was the never-ending problem of compensation.

Becca Roux offered much more than an ear for complaining. At the meetings she got the women talking to each other rather than just to her. In order to channel players' concerns into a call for action, she used a common McKinsey strategy. Players listed all their concerns on a poster board. Then each player placed three sticky dots on the issues they cared about most. There was a lot of agreement.

Becca Roux and the players discussed a vision for the team too. They began to think of themselves as a powerful start-up with enormous potential to be the most successful team in sports. One obstacle was that U.S. Soccer did not see them that way; it didn't value the team as highly as the women valued themselves.

The membership held union elections, picking three players, Becky Sauerbrunn, Christen Press, and Meghan Klingenberg, as union executives. They broadened the group of players who would negotiate the new contract to include Christen and Becky as well as Kelley O'Hara, Sam Mewis, Megan Rapinoe, and Alex Morgan. Other players got involved by working on engaging past players and getting new players up to speed. The goal was to involve as many players as possible and make the negotiations more player driven.

In February 2017, Becca Roux and the collective bargaining committee headed to New York City with their newfound focus and energy to restart talks with U.S. Soccer. They were ready to get creative with their proposals. It would not be simply a matter of the women asking for higher pay, U.S. Soccer countering with low pay, and the two groups settling somewhere in the middle. The players would base their proposals on their vision and their priorities.

The women began by asking for rates of pay at least equal to the men's team. Athletes at the top of their game and the top of their sport should not accept any less than what justice required, the team believed.

"Part of the problem for women is that when it comes to asking for raises, we've been socialized to not make 'selfish' demands," Megan Rapinoe said. "We can advocate for our families, or in the services of a cause or campaign, but if we're simply asking for our own money on our own behalf and because we have the temerity to believe we deserve it, we are liable to be called greedy." But money matters. It buys health care. It buys stability for players. It provides stability for families. It can buy a college education. It provides secure retirement. It buys freedom to relax or to spend time (and money) to make the world a better place. Why should men be the only ones to have those choices, that freedom?

U.S. Soccer said no to the women's first proposal. The mantra was the same: the team didn't deserve equal pay because historically they didn't bring in as much revenue as the men. Plus, U.S. Soccer said that equal pay would be too much of a burden on the organization financially, cutting into funds they wanted to allocate toward coaching or developing younger players.

The women tried another approach—revenue sharing, a creative idea the men also backed. The men's and women's teams would each get 35 percent of the revenue their team brought to U.S. Soccer. The women believed in themselves and their growing public appeal. It seemed like a possible win-win. U.S. Soccer would never have to pay the women more than a portion of what they brought in, so there was little financial risk. And the women were excited to turn their faith in themselves into growing earnings.

U.S. Soccer rejected the proposal too. "We're nonprofit," it said, "so we don't do revenue sharing."

Becca Roux was outraged. "You can't have it both ways," she said. "You can't say you won't do equal pay because of revenue and then, when we are willing to bet on ourselves, you won't do a revenue share." The women could tell that the real issue was not revenue. It was a complete refusal to equalize pay. "We weren't even operating in the same world yet," said Becca.

The resistance to equal pay was deeper than Becca expected. "I thought if you put a bunch of data in front of people and showed them their own bias that they'd see the light and get this done," she said.

But it would be much harder than that.

The next day the federation offered a totally different proposal, a combination of salaried players and players who would only be paid when they played. And the pay, as usual, was low compared to the men.

The women were frustrated but made a counterproposal with the same structure but with higher pay. U.S. Soccer turned it down.

Negotiations moved to Portland, Oregon. The two sides debated every line item, proposing changes, countering, making only slow incremental adjustments as they went. The whole process was becoming wearying, discouraging, and repetitive. "I think so many women can understand what this feeling is of going into a negotiation knowing equal pay is not on the table," Megan said, "knowing anywhere close to your male counterparts is not even on the table."

Becca Roux and the players on the collective bargaining committee wrangled over each word in the contract and planned out exactly what they would say in negotiations. At one point, Becca realized that U.S. Soccer thought that the women's group-licensing rights were worthless. Group licensing allows a company to use the name, image, and likeness of multiple players on a team for things like trading cards or video game characters. So the team asked to add ownership of those rights to their contract, hoping they could earn some money by selling them. U.S. Soccer agreed. The women asked whether U.S. Soccer thought the team could land more sponsors. The federation said no, so the women asked to control revenue from sponsorship categories, such as nutrition snacks, that had not already been sold. U.S. Soccer agreed.

"Sometimes you'd feel like you're making progress," Becca said. "Then you'd hit a snafu and you're like, 'We're never going to get this done.'"

Negotiations in Portland and, later, Chicago were dragging on. "There were some dark days," Becca said. "It's hard to get told to your face over and over again that you are not worth that much."

Hardball

Early 2017

U.S. Soccer put pressure on the team to come to agreement. They even scheduled negotiations while the team gathered outside Dallas for a training camp. "It was a shitty thing to do," Becca Roux said. Training camps were already high-pressure situations for players. With more athletes called for camp than would make rosters for matches and tournaments, camps were essentially high-stakes tryouts. So, while engaged in these negotiations, the players were also actively fighting for their jobs on the field.

The days were long and draining. The women faced demanding workouts and drills. Then, instead of resting and recovering, they hunched over papers at a conference table. Then they were off to afternoon training, followed by another session at the negotiating table, sometimes till midnight. To star defender Becky Sauerbrunn, it felt like an intense chess match.

But forcing the negotiations to happen at camp brought the players together in a way that U.S. Soccer hadn't anticipated. Instead of just the player reps showing up to negotiation sessions, the whole team gathered in the conference room around the long table. Donning matching T-shirts that said EQUALITY, they filled chairs along the wall surrounding the table. Alex Morgan, who was playing for a pro team in France, rang in. Midfielder Julie Ertz dialed in from her honeymoon.

Players who had not been in the negotiations before were shocked at the tone, how toxic it felt. After one session, a player approached

Becca Roux and said, "You are getting abused in there."

"It's okay," Becca replied. "As long as it's not turning toward you guys."

Back and forth went the discussion, for five hours on Saturday and six hours on Sunday. The player reps asked to increase the tournament bonuses. U.S. Soccer allowed them a few thousand more dollars per game but wouldn't go any higher. They made some progress on side issues such as equal per diems and equivalent travel and accommodations. But they couldn't agree on basic pay.

At one point, the women were scheduled to play in a scrimmage. U.S. Soccer president Sunil Gulati had a flight to catch and wanted the deal done before he left. "He physically stood in the door and tried to prevent the players from going to the scrimmage, doing their jobs," Becca Roux said. When he finally let the players go, the scrimmage did not go well.

With the contract still not resolved and the training camp over, the players scattered to their homes. Most of the women on the national team played for teams in the U.S. women's professional league, called the National Women's Soccer League, or in other new pro leagues around the world. But they remained united, discussing issues over the phone and via text message.

"Sometimes the suggestions arrived in an overnight email from forward Alex Morgan in France, or a late-night one from midfielder Megan Rapinoe on the West Coast," wrote Andrew Das of the *New York Times*. "They sent out anonymous surveys to their teammates, to better gauge what people prioritized but might not want to say aloud, and weighed in on legal language and PowerPoint slides in a cache of shared Google Docs."

Then the federation played hardball.

This is our last, best, and final offer, they said. Either you accept it immediately, or we shut down the team.

Concede or Strike?

April 2017

Facing a lockout, the women had to think strategy. If they stood their ground, they might not be able to play in any more games for some time. There was no other employer that could hire them to play international soccer. A pause in play would be sad and scary on its own. But it could also hurt their fans. It could hurt the sport they loved so much.

If they agreed to the unequal pay deal, the EEOC could still rule in their favor and compel U.S. Soccer to equalize their pay.

But that was uncertain too. Lawyer Jeffrey Kessler thought the dynamics were too complex to predict an outcome. "In my perception, there was a conflict between the staff of the EEOC, who really thought we had a great claim and wanted to pursue it," he said, "and the Trump administration, which was not generally supportive of these types of equal pay issues."

On April 4, 2017, the players on the collective bargaining committee gathered in a hotel room to review the proposal. The women had some wins. Base pay would increase 30 percent, and match bonuses also got a bump. The federation would equalize per diems and reimburse the women for two years of unequal per diems. They had negotiated some protections related to health and safety, return to play after injury, minimum medical staffing, and control of some licensing rights.

But going forward, their pay was still not equal to the men's pay. And the men's pay would likely increase in their next negotiations, widening the gap again.

The women thought hard, weighing their options.

"Maybe we have done the best we can," someone said.

"For now," Becca Roux agreed.

Finally they decided that the best strategy was to accept the offer with a few changes, keep playing, and hope that the EEOC would come through for them, closing the gap.

Four players, clad in jeans and sweatshirts, gathered around a coffee table. Kelley O'Hara called U.S. president Sunil Gulati on her cell phone and put him on speaker. She and Christen Press went over a few details with him as Meghan Klingenberg and Megan Rapinoe listened in.

"So we have a deal?" Sunil said.

"We have a deal," Kelley replied. She hung up, and Megan Rapinoe leapt out of her chair, arms spread over head in a wide V. Kelley dropped her head to her knees and Meghan Klingenberg dropped her head onto the coffee table. Christine grinned. It had been a long road, but they had a deal. It wasn't perfect, but it was a huge relief.

All twenty-two voting players approved the deal. "When we settled on a less-than-perfect deal, it was partly a matter of expediency," said Megan Rapinoe. "It was clear U.S. Soccer wasn't willing to give us more, and the team wasn't in a place—politically or emotionally—where we were ready to strike."

Federation officials gathered separately on a conference call and also approved the contract.

When the deal was announced the next morning, U.S. Soccer president Sunil Gulati was proud. "We've always had the most highly compensated women's team in the world, and this puts them at an even higher level," Sunil said. "Their performance over the last quarter-century has put them at the top of their game. Financially, the agreement gives the players security in a way that they haven't had before and adds a number of other things that were very important to them."

But being the most highly paid women's team in the world did not mean equal pay for equal work. And security is not the same as equality either.

This fight was far from over.

Time's Up on the Men's Contract

Spring 2017

"This is horrendous," Mark Levinstein, acting director of the men's players union, thought when he saw the women's new contract. While the terms of the women's collective bargaining agreements were not public, the women's and men's players unions had begun sharing details with each other. "This is worse than our 2011 to 2018 deal, and U.S. Soccer now has three times the revenue!"

Some observers suspected that the women's 2017 collective bargaining agreement was designed to punish the team for speaking up. No matter the reason, it left the men's team in a tough spot too. Their contract was due to expire at the end of 2018, so the men faced negotiations of their own. With U.S. Soccer's growing stability and success, the men expected—and would fight for—a much better contract. But players on the U.S. men's national team also had a growing awareness of the plight of their female counterparts.

Young, dynamic midfielder Tyler Adams served on the men's collective bargaining team. A natural leader, Tyler had become the connective tissue on the national team. "He makes everyone's job a little easier," veteran defender Tim Ream said. "As he goes, the team goes."

While working through their numbers and comparing them to the women's numbers, Tyler felt shock and discomfort. He considered all the trophies the women's team had brought home. "It was quite evident that what they've done and the success they've had and how hard they work, just as hard as us, that they deserve the opportunity to get paid as much as, if not more," he thought. "It doesn't matter about gender or anything like that. Their success speaks for itself."

The men's team delved deeper into the situation: "What is right? What is the right thing to do in this scenario?"

"The right thing is for the women's national team to get paid," Tyler realized. "That's the bottom line."

But the players were not sure what to do about the problem.

"I'm Going to Make a Change"

2017–2018

Around the same time, elementary school students in several viral international videos grappled with the question of what is right when it comes to pay for males and females doing equal work. Filmmaker Ann-Helen Hopland, who worked for a Norwegian trade union, scattered colored balls around a room. With a camera rolling, she invited pairs of elementary schoolchildren—a boy and a girl—to put the blue balls in one container and the pink ones in another. The kids went to work, deciding where the balls should go and hustling around to gather them up. When they finished, they smiled and high-fived.

Then they got their rewards, eyes closed, cupped hands held out. The boy got a tall glass overflowing with candy. The girl got the same tall glass filled only halfway with candy. The children opened their eyes and glanced back and forth between the glasses, their smiles fading, the boys sheepish, the girls hurt and angry.

"The reason you got less," the filmmaker explained, "is because you are a girl."

Eyes widened and jaws dropped.

"That's just weird," one kid said.

"That's not good! That's so unfair!" said another.

"We did the same job, but we didn't get the same amount," said one girl sadly. The boy next to her looked like he was going to cry.

Ann-Helen's video went viral, with more than 65 million views in more than eighty countries. Hollywood stars Amy Schumer and Ashton Kutcher touted it on social media. Requests asking permission to use it for employee training poured in from companies around the globe.

A similar video was produced in Australia and New Zealand, where siblings were paid unequally for doing chores together. A girl declared, "It should be flat-out illegal! I'm not joking. I'm not being unreasonable."

Another girl said, "If the men notice that they were being paid more than the woman, maybe they should speak up about it."

A little boy, looking serious and determined, said, "When I am older, I'm going to make a change." Then he whispered, "If I don't forget."

Though the U.S. government was conducting studies on the pay gap, convening task forces, and asking companies to sign an Equal Pay Pledge, lawmakers in several other countries were making more concrete legislative progress. In 2017 and 2018, the United Kingdom, Canada, and France passed measures requiring companies to report on differences in pay between male and female workers. Iceland had been keeping close track of the gender pay gap for years and in 2018 made a huge change. Instead of relying on women to enforce the law by proving that they were being paid less, the small island nation passed that burden to employers. Starting at the end of 2018, companies would have to demonstrate that they paid men and women equally—or face fines.

Elin Eggertsdottir, an Icelandic arts and entertainment executive living in the United States, told *Forbes* that in America, the dialogue around equal pay put too much onus on women. "In Iceland, the conversation has moved beyond that," she said, "and this legislation acknowledges that the responsibility to close the wage gap ultimately lies with the employer."

A New Leader for U.S. Soccer

Early-2018

On February 10, 2018, U.S. Soccer elected a new president to replace the retired Sunil Gulati. Carlos Cordeiro had been in the United States since age fifteen, when he and his Colombian mother and three siblings moved from India. A graduate of Harvard College and Harvard Business School, Carlos spent thirty years in finance, rising to partner at Goldman Sachs. A soccer fan his whole life, Carlos served many roles at U.S. Soccer before filling the unpaid position of vice president and then the unpaid presidency.

In interviews, Carlos promised, among other things, to grow the sport, expand diversity, and "implement equal pay between the men's and women's teams while providing both with the same training support."

The U.S. women's national team—and the men's team—hoped the new leadership would change things. They hoped Carlos would be less tied to the past and more willing to move forward.

But union leader Becca Roux also knew that when anyone took over an institution accused of wrongdoing, the new leader could either blaze a new path forward or circle the wagons to protect the institution's reputation.

Only time would tell which way Carlos Cordeiro would go.

A Tale of Two World Cups

2015–2019

In 2018, Russia hosted the men's World Cup, with a prize pool of $400 million.

In 2019, France would host the women's World Cup, with a prize pool of $30 million.

FIFA justified the difference by noting that men drew a bigger global TV audience and made more revenue. But even FIFA's own numbers did not justify the wide gap.

The 2015 women's World Cup viewership worldwide was 850 million.

The 2016 men's World Cup viewership worldwide was 1.1 billion.

In other words, the women's audience was 75 percent of the men's. A proportional prize allotment for the women would be $300 million—ten times what FIFA was offering.

Plus, FIFA was the *international* governing board of soccer. They did not employ the U.S. men's and women's soccer teams. U.S. Soccer did, and U.S. Soccer ultimately controlled their pay. And in the United States, the most recent women's World Cup had drawn a larger audience.

The 2015 women's World Cup final drew 25 million American viewers.

The 2016 men's World Cup final drew 14 million American viewers.

So did U.S. Soccer pay the women more?

They did not.

And would they pay them more for the upcoming World Cup tournaments?

They would not.

If the men won their World Cup, U.S. Soccer would pay the team $38 million.

If the women won their World Cup, U.S. Soccer would pay their team $4 million.

In October 2017, the men's national team failed to qualify for the World Cup, losing to Trinidad and Tobago, the weakest team in their group.

In 2018, the women's national team won decisive victory after decisive victory, dominating other teams. They did not lose a single game the entire year.

They easily qualified for their World Cup.

Freaking Out

February to March 2019

Jessica McDonald was one of the new players called up to the national team before the 2019 World Cup. Like others on the national team, Jessica was a pro athlete at the top of her game, yet she had friends who were restaurant servers who earned three times more than she did. She worked multiple jobs—coaching and stacking boxes in an Amazon warehouse—while trying to parent and train. There were times when childcare cost more than her paycheck, times when she had to bring her young son to training, times he pooped in his diaper and she would have to stop training to change him. Sometimes Jessica was so busy, she struggled to find time in the day to eat a meal.

Friends relieved some of Jessica's stress when they invited her and her son to move into their home. It was an important break that allowed her to focus more on soccer. But during a meeting with the U.S. National Team, Jessica worried that even that precarious stability could be in jeopardy. In February, the team's lawyers had received a letter from the EEOC. After reviewing documents and interviewing officials and players, the agency was unable to determine conclusively whether there had been discrimination. The agency would take no action against U.S. Soccer.

The team leaders had been on a late-night call with their lawyers, who laid out the situation for them. "We're running out of options," the lawyers told them. "We tried [collective bargaining] negotiations and that didn't work. We filed this grievance with the EEOC, but that didn't work. The only other available option to fight this is to sue U.S. Soccer."

As team leaders updated the players, Jessica, who has a broad smile and long dreadlocks, stopped smiling. "Lawsuit?" she thought. "I don't know anything about lawsuits."

The players fired a barrage of questions. What would it cost? How long would it take? What were the risks of doing this? Could they lose? Many also wondered how U.S. Soccer would react. Would there be retaliation, especially against the handful of players who agreed to represent the team in the lawsuit? What would it be like the first day after the lawsuit was filed? How would their coach treat them in practice? How would U.S. Soccer treat them if they needed something unrelated to the lawsuit, like time off or support for an injury, access to a special diet, or emergency family leave?

Jessica started "freaking out." Being so new to national-level play, she felt vulnerable. "I just got here," she thought. "Is this gonna kill my position on the team?"

The possibility that U.S. Soccer would just shut down the team also remained a danger. That would leave only one possibility for playing at a high level—the domestic, professional National Women's Soccer League, which was struggling to survive. "Let's pump the brakes," Jessica said. "We're going to sue our employer that gives us a job? And this is the job we all want? And that we all strived our entire lives for?"

It wasn't just the national team that could be endangered. U.S. Soccer was quite involved in supporting the professional league. The lawsuit could put that support at risk as well. Once again, the women discussed how U.S. Soccer had so much power and that the only way to fight that power was to stand together.

Jessica realized that in the long run, the lawsuit could make things easier for her and her son. But in the short run, it could be costly. The EEOC filing had been simple and free. The agency did not charge for its investigation. A complicated lawsuit would mean paying investigators and experts and accumulating hefty attorneys' fees. The players, though they were world champions and quite famous, were far from rich. It was a sad irony that if the players had been paid equally to the men, they would have been able to afford the lawsuit. Because they were underpaid, fighting for equal pay could empty their bank accounts.

The women were also aware that U.S. Soccer had deep pockets. In fact, the organization had tens of millions of dollars of revenue, generated from the women's work, to use to fight the women's lawsuit if it wished.

The team leaders made a strong case for the lawsuit. They pointed out how much more successful the women's team was compared with the men's team—and yet the women made so much less money. They reminded players how long they had been asking U.S. Soccer for more pay, for equal pay. They connected the lawsuit to the bigger issue, that women everywhere faced pay discrimination. In 2017, the wage gap in the United States did not close by even one cent. In fact, the pay gap between women of color and the average man actually increased by two cents.

We have a platform, the team leaders argued. We should use it.

Still, Jessica and others voiced serious concerns about the timing. The World Cup coming up in June could be the pinnacle of their careers—even their lives. The lawsuit would be so public. Their claims about their excellence would be so public. As would their success or failure at the World Cup. What if they didn't do well? The lawsuit would put enormous pressure on them all.

But others pointed out that the World Cup would bring even more attention to the gender pay gap in soccer and in society at large.

"Okay, we're gonna do this really scary thing together that's really important and can impact the world at the same time we put our entire life and career on the line for each other?" Jessica asked.

Some of the women grinned.

"We're all in this together," someone said.

"Let's do it!" another player yelled. And they all joined in.

Preparing a Lawsuit

Early 2019

The players formed a litigation committee, athletes from the team who would supervise the lawyers and keep their teammates informed at every step.

The women decided to focus on more than just salaries and bonuses. They wanted to address the fact that men flew to games on convenient and comfortable charter flights, arriving to games loose and well rested, while the female athletes were stuck in tight economy seats on slow trains and even crowded buses. The men consistently played on higher-quality grass fields, while the women often were forced to play on more dangerous artificial turf. The team wanted the lawsuit to include how even their coaching, medical, and support staff teams were smaller and less well paid than the men's. The women decided that the lawsuit would contest *all* the ways U.S. Soccer treated them differently because of their gender.

Preparing the complaint, the women and their lawyers drafted, reviewed, and rewrote the document so that the lawsuit reflected what the players really experienced, what they really believed. There were many late nights going back and forth over the material. The team worked together like this on the field, but this felt different, more important.

The team decided that if they were going to go for it, they were going to go big. They wanted to make their case not only in court, but also in the court of public opinion. They brought in a top public relations team, headed by Molly Levinson. They wanted their message of equality and fairness to ring out everywhere, on the front page of every newspaper, on TV, and on social media. Molly and her colleagues spent a lot of time talking with players one-on-one, homing in on why they were filing the lawsuit, what they had suffered, what they cared about, what they hoped to get out of it.

The players, lawyers, and PR team hashed out the best time to file the suit. Should they wait till after the next World Cup, so they could go into the tournament without the distraction of the lawsuit? No, they decided. They could handle the extra pressure. And the World Cup would give them a global platform to highlight the pay gap problem. "It was like, dang," Megan Rapinoe said. "This is really not great timing, but we were like, but this has to be done."

The legal team considered where to file the lawsuit. U.S. Soccer's headquarters were in Chicago, Illinois. But the players lived all over the country. They could file in any district where a player lived. They wanted a community that would be supportive of equal pay. That mattered a lot if the case went to trial, as the jury would be drawn from the community. Jeffrey Kessler and his co-council on the case, Cardell Spangler, reviewed rulings in various circuits. The Central District Court of California in Los Angeles had a good interpretation of the meaning of equal pay. It also seemed amenable to allowing class actions, where people in the same circumstances banded together in one lawsuit. So Los Angeles it would be.

Finally they settled on a date—International Women's Day—which would put the lawsuit in the context of the broader global battle for women's rights around the world.

Lawsuit Filed

March 2019

On March 8, 2019, just three months before heading to France to defend their World Cup title, at a time when players usually try to minimize distractions as they intensely train and prepare, all twenty-eight members of the U.S. Women's National Team filed a class-action gender discrimination lawsuit against their employer, the U.S. Soccer Federation.

The lawsuit, *Alex Morgan et al. v. U.S. Soccer Federation*, stated the situation simply: "The USSF discriminates against Plaintiffs, and the class that they seek to represent, by paying them less than members of the MNT for substantially equal work and by denying them at least equal playing, training, and travel conditions; equal promotion of their games; equal support and development for their games; and other terms and conditions of employment equal to the MNT."

The lawsuit charged that U.S. Soccer violated the Equal Pay Act, which stated, "No employer . . . shall discriminate . . . between employees on the basis of sex by paying wages to employees . . . at a rate less than the rate at which he pays wages to employees of the opposite sex . . . for equal work on jobs the performance of which requires equal skill, effort, and responsibility, and which are performed under similar working conditions."

They charged that U.S. Soccer also violated the Title VII of the Civil Rights Act of 1964, which stated, "It shall be an unlawful employment practice for an employer . . . to discriminate against any individual with respect to his compensation, terms, conditions, or privileges of employment, because of such individual's race, color, religion, sex, or national origin."

The complaint described how U.S. Soccer "centrally manages and controls every aspect of the senior national team program for both teams and their female and male members."

It detailed the women's successes: they had won three World Cup titles and four Olympic gold medals. They had been ranked number one in the world for ten of the last eleven years. Their 2015 World Cup final drew 23 million viewers, the biggest American audience for a soccer game on TV.

The complaint detailed the similarity of the jobs of the team members: the training, the games, the travel, the conditioning and skills, the promotional activities, media engagements, and autograph signing sessions. It noted that the rules of their soccer matches were the same. "They play on the same size field; use the same size ball; have the same duration of matches and play by the same rules regarding start and restart of play, offside, fouls and misconduct, free kicks, penalty kicks, throw-ins, goal kicks, corner kicks, etc."

And they highlighted important differences: "In light of the WNT's on-field success, Plaintiffs often spend more time practicing for and playing in matches, more time in training camps, more time traveling and more time participating in media sessions." From 2015 through 2018, the women's national team played *nineteen* more matches than the men's team. That, they pointed out, was almost a year's worth of games.

The complaint described how long the women had been asking for, and how long U.S. Soccer had been denying them, equal pay. They quoted a U.S. Soccer representative who allegedly told the women in

2016 that "market realities are such that the women do not deserve to be paid equally to the men," even though the organization "already had conceded that the WNT outperformed the MNT in both revenue and profit the prior year."

They asked the court to certify the lawsuit as a class action, which meant that if the court approved the class, the lawsuit could be on behalf of all USWNT players on the roster during the time of the lawsuit. They wanted the court to declare that U.S. Soccer's actions were unlawful and to issue an injunction to keep the federation from continuing the unlawful discrimination. And they wanted the court to award back pay and punitive damages.

When former player Julie Foudy first heard about the lawsuit, she immediately reached out to friend and teammate Mia Hamm, who had kicked off the fight for equal treatment with her. "Wow, that was ballsy," Julie said. "Pun intended." Mia laughed.

"Really, to throw a lawsuit down against your employer," Julie continued, "who you're going to the World Cup with in three months' time?"

"Yeah, incredibly bold and brave," Mia agreed.

Union leader Becca Roux also marveled at the team's courage. "It just shows you who these women are and their mindset," she said. "A lawsuit is not something every professional athlete could handle, but accepting pressure and challenge while still succeeding in their jobs is just part of the DNA of this team."

The players were deeply motivated by the message the lawsuit sent to women and girls everywhere, said Megan Rapinoe. "Always believe in yourself. Fight for what you're worth. And never accept anything less. Never."

The Response

March 2019

The men's team backed the effort almost immediately. "The United States National Soccer Team Players Association fully supports the efforts of the U.S. Women's National Team Players to achieve equal pay," they wrote in their public statement, which also noted that their own contract had expired. "We wait on U.S. Soccer to respond to both players' associations with a way to move forward with fair and equitable compensation for all U.S. soccer players."

Rather than moving forward, on May 6, 2019, U.S. Soccer filed their answer with the court, largely denying the allegations of discrimination. The work of the two teams, they argued, was not comparable. The two teams "play at different times, in different locations, against different opponents . . ."

They denied that the obligations and responsibilities of the two teams were similar.

They denied that anyone could even compare the two teams' compensation because the women earned guaranteed salaries and benefits while the men were paid based on match appearances. Differences in pay, they claimed, were based on "legitimate business reasons" and differences in revenue.

U.S. Soccer also argued that the women's pay was a result of collective bargaining, so it couldn't be illegal. They even claimed that the women made more than the men.

"The answer was kind of predictable," lawyer Jeffrey Kessler said. "They made a whole bunch of excuses." But to him, it boiled down to this: "They refused to pay women equally because they could get away with it. But you can't treat women like this in the workplace and get away with it. If I didn't think we were going to win, I would never have taken this case."

The battle lines were drawn.

Four-Star World Cup

France, 2019

"For what felt like the umpteenth time, we found ourselves approaching a major tournament with a pay dispute hanging over our heads," Megan Rapinoe said. It no longer felt like the team was just playing for the United States. "We were playing for diversity, democracy, inclusion," said Megan, who had been named co-captain in 2018. "We were playing for the right to be different and still respected. We were playing for equal rights, equal pay, and the glory of the women's game."

The night before leaving for the tournament, Megan dyed her hair bright pinkish lavender. She wouldn't even let her hair be quiet.

In the first game on June 11, 2019, against Thailand, the players were riled up, ready to make a statement that would buoy them throughout the rest of the tournament. They came out strong, savvy, fast, and furious, and pounded balls into the goal, 1–0, 2–0, 3–0, 4–0, 5–0, 6–0, 7–0. Alex Morgan scored a stunning five goals, and four of her teammates scored their first-ever World Cup goals. The game ended at 13–0.

Some criticized the team for the lopsided score and for celebrating every goal. But if there is a tie between teams at the end of the group stage of a World Cup, goal differential determines who moves on to the elimination round. Alex also pointed out that "It was important to celebrate with each other." For some players like young Mallory Pugh Swanson, who had turned twenty-one the month before, it was her first World Cup. Scoring on such a big stage was momentous.

Washington Post columnist Sally Jenkins was angered by the whole discussion. "I don't want to hear another word about whether the Americans scored too much or overcelebrated," she wrote. "This is a team in full attack mode, fighting not just to win the World Cup but to prove a larger point about their worth. . . . You don't make up a chronic pay gap with ladylike restraint. You do it by kicking through a wall."

After beating Spain in the first elimination round, the U.S. faced host nation France in the quarterfinals. A crowd of 45,000 gathered in ninety-degree heat for the match. The game was sold out, and scalpers roamed outside the gates hoping to capitalize on demand.

The starting whistle blew, and all the pent-up tension and energy the players felt began to unfurl.

Five minutes in, Alex was fouled.

Megan stepped up to take the kick twenty-two yards out. French players made a human wall to block it, but the ball soared through the defenders, past the goalkeeper, and into the far-right corner of the net.

Fans leapt to their feet, clapping and screaming.

Megan, who teammates said brought "the confidence, the swagger, the bravado," to the field, faced the crowd and threw her arms wide open as if to take a dramatic bow. But instead of bowing, she stood there and grinned proudly at the crowd, her arms stretched out in a V.

France emerged strong in the second half, but twenty minutes in, Alex touched the ball to Tobin Heath, who passed it to Megan, who tapped it in for a second goal. "Purple-Haired Lesbian Goddess Flattens France like a Crêpe," chortled the sports website *Deadspin*.

The French grabbed a goal with a beautiful head ball, but the score stood at 2–1 and the U.S. advanced. After beating England in the semifinal, the U.S. team was once again just a game away from taking home the trophy.

A Greater Goal

July 2019

The U.S. went into the final confident, perhaps overconfident. They fully expected to hit the Netherlands hard from the beginning, racking up goals early. When the opening whistle blew, they did manage to move the ball up the field toward the goal again and again, but they could not break through. They didn't even get one shot off in the first thirty minutes. The half ended scoreless.

The team tried to regroup and come out stronger in the second half.

Early on when they won a penalty kick, captain Megan Rapinoe hoped it would change everything.

The crowd roared; it sounded like 60,000 were screaming her name. She couldn't block out the chanting. Instead, she tried to "take the noise and energy and push it down into a blade of concentration."

She drew a deep breath.

She ran at the ball.

And she blasted it, slightly to the right of the keeper and into the back of the net. She threw out her arms in what was now her signature pose, and her teammates swarmed her.

The U.S. was up 1–0.

Eight minutes later, Rose Lavelle dribbled the ball from the back, dodged and outran defenders, and struck the ball into the goal.

At the final whistle, Megan collapsed to the ground. Tears poured down her face. Teammates flew into each other's arms, squeezing one another tightly.

As the team was awarded the World Cup, blue and gold confetti rained down. The stadium rocked with chants of "Equal pay! Equal pay! Equal pay!"

When FIFA's president held up the trophy, the stadium echoed with boos. The fans knew how wildly unequal FIFA's awards were for the men's and women's tournaments. In fact, U.S. Soccer and fans all around the world had begun pressuring FIFA to equalize prize money.

Megan didn't mind the booing. "A little public shame never hurt anybody," she thought.

When the players had the trophy in hand, the stadium erupted with support again. The women celebrated exuberantly and playfully, even lying down in the sparkles on the field to make confetti angels.

Winning was amazing, but Mallory Pugh Swanson was most proud to be part of a group that had the potential to change women's sports and people's views on what women could accomplish. "The way I like to look at it is the 99ers [early pioneers such as Julie Foudy] started and kicked off soccer in America," she said in a podcast. "And we started, like, a whole other kind of narrative about women's football around the world." She paused. "It's gonna make me cry."

Sponsors Step Up

Summer 2019

The lawsuit was on everyone's minds on the plane ride home to the United States. "We—all players, every player at this World Cup—put on the most incredible show that you could ever ask for," Megan Rapinoe told the *New York Times*. "We can't do anything more, to impress more, to be better ambassadors, to take on more, to play better, to do anything. It's time to move the conversation forward to the next step."

In the wake of the women's stunning victory, many of the companies that sponsored U.S. Soccer and the two national teams lined up publicly to side with the women on the equal pay fight. Visa, the credit card company, announced that it wanted at least half of its five-year sponsorship to go to the women's program. Luna Bar offered every woman who made the roster a $31,250 bonus to make up for the pay gap between the men's and women's teams. Proctor & Gamble, makers of Secret deodorant, bought a full-page ad in the Sunday *New York Times* urging the federation to "be on the right side of history."

"Inequality is about more than pay and players," the ad said. "It's about values." Proctor & Gamble backed up their support with a donation of more than a half million dollars—$23,000 for each of the twenty-three players—to their players' association, to support their fight for equal pay.

Nike released a one-minute ad focused on equality. Volkswagen expressed its support for "equality, inclusion, and access." AT&T told the *New York Times* that it had "clearly communicated our position that we expect players to be equally compensated."

With more than a dozen sponsors openly siding with the team, with popular support heavily on their side, with their fourth World Cup win behind them, the women hoped that the moment for real change had arrived.

Invested More Than Any Country in the World

July 2019

The team returned to the United States as heroes. New York City threw another ticker-tape parade on a lovely summer day. The players rode up the Canyon of Heroes on floats to deafening cheers.

An NBC reporter handed defender Crystal Dunn a microphone. After thanking everyone, she threw her fist in the air and yelled, "Equal pay!" The players around her came to life and joined her, chanting, "Equal pay!" Fans lining the sidewalks joined in: "Equal pay! Equal pay!"

The cheers and chants followed them all the way up Broadway to City Hall.

The players clambered onto a platform in front of the imposing white limestone façade and settled into chairs. Crowds packed the park to hear them speak.

U.S. Soccer's president, Carlos Cordeiro, spoke first.

"To our women's national team and the millions who support them, in recent months, you have raised your voice for equality. Today, on behalf of all of us at U.S. Soccer, I want to say, we hear you . . ."

The players wondered if, finally, U.S. Soccer really did hear them. They were equal parts skeptical and hopeful.

"We believe you. And we are committed to doing right by you. . . ."

Could this be the opening they had hoped for? Was it possible that Carlos would make a public commitment to equal pay now, in front of this crowd?

"And that's why over the years, U.S. Soccer has invested more in woman's soccer than any country in the world."

"Not exactly what we want to hear," Megan thought. "Just because you're better than someone who's bad doesn't mean necessarily that you're good."

"And we will continue to invest . . ."

The crowd did not miss the dodge. The president of U.S. Soccer was not promising equal pay. He was promising more of the same.

Boos filled the air. Carlos quickly finished his remarks, with the boos drowning him out.

Then New York City's mayor, Bill de Blasio, came forward. Under a banner that stated U.S. Soccer's motto, ONE NATION, ONE TEAM, the mayor presented the keys of the city to captain Megan Rapinoe.

She took to the mic wearing round sunglasses and a wide grin. She voiced some support of Carlos, while also calling him to task. "I think he's gonna make things right," she said. And she promised that the team would hold his feet to the fire. "It's time to come together. It's our responsibility to make this world a better place."

She explained the players' point of view and implored Carlos and the wider world, "Yes, we play sports. Yes, we play soccer. Yes, we're female athletes, but we're so much more than that. YOU are so much more than that. We have to collaborate. It takes everybody. Please."

A month later, the team set off on a five-city U.S. victory tour, playing Ireland, Portugal, and South Korea. Throngs of fans showed up to game after game. And after the victory tour, Megan kept going, visiting schools, colleges, nonprofits, companies, sharing the microphone with other activists fighting sexism, racism, and homophobia—and unequal pay. "Caring is cool," she told them. "And lowering the ladder can raise your own game."

People approached her at airports, before and after matches, lining up to congratulate her after speeches. They cheered on the team's equal pay efforts, as well. "You need to get paid," they told her. "You get your money!"

Settlement?

July 2019

The team and their lawyers saw an opening. With the outpouring of support at the World Cup, in New York City, and during their victory tour around the United States, the players felt well positioned to enter into settlement discussions. Megan Rapinoe was hopeful that U.S. Soccer would change its tune and take this opportunity to be the equal pay heroes. She thought, "Surely you're not going to mess this up—like, it's laid out for you."

But right before the sessions were about to begin in New York City, U.S. Soccer president Carlos Cordeiro published an open letter on the federation's website. The letter said that U.S. Soccer had "spared no expense" supporting the team.

Union leader Becca Roux was frustrated that Carlos continued to be so defensive instead of forward-thinking. She wanted to say, "Stop assuming that the sins of the past are your sins. Instead, let's work to fix them."

U.S. Soccer continued to offer the same excuses. "In the case of our men's and women's national teams," Carlos wrote, "they have different pay structures, not because of gender, but because each team chose to negotiate a different compensation package with U.S. Soccer. Separately, FIFA competitions for men and women include a different number of games each year, at different times, in different locations, against different opponents with different FIFA rankings and different tournaments with different qualifying criteria and different prize money."

"Really?" Megan thought as she read the letter. "This is what we're gonna do?" She couldn't believe that he wouldn't acknowledge how similar their jobs were. "It was really irritating and really frustrating," she said. "Honestly, I'm just so fucking sick of debating my own worth with the federation."

Carlos called "direct comparisons between their pay extremely difficult," but announced that U.S. Soccer had hired an accounting firm to review a fact sheet his staff had pulled together on the last decade of U.S. Soccer's pay to players on the two teams. "As you'll see," he wrote, "separate and apart from any prize money awarded by FIFA—U.S. Soccer has, over the past decade, paid our Women's National Team more than our Men's National Team in salaries and game bonuses."

The women and their lawyers picked the fact sheet apart. To begin with, the ten-year analysis didn't even match the time period of the lawsuit. Megan and her teammates worried that the letter and fact sheet would confuse the public and possibly cause people to question the women's efforts.

The most troubling part of the missive came near the end, where the president suggested that U.S. Soccer didn't have the resources to do any more. "After all, our federation is a 501(c)(3) nonprofit with the mission of making soccer the preeminent sport in the United States by developing players, coaches, and referees at all levels, including youth. As such, we have a responsibility to use our resources wisely to serve all our members and to plan prudently for the future."

53 Support and Derision

July 2019

The men's national team players association responded publicly to Carlos Cordeiro's letter the day after it was posted. They wrote that they "stand with the members of the world champion Women's National Team" and that the female players "deserve equal pay and are right to pursue a legal remedy from the courts or Congress."

They blasted Carlos for being misleading, taking particular issue with the part of the letter where the president wrote, "Here in the U.S. and around the world, the more tickets to women's matches we buy and the more games we watch on TV, the more revenue we can generate for the women's game, including FIFA prize money. That, we believe, is the best and most sustainable path to true and lasting equality."

The men's statement countered, "The only solution Mr. Cordeiro proposes is for fans to buy more tickets and watch more games on television. He conceals the fact that the money will not go to USWNT players." When fans buy more and higher-priced tickets, when sponsors pony up more funds, and when companies pay more for broadcasting rights, "those revenues line U.S. Soccer's pocket, not the pockets of the players."

Though the current men's team backed the letter, not all of their former players held the same view. A few days after the players' association's public support, former USMNT midfielder Jermaine Jones posted a video where he declared, "There is a big difference between men's sport and women's sport. Give me one country where the girls get paid the same as the men. There is just no country. Of course, as men, we know it's tougher to win a World Cup than the girls."

Mediation

Summer 2019

Despite the opposition the women's team so clearly still faced, their leadership optimistically set aside three days for mediation. Maybe the letter was just a negotiating tactic to keep the back pay damages low, they thought. Maybe U.S. Soccer would come through for them.

The women, dressed in business casual, made their way through the New York City streets with buses squeaking by, cabs honking, and people hustling down the sidewalk.

The opposing sides gathered at the law offices of Winston and Strawn on Park Avenue. In one large conference room, the women and U.S. Soccer could meet together. Two other smaller breakout rooms would give each side a place to discuss developments in private.

The players were equal parts skeptical and hopeful. Public sentiment was with them. U.S. Soccer had made many public statements about how much they supported the team. Despite Carlos Cordeiro's letter, the women were under the impression that U.S. Soccer might offer some version of equal pay.

Then they got the federation's proposal.

"It wasn't even close," Jeffrey Kessler said.

The two sides negotiated until the sun set, and the New York City lights twinkled from all the skyscrapers. Megan admitted to a moment of just wanting to punch someone in the face.

On day two, some players had to return to their home cities to play for their professional teams. A group text about the negotiation went something like this:

Any movement from them?

No

Nothing tangible.

We just gave them a presentation to consider.

We're waiting for their response.

. . . sadly, my compatriots, it was rejected.

Day three dragged by with no progress. The women were frustrated and angry. Becky Sauerbrunn noticed that Kelley O'Hara, the player who the team said "brought the crazy" looked like she wanted to upend the whole conference table.

"To do so much to set this moment up," said Becky Sauerbrunn, "and for them to just kind of like shit the bed, basically, we were kind of blown away."

But these women had faced difficult setbacks before. They were determined to continue the fight.

While they were in New York City, the players hit the morning TV shows to make their case to the public. The *Good Morning America* host asked what was holding up the negotiations. Forward Christen Press answered mildly, yet damningly. "Unfortunately, it was just the concept of paying us equally. We never even got past that."

Megan added, "There is no social equality without financial equality. So that means we're going to trial . . . we won't accept anything less."

Class Action?

2011 and 2019

Before the lawsuit could move toward trial, the judge had to certify the class. In other words, he had to agree that a handful of players—Alex Morgan, Megan Rapinoe, Carli Lloyd, and Becky Sauerbrunn—could represent the interests of the other past, current, and future USWNT players in a class action suit against U.S Soccer.

Class actions are a powerful tool for people challenging widespread injustice. Individuals suing on their own may have to shoulder hefty legal fees alone. Being the lone voice of protest also leaves individuals vulnerable to retaliation.

Employees fighting discrimination as a group are harder to punish. Working together offers support and protection. And the rewards of a group action can be much higher. Lawyers are more likely to take on class action cases as they can recoup hefty legal fees from the court in the judgment or settlement.

Group actions also make a bigger difference. Instead of correcting one instance of discrimination suffered by one person, class actions can ask the court for injunctive relief to end institutional and companywide discrimination.

The players had sued U.S. Soccer under two laws: the Equal Pay Act, which says it is illegal to underpay someone because of their gender; and Title VII of the Civil Rights Act, which says that not only is unequal pay illegal, but it is also illegal to offer unequal working conditions. The women needed to persuade the judge to certify their case as a class action under both laws.

Gaining class certification for pay discrimination had become more difficult in 2011 when a case called *Wal-Mart Stores v. Dukes* made it to the U.S. Supreme Court. The case involved a group of women working at Wal-Mart stores across the country who sued their employer for gender discrimination in pay and promotion.

Edith Arana had years of retail experience when she applied for a job at Wal-Mart. She was excited because she had heard that if you worked hard, the sky was the limit for growth within the company. She worked as a test scanner, checking prices; then as a universal product code clerk, putting in the UPC for each product; then invoicing; and then a support manager. And all the while, she kept applying for the company's assistant manager training program. She was repeatedly turned down. Though her shift was forty hours, she often worked five hours longer, to learn more about the store and the assistant managers' role.

This extra time was time away from her three children. "I knew I was spending a lot of hours, but I had something in mind," she said. "I'm going to work hard and make that assistant management position and it is going to make up for all those times I wasn't there for homework or for soccer." Little by little she began to notice that men with just a year or two of experience, significantly less than she had, were getting promoted above her. "Then they would have the women, who already knew the job, train the guys!" she observed.

Edith joined Betty Dukes, a greeter at Wal-Mart, and other women who had faced similar discrimination, to seek certification for a class action lawsuit against Wal-Mart that would represent 1.5 million current and past female employees. Data showed that the plaintiffs' experiences were not anomalies. Women at Wal-Mart were paid less at every level. Promotions were given to men with less tenure and lower performance ratings. Female hourly employees earned roughly $1,200 less per year than men. Salaried women employees earned $15,000 to $20,000 less.

Ultimately, the U.S. Supreme Court ruled that the women didn't have enough in common to be considered a class. Even if widespread discrimination existed, such a large company couldn't be held responsible for the workplace decisions of thousands of local managers exercising their own discretion. Each woman would have to bring her own case. Edith was distressed. "It can't just be you out there," she said. "No one person, no one attorney, no one support system is enough."

In the case against U.S. Soccer, Jeffrey Kessler felt hopeful about the players' chances at class certification. In the Wal-Mart case, the women couldn't point to specific discriminatory policies. In the soccer case, one collective bargaining agreement dictated exactly how much every female player would be paid, and another CBA dictated exactly how the men would be paid.

"We did not have a Wal-Mart-type problem," he said.

Can Four Players Represent the Class?

Fall 2019

On September 30, 2019, U.S. Soccer filed its opposition to class certification. Their brief started out with a bang: "Plaintiffs' motion for class certification should be denied because the proposed Class Representatives Alex Morgan, Megan Rapinoe, Carli Lloyd, and Becky Sauerbrunn were paid more than even the highest-earning MNT members and therefore have suffered no injury." The brief noted that "the Class Representatives did not suffer injuries under Title VII and thus cannot represent class members who allegedly *did* suffer injuries."

"Utterly frivolous" is how the women's lawyers characterized the claim that the female athletes suffered no injury. U.S. Soccer's argument was based on "the illogical proposition that a female soccer player does not suffer any injury from a discriminatory compensation policy in favor of male soccer players as long as she can achieve an equal amount of total compensation by playing many more games and being far more successful in those games."

Yes, the four representatives made more money than the top male national team players. But that was because they played more games than the men, won more games, and won more high-profile games, such as the World Cup, which paid more.

A ruling in an earlier equal pay case established that *total* pay "cannot be the proper point of comparison." If it were, "an employer who pays a woman $10 per hour and a man $20 per hour would not violate the EPA . . . as long as the woman negated the obvious disparity by working twice as many hours." Such a result, the ruling said, would be "absurd."

Indeed, the four class representatives would have made millions more if the pay rates were equal. The women's brief included a chart that showed what the four players made from March 30, 2014, to October 7, 2019, and what they would have made if they had been paid the same rates as the men's team.

Player	**Pay Under WNT Rate**	**Pay Under MNT Rate**
Alex Morgan	**$1,201,449.64**	**$4,104,920.65**
Megan Rapinoe	**$1,159,099.64**	**$3,722,625.00**
Carli Lloyd	**$1,204,049.64**	**$4,168,420.65**
Becky Sauerbrunn	**$1,188,249.64**	**$4,172,670.65**

To the women and their lawyers, the discrimination was clear and obvious. They hoped that the judge—like a referee checking the video review in a game—would rule in their favor.

A Ruling

Fall 2019

On November 8, 2019, the women won class certification. That meant that the national team players could fight together rather than as individuals. And though twenty-eight players filed the lawsuit, the judgment would cover a larger "class" that included all the women who played during specified dates. Any ruling requiring U.S. Soccer to pay equal wages would apply to all the women on the national team at the time the case resolved—and everyone going forward. Back pay could be awarded to players on the team from March 8, 2016, to November 8, 2019. Women on the national team between June 11, 2015, and November 8, 2019, would split any damages awarded.

Judge R. Gary Klausner distinguished between total pay and rates of pay in his order, writing that "The EPA [Equal Pay Act] provides that an employer may not 'discriminate . . . on the basis of sex by paying wages to employees . . . at a *rate* less than the rate at which he pays wages to employees of the opposite sex.'" He added the italics for emphasis.

He also wrote that "The failure to provide the WNT with equal working conditions is a real (not abstract) injury which affects each Plaintiff in a personal and individual way."

The ruling did not mean that the women had won their case. But they had the judge's blessing to head to trial as a class action with

Alex Morgan, Megan Rapinoe, Carli Lloyd, and Becky Sauerbrunn appointed as class representatives.

For now, this win felt good.

But the question of who earned more, the women or the men, would come back to haunt them later.

The Search for Evidence

Late 2019

With class certification granted, the trial for *Alex Morgan v. U.S. Soccer* was scheduled for May 5, 2020. The players and U.S. Soccer embarked on discovery. Discovery is a process required before a trial, where both sides search for evidence supporting their claims. They also share with each other information about what evidence and witnesses they will present at trial. This allows both sides to make their best case before the jury.

Discovery is a huge undertaking. The players' lawyers asked U.S. Soccer to turn over all the emails, letters, and documents with discussions about the men's and women's negotiations, pay, and revenues. The women's players' union had to turn over notes and documents from bargaining sessions. U.S. Soccer demanded that the female athletes turn over emails and texts from their personal phones and computers. Kelley O'Hara found that really uncomfortable, "like an invasion of privacy."

During this period, the women remained open to settling the case out of court. But they would only settle for equal pay, and U.S. Soccer would not offer equal pay. So they continued accumulating evidence.

The players were in constant communication, talking and sending texts and emails to each other and to their lawyers. To make their case, the women had to document all the inequalities they faced. In a documentary called *LFG,* after the team's rallying cry, "Let's Fucking Go!,"

Megan Rapinoe said it took "hours and hours and hours and hours and hours and hours and hours of our time."

The documentary caught a video call between forward Christen Press and Megan during trial prep.

"You need to slow down, I think," Christen said.

Megan laughed and rubbed her forehead. "Oh yeah? How?"

"You're gonna lose yourself. You need to say no."

"I know, it's crazy, I have to stop. . . . It's a lot. This is too much." Megan shared how she had worked on the case from two p.m. to midnight every night and her to-do list just got longer and longer.

Christen repeated, "Don't lose yourself."

Megan paused. "I'm not going to."

"Okay, well listen, we'll talk tomorrow."

"Love you," Megan said.

"Okay, love you."

They hung up, and Megan got right back to work.

Both sides began depositions. A deposition is like testifying at trial. Witnesses swear to tell the truth, the whole truth, and nothing but the truth. The opposition interrogates them with questions and a court reporter transcribes everything they say for use as evidence in the trial.

Depositions can be perilous, the players' lawyers warned the women. When co-council Cardell Spangler sat down with Christen Press to prepare her, she explained, "One thing the lawyer will try to do is make it seem like it's really informal, just really conversational. We're just here having a nice little chat." That's to trick you to let your guard down, she said. "Depositions are never informal. It's as if you're testifying at trial."

She wanted Christen to keep in mind at all times that the person across the table was not her friend. "Their whole goal is to get information from you that will hurt your case and help their case." Concentrate, the women's lawyers advised. Listen carefully to the question and only answer the question asked.

Kelley O'Hara dreaded the deposition but also felt philosophical about how, once again, the team was facing something difficult together. "When we do come together as a collective, and we decide we're doing this with one voice and we're all making the same decision, that's when we've gained the most progress."

The women, though accustomed to pressure-cooker situations in many big games, found the depositions stressful. They had no experience with depositions or court proceedings, so they walked into the conference rooms worried, nervous, and tense. Some said it was one of the most difficult things they ever had to do.

The depositions lasted for hours, with the opposing lawyers trying to get the witnesses to say something that could be bad for their case.

But the women stood strong. "They did great," Jeffrey Kessler, their lawyer, said. "And the reason they did great is because telling the truth is easy. Lying is hard."

Jeffrey was shocked by what some of the U.S. Soccer officials said in their depositions. They admitted, under oath, that U.S. Soccer never offered the women the same deal as the men. They admitted that the women asked for equal pay and that they refused to provide it. In his deposition, President Carlos Cordiero confirmed that "our female players have not been treated equally" and that "we clearly need to work toward equal pay for the national teams."

That was strong evidence that would help the women make their case.

Questioning the Media

December 2019

At the end of 2019, *Sports Illustrated* honored Megan Rapinoe as the Sportsperson of the Year. She graciously accepted the award but used the spotlight to illuminate the role the media played in the inequities she and other female athletes were battling. Sports writing and commentating had long been, and continued to be, an old boy's network. Women's sports received roughly 5 percent of mainstream media coverage, according to a report out of the University of Southern California and Purdue University. In fact, the report found that 80 percent of sports news programs devoted zero time to women's sports. They also observed that when women's sports were covered on television, they were described in a "boring, inflection-free manner" that the researchers dubbed "gender-bland sexism."

Written coverage was skewed as well; the Women's Media Center found that 90 percent of sports articles were written by men.

The content of the media coverage showed bias too. Interviews with female athletes focused *less* on strength, skill, teamwork, and training, and *more* on their appearance, body shape or size, and dating or personal family matters. Female athletes, when compared with their male counterparts, were also much more likely to be portrayed off the field or court, out of their uniforms, and in sexualized poses, research out of the University of Minnesota found.

In her speech at the *Sports Illustrated* award ceremony, Megan asked some tough questions:

Was I, really, only the fourth woman in the award's sixty-six-year history who deserved this honor?

Were the only people qualified to write for *Sports Illustrated* white men?

Why did so few writers of color deserve to be featured in the publication?

Why did so few women's voices deserve to be heard and read in this publication?

She and the other players, and their agents and PR people, couldn't help but wonder how support for women's sports would blossom if they were covered in the media with the same excitement and commitment as men's sports. How would that in turn affect how many people filled stadiums for games and watched regularly on television?

Massive interest in women's soccer was currently untapped, according to a survey by the Collective Think Tank. Nearly 90 percent of those surveyed internationally would watch more women's soccer if it were more accessible. U.S. Soccer talked about market forces determining pay, but why did those market forces exist?

A Dangerous Virus

Winter 2019–2020

Meanwhile, a deadly virus had been silently circulating across the globe for at least a month. Sometime at the end of 2019, a seafood vendor and several other people at an animal market the size of a soccer field in Wuhan, China, fell ill. The Huanan Seafood Wholesale Market, where poultry, meat, and wild animals were also sold, was dank and poorly ventilated, so the new virus spread through the crowds easily. Some who caught the virus ended up in the hospital with fever, tightness in the chest, and difficulty breathing.

On January 9, 2020, forty-one people were in the hospital with Covid-19, seven in serious condition, and a sixty-one-year-old man died. By January 19, several hundred people in China were diagnosed with Covid, and it had spread to Thailand, Japan, and the Republic of Korea. A man who had returned from a trip to Wuhan to his home near Seattle checked into the hospital with symptoms. It was the first reported case of Covid in the United States.

By February 10, reports indicated that more than 1,000 people had died of Covid worldwide. The U.S. had fifteen reported cases. China and Italy went into lockdown.

The 2020 Olympics in Tokyo were scheduled to begin in July, but sporting events in Japan and other countries were being canceled. A professor of infectious diseases in Japan wondered whether it made sense to have thousands of people from around the globe gather together so closely, creating "a hub to disseminate the virus to other countries." Other experts countered that the spread of Covid would be suppressed in warmer months.

The Olympics had only been canceled in 1916, 1940, and 1944, during world wars. So far, Japan and the 2020 Olympic organizing committee said the games would proceed "as planned."

The U.S. women's team hoped that was true.

A Word from the Men's Team

February 2020

On February 12, 2020, the men's team, which was in negotiations with U.S. Soccer over its expired contract, stepped further into the equal pay fray with an open statement on the website of their union. They began by explaining that up until this point, they had kept their negotiations with U.S. Soccer confidential. "However, the federation has been working very hard to sell a false narrative to the public and even Congress," they wrote. "They have been using this false narrative as a weapon against current and former members of the United States Women's National Team."

They urged people to think differently about the women's and men's contracts. The men's contract from 2011 to 2018 was artificially low because it was negotiated in the wake of a nationwide financial crisis, when the federation argued that it was uncertain of its financial future. Since then, U.S. Soccer's revenues had tripled.

Given the increase in revenues, the men's team argued, both the men's and women's teams deserved to be paid much more. Instead, U.S. Soccer had pressured the women to accept less. And for the record, "yes, the federation continues to discriminate against women in their wages and working conditions."

In fact, the men's union charged, "Rather than share the massive surpluses the women helped generate with the players, they are using those funds to dramatically increase the federation's annual legal fee budget to over $10 million to try to impose massive legal fees the women cannot afford. They're lobbying and using every legal trick in the book to distract Congress, the judge, and the soon-to-be-empaneled jury.

"It's time for this to stop," the statement declared.

Asking for Judgment

February 2020

On February 20, 2020, with all the evidence collected, both sides filed motions for summary judgment, which asked the judge to resolve the case without a trial.

Juries in a trial decide which facts to believe. With these motions, both the women and U.S. Soccer were arguing that there were no facts under dispute, so there was no need for a trial. In their briefs, each side tried to convince the judge to rule in their favor based on their view of the evidence collected. Both sides dug into the statements and data, emphasizing the facts that proved their points. The judge could agree with either side, or rule that there were disagreements about facts that a jury would have to resolve at trial.

To persuade the judge to take their side, the women's twenty-six-page brief opened with: "This is the rare case where it is Plaintiffs who are entitled to summary judgment in a wage discrimination case because the undisputed fact of the rate of pay discrimination against the female employees is contained in written collective bargaining agreements and the common defendant employer has not come forward with evidence to meet its burden of proving that this indisputable discrimination is the result of a cause other than gender." In other words, just look at the teams' contracts. The men and women are paid unequally.

Quoting U.S. Soccer's own website, the brief pointed out that the Women's National Team was "one of the most dominant squads in the history of sport—men or women." Undisputed facts included that the two teams had a common employer and did substantially similar work and that the WNT brought in more revenue than the MNT during the period covered by the suit.

They reiterated that the laws are concerned with *rate* of pay rather than *total* pay and that "WNT players received a lower rate of pay than the MNT even when all the fringe benefits are taken into consideration."

The women had to prove that they did "equal work" to win summary judgment. The Equal Pay Act considered skill, effort, and responsibility. Numerous U.S. Soccer witnesses admitted that the female national team players were equally skilled as male national team players, with enormous "athleticism, tactical IQ, tactical proficiency, and mental fortitude." The past and current U.S. Soccer presidents testified in their depositions that WNT players worked as hard as MNT players. Coaches of both teams said that their responsibilities were the same.

The women's lawyers also took issue with another U.S. Soccer argument that came up in deposition—that men's soccer was more "competitive" than women's soccer. Actually, the brief noted, "Since 2014, the WNT has played, on average, teams with *higher* FIFA rankings than the MNT team every year except 2018." (Emphasis theirs.) And, more importantly, "this argument is exactly the type of pernicious and offensive gender stereotyping that the EPA does not permit as a justification for wage discrimination."

The women also countered U.S. Soccer's argument that because the jobs were segregated by gender, they could not be equal. They cited a case, *Marcoux v. State of Maine*, where a court ruled that female prison guards in a female prison deserved the same retirement benefits as male prison guards in a male prison.

The women wanted the judge to rule that U.S. Soccer had violated wage discrimination laws and to order U.S. Soccer to pay both teams equally. If that part of the lawsuit was resolved, they could go to trial to determine whether and how much back pay and damages the players deserved, and whether U.S. Soccer also violated laws by offering unequal working conditions.

On the other hand, U.S. Soccer wanted the judge to "dismiss this lawsuit in its entirety." On working conditions, they offered reasons for chartering more flights for men and for scheduling women to play on artificial turf, but they also pointed out that those conditions had been recently equalized.

On the equal pay issue, they made many of the same arguments as before:

- that the men and women "perform different work in different jobs" and do not even work in the same place.
- that the two World Cups were "completely different tournaments," so equal pay for them was not required. And they blamed FIFA for differences in prize money.
- that any pay differences were based on factors other than gender, including "the difference in revenue (and potential revenue) generated by U.S. Soccer from the two teams' matches." They added that "the WNT's games ended up generating more revenue during the last five years than the MNT's games, but this includes only one World Cup cycle compared to two for the WNT."
- that the women fought for different terms in their collective bargaining agreement and in fact won terms that the men's team did not enjoy.

- that the two collective bargaining agreements were too different to compare. "The MNT has a high-risk, high-reward agreement whereas the [WNT] negotiated a deal more heavily focused on stability and security."

But the heart of U.S. Soccer's arguments was—yet again—that "it did not pay the MNT more than the WNT."

Dueling Experts

February 2020

To make their case on summary judgment, U.S. Soccer put forth an analysis conducted by their expert witness, accountant Carlyn Irwin. She added up all the earnings paid to each team from 2015 to 2019 and then divided those earnings by the number of games each team played.

$$\frac{\textbf{WNT: \$24,503,863}}{\textbf{111 games}} = \textbf{\$220,747 per game}$$

$$\frac{\textbf{MNT: \$18,499,615}}{\textbf{86 games}} = \textbf{\$212,639 per game}$$

Thus, she concluded, "USSF paid more to members of the WNT and the WNT Players Association both in total and on a per-game basis," than the men's team. U.S. Soccer again argued that there could be no wage discrimination if the women earned more.

The woman's national team offered an expert witness as well, economist Finnie Cook. She added up all the compensation all the players on the women's team would have earned from 2015 to 2019 if they had been paid under the men's contract. Then she subtracted what they were actually paid. The difference: $63,822,242. Based on her analysis, the USWNT was entitled to nearly $64 million in back pay.

The women's team also submitted a rebuttal to U.S. Soccer's expert's report, pointing out that those calculations did not consider how differently the two teams performed. Their contracts established performance bonuses based on wins and losses, the rank of the opponent, and whether the game was part of an important tournament. Any comparison of earnings should reflect these factors as well, the women's expert pointed out. Calculations that compared the rate of pay for each kind of game (World Cup tournament, other tournament, friendly) and result (win, lose, draw) would clearly show that the women earned lower rates of pay.

The judge had at least three options. He could dismiss the case if he concluded that there was no pay discrimination. He could find that the women did suffer pay discrimination and award $64 million in back pay and possibly damages. Or he could hand the case over to a jury to figure it out.

Michael McCann of *Sports Illustrated* thought the judge would send the case to trial, "Particularly since the two sides have offered very conflicting empirical data about pay and revenue—and this is a case where economic analysis is crucial to determining the correct application of law—the judge might be inclined to let the jury hear the case," he wrote.

Andrew Das of the *New York Times,* who had been following the lawsuit, had a similar take. "Both the players and U.S. Soccer expect [the judge] to allow the case to proceed to trial rather than pick a winner now on one side's terms."

But judges in courts are like referees on the field. And like players who try to sway a referee's call, each side would try to affect the outcome of the case by responding directly to the other's motion for summary judgment. Work on the reply briefs, where each side counters the other's arguments, began.

A Pandemic Brewing

March 2020

By early March 2020, the worldwide Covid death toll surpassed 3,000 people.

The media began speculating about what would happen with the summer Olympics. Would the games be canceled or postponed? Would the Olympic Committee bar travel from certain countries or hold the events but close them to spectators?

The president of the International Olympic Committee reported after a meeting that "neither the word 'cancellation' nor the word 'postponement' was even mentioned." When asked what might happen if the outbreak worsened, he answered, "I will not add fuel to the flame of speculation."

The equal pay trial, too, was still set to begin in a couple of months. Settlement discussions continued, with U.S. Soccer offering $9 million to settle, less than one-sixth of what the women calculated they were due.

A reporter asked Megan Rapinoe what it would take to avoid a trial. "An actual offer for equal pay," she said, "and some considerable damages as well."

That did not appear to be forthcoming, so the women continued to hurtle toward the trial and the Olympics. But they had another tournament to tackle first.

What He Believes

March 2020

In March 2020, the U.S. women headed off to play in the SheBelieves Cup, a four-team international tournament hosted by U.S. Soccer in Florida, New York, and Texas. In the opening match on March 5, the U.S. shut out England 2–0.

On March 8, the anniversary of the filing of their lawsuit, the team would face Spain.

The day before the game, U.S. Soccer president Carlos Cordeiro posted an open letter on Twitter, providing an "update" on the federation's efforts to "chart a new path forward" with the women's team. He explained that U.S. Soccer had obligations to millions of players, coaches, and referees at all levels and that making up the gap in the World Cup prize money offered by FIFA was not "reasonable or fiscally sound." And he touted U.S. Soccer's offers of "multiple contract options," including "identical compensation to our [female and male] players for all matches controlled by U.S. Soccer."

This infuriated the women, because U.S. Soccer had never offered equal pay, not even for friendly matches and tournaments such as the SheBelieves Cup hosted by U.S. Soccer. And any pay rates the federation did match in their offers were tied to rates set years ago, in 2011, with no commitment to match the men's rates in their new contract going forward. Players called the letter "misleading," "dishonest," and "distracting."

Still, the team was excited for the game against Spain. It would be Crystal Dunn's one-hundredth game with the national team. In the locker room before the game, the players cheered and hugged their visionary and versatile defender.

Crystal was all smiles as she strode through the tunnel and into the filled-to-capacity stadium. On the field, Team USA lined up next to the Spanish team, facing their fans. The announcer called Crystal forward. Her family, with her mom carrying a bouquet of flowers, met her. To echoing cheers, Carlos Cordeiro presented Crystal with a framed shirt, with Dunn and 100 on the back.

Crystal smiled graciously.

The team went on to beat Spain 1–0. The U.S. women hadn't lost a game in fourteen months, and their unbeaten streak was now thirty games. They had already racked up twenty-eight goals this year, and had not allowed their opponents a single goal.

The next day, Carlos tweeted, "It was an honor to recognize @ crysdunn_19 for her 100th National Team cap before last night's @ USWNT victory over Spain. Thank you, Crystal, for all you have done and continue to do for this team."

Fans posted dozens of replies, such as:

"You know what you can do to actually recognize @crysdunn_19 and the @USWNT? EQUAL PAY!!!"

"Equal Pay dude."

"#TimesUp #EqualPay"

But the comments became much more strident the next day. Word had gotten out about what U.S. Soccer had written in the response brief they'd filed with the court. U.S. Soccer had claimed "that ***the job*** of MNT players (competing against senior men's national teams) requires a higher level of skill based on speed and strength than does

the job of WNT players (competing against senior women's national teams)." Emphasis theirs.

They also wrote that "MNT players face tougher competition." And they disputed that "the job of the WNT players and the job of MNT players carry equal responsibility." Because men compete in tournaments with bigger cash prizes, U.S. Soccer argued, their level of responsibility was higher. They also asserted that "there is simply more prestige" involved in winning the men's tournaments compared to the women's tournaments.

The women were shocked. "My god, they had said out loud what they had always been thinking," Megan Rapinoe marveled. "You'd think there would be nothing they could say at this point that would surprise us. But even by the standards of the federation, their words were bald-faced misogyny."

The skills required for world-class soccer—such as precise ball handling, quick and clever passing and shooting, strategy and playmaking, teamwork and mental toughness—were not tied to gender. Neither were the components that made watching the sport so mesmerizing: the thrill of the competition, the grace and power of individual performances, the rhythm of skilled athletes working passionately and smoothly together toward a common goal.

Players called the brief "a slap in the face." It made them feel like they were back in the 1950s. The women's public relations representative, Molly Levinson, told the press that the argument "sounds as if it has been made by a caveman" and that this kind of thinking "belongs in the Paleolithic Era."

Becca Roux, the union leader, was also stunned. She had been working with the very same lawyers who had drafted this offensive brief. "How are we ever going to negotiate a CBA?" she wondered. "They have gone down a path that was almost unreconcilable."

"Sadly," Jerry Brewer of the *Washington Post* commented, "I'm not sure everyone in the world understands the sexism of U.S. Soccer's argument. That's why the tone of that motion is as dangerous as it is disappointing. It legitimizes stereotypes and ignorance and, if not shot down forcefully, creates the risk of setting back the inspiring work that the U.S. women's team and many others have done to illuminate the strength, power, and possibilities of women's athletics."

Former player Julie Foudy said U.S Soccer's argument that "you shouldn't make an equal amount because you are inherently inferior" was soul-crushing. "Women are spending an equal amount of time, work equally hard, and show the same level of commitment doing the same things the men are doing," she said. Plus, the women's team offered fans something really special. As athletes who came up playing on local teams with their friends, they were relatable. The team also had a joy and playfulness, as well boldness and flair, which was fun to watch. "And we win," Julie said, "and America loves a winner."

Taylor Twellman, a former men's national team player, ripped U.S. Soccer on *Banter*, his show on ESPN. "Using [women's] biological differences to define their stance makes me want to puke," he said. "U.S. Soccer is supposed to be the leader, uniting everything in this country from coaching, refereeing, youth, professional, amateur soccer, and yet does anyone believe they are leading in this moment? I don't."

Longtime U.S. Soccer sponsor Coca-Cola released a statement calling the filing "unacceptable and offensive," and asked to meet with U.S. Soccer immediately to express its concerns. Visa also demanded a meeting, saying that U.S. Soccer's position is "one which we do not share." Deloitte, another sponsor, said it was "deeply offended by the views expressed by the USSF."

Twitter comments related to Carlos Cordeiro's tweet about honoring Crystal Dunn blew up with outrage.

"Did you happen to tell her that she wasn't as skilled as the men?" someone asked.

"Stop stealing the shine from the USWNT while you are actively trying to deny them equal pay," tweeted another.

"The balls you have to stand out there sharing their glory while you call them inferior behind their backs. Shameful!" wrote a third.

Some people could not quite grasp what all the hoopla was about. "Words matter more in this case than in the inane sports debates that occupy most of our time," Jerry Brewer of the *Washington Post* tried to explain. "The way we talk about these women and their pursuit of fair compensation can elevate the minds of many, or it can send us sliding back down into the exasperating, sexist mud."

This was what concerned the women's team the most.

"It's so dangerous to teach young boys that girls aren't as good as them," Becky Sauerbrunn, a star defender and president of the players union, worried. "It's like leading us all down this bad path to perpetuate sexism that's been around forever."

The women would not, could not, let this stand. They had to do something to voice their outrage at their match against Japan the next day, but they didn't know what. Becca Roux booked a flight to Texas to be with the team. As they banged around different options for protesting, Becca checked their collective bargaining agreement to make sure any protest they planned wouldn't break their contract.

What She Believes

March 2020

On March 11, 2020, a crowd of nearly 20,000 people filled Toyota Stadium in Frisco, Texas, to watch the last match of the SheBelieves Cup between U.S. and Japan. A pall hung over the game, not only because of U.S. Soccer's offensive arguments in the lawsuit, but also because of Covid worries.

That day, with nearly 120,000 cases in 114 countries and more than 4,200 deaths, the World Health Organization declared Covid a global pandemic. Earlier that week, infectious disease expert Anthony Fauci recommended to Congress that professional sporting events should be played without spectators. But there they all were in Texas, the athletes and fans.

The mood in the tunnel before the game was somber. The women were angry and determined. "We were so ready to show the world what real talent, what real energy, what real competitive drive is," Becky Sauerbrunn said. "Like, all those things they argued against us? We were gonna prove them wrong."

The U.S. team was called to the field to a roar of support. The women strode out, faces serious, heads held high. But something was off.

Julie Foudy was commentating on the game for ESPN with Sebastián Salazar. "I notice something different about their warm-up," Sebastián said. "This looks intentional."

All twenty-eight players had turned their warm-up shirts inside out. Where the U.S. Soccer logo should have been, there was only a faint outline. From a distance, one could only make out the four stars signifying their World Cup wins. The message: U.S. Soccer, you don't respect and honor us, so we are not going to respect and honor you.

The players did not smile as they came out on the field. They did not smile for photos.

The opening whistle blew, and the U.S. team scored in the opening minutes. Instead of looking joyful and jumping into each other's arms, the women look angry, their arms crossed.

Midway through the game, as Julie and Sebastián narrated the quick passes and maneuvers, someone gave Sebastián a piece of paper.

"Julie, I have just been handed a statement from USSF president Carlos Cordeiro," he said.

And he read it aloud. "On behalf of U.S. Soccer, I sincerely apologize for the offense and pain caused by the language in this week's court filing, which did not reflect the values of our federation and our tremendous admiration of our women's team. . . ."

Julie took a deep breath and a fifteen-second pause. "I'm going to need some time, so I don't lose my mind on this," she thought. She managed to stay calm and continue analyzing the game.

On the field, the women played on. They cracked some smiles when they won 3–1, their thirty-first straight victory and their third time winning the SheBelieves tournament. But the scene after the game felt constrained and fraught with conflict.

Postgame, fans were barred from direct access to the players. Even the media was restricted. As the women waited to receive their medals, staff members told them that several NBA players had Covid, and the NBA was shutting down.

"It was surreal," Carli Lloyd said.

After the game, Julie interviewed Megan Rapinoe, who blasted U.S. Soccer for its "blatant misogyny and sexism."

"I know we are in a contentious fight," Megan said. "But that crossed the line completely."

And she had a message for all the kids watching. "It's false.... You are not less just because you are a girl, and you are not better just because you are a boy. We are all created equal, and we should all have equal opportunities to go out and pursue our dreams."

Pressure Builds

March 2020

Almost immediately, the U.S. Soccer lawyer on the case resigned, and the federation fired its outside law firm and hired another one.

"They didn't give up, by the way, and say, 'Yes, we will provide equal pay,'" the women's team lawyer, Jeffrey Kessler, pointed out.

All the presenting sponsors of the SheBelieves Cup publicly condemned U.S. Soccer. Even Volkswagen, whose logo on the warm-ups had been hidden by the women's protest, declared, "We stand by the USWNT and the ideals they represent for the world." Their statement said the company was "disgusted" by U.S. Soccer's position and found it "simply unacceptable."

On Twitter, the comments on Carlos Cordeiro's first tweet about Crystal Dunn became more pointed.

"You're ridiculous and your apologies are lip service only. Pay these women their true worth and then do us all a favor and RESIGN. Disgraceful."

"Nice try bud. Resign now."

"I need you to resign. Like yesterday."

"Resign."

"Do the right thing and please resign."

On March 12, 2020, U.S. Soccer president Carlos Cordero did just that.

"The arguments and language contained in this week's legal filing caused great offense and pain, especially for our extraordinary women's national team players, who deserve better," he wrote in his public resignation letter. "It was unacceptable and inexcusable."

He explained, "I did not have the opportunity to fully review the filing in its entirety before it was filed, and I take responsibility for not doing so. Had I done so, I would have objected to language that did not reflect my personal admiration for our women's players or our values as an organization."

The players were skeptical. "What do you mean you didn't know what's being filed?" Becky Sauerbrunn said. "You're the president of U.S. Soccer and your eyeballs didn't see this?"

Jeffrey Kessler thought Carlos's excuses were disingenuous. He noted that all of the sexist arguments had already been made during depositions. "It struck me as so offensive and, frankly, a stupid legal decision to put these arguments in the brief," he said.

Many observers worried that Carlos stepping down would change little. As Meredith Cash of *Business Insider* put it, "it's undoubtedly misguided to pin all of U.S. Soccer's problems on one man. Yes, he undoubtedly oversaw and was, at best, complicit in the mistreatment of the USWNT. Sure, his rebuttals of the women's statements were often ill-timed and tone-deaf. And yes, at the end of the day, we will find him on the wrong side of history. But does that mean that the problems the USWNT has been enduring since long before the start of Cordeiro's reign are suddenly solved? Almost certainly not."

The arguments in the brief mirrored the logic of detractors of women's sports generally, whether in sports bars, in locker rooms, or on social media. Women, some people believe, will never be strong enough, fast enough, skilled enough—and entertaining enough—to merit more investment, more media coverage, or more pay.

Thus, the fight is bigger than equal pay, Cash continued. "Whether the USWNT players—and their supporters—explicitly know it or not, their battle is against an opponent far bigger and far less concrete than Carlos Cordeiro . . . or the U.S. Soccer Federation. It goes beyond both the soccer pitch, the country they represent, and their individual bank accounts. And while the world of athletics is certainly a microcosm for the larger issue at hand, I would argue that the USWNT players' fight transcends sports. By engaging in this conflict, the team is pushing back against the traditional understanding of what women can do. They're battling the learned understanding that women are inherently less capable and less deserving than men. They're fighting against misogyny and sexism itself."

And with an out-of-control virus strangling the globe, these were not the only forces the women faced.

March Madness

Spring 2020

By March 12, 2020, the whole sports world had imploded. College women's and men's basketball tournaments were canceled. Major League Baseball canceled all remaining spring training. The National Basketball Association and the National Hockey League suspended their seasons.

Infectious disease experts feared that the Olympics could become a massive super-spreader event. More than 10,000 athletes from two hundred countries and nearly that many members of the media were due to descend on Tokyo. Eight million tickets had already been sold.

In Japan, a member of the local Olympic organizing committee told the *Wall Street Journal* that he thought it made sense to postpone the games. His comments caused an uproar, and the committee quickly countered. "He certainly said an outlandish thing," the chair of the committee said. "Our basic stance is to proceed with our preparation and hold a safe Olympics."

Two U.S. senators, a Republican and a Democrat, sent a letter to the Olympic committee stating, "If not handled properly, this year's Olympic games present a dangerous opportunity for Covid-19 to spread at unprecedented levels throughout the globe."

President Donald Trump recommended that "all Americans, including the young and healthy, work to engage in schooling from home when possible, avoid gathering in groups of more than ten people, avoid discretionary travel, and avoid eating and drinking at bars, restaurants, and public food courts."

Then, on March 17, the vice president of Japan's Olympic committee came down with Covid. He had attended the March 5 SheBelieves tournament. The USWNT's medical staff began monitoring players closely for symptoms.

Postponement or cancellation of the Olympic games seemed inevitable. But the organizers still didn't make the call.

The members of the women's national team were of many minds about the situation. They lived to compete. They were eager to reclaim the gold medal that had slipped out of their grasp in 2016. Their team and their sport needed to keep up the momentum in order to continue to grow their fan base and to draw attention to their fight for equal pay. Many of the veteran players were in their thirties, nearing retirement age. This could be their last Olympics.

But like the overwhelming majority of athletes polled, national team players worried about jeopardizing their health and the health of millions if the games went on. They worried about how they would train during lockdown. They worried about doing anything that would potentially contribute to the growing tragedy of the pandemic.

The team was stuck in limbo. Courts were also shutting down across the country. As athletes around the world waited to see whether or not they would get to compete, the national team players also waited to see how the shake-up at U.S. Soccer would affect their chances for justice.

A Teammate Takes the Helm

2004 to 2020

Being the president of U.S. Soccer was never part of former player Cindy Parlow Cone's plan. She didn't necessarily want the job. When Cindy retired from the USWNT in 2004, because of multiple concussions, she returned to college to finish her degree and began coaching, leading youth teams, the University of North Carolina, and the Portland Thorns to championship victories.

Early on, Cindy had been recruited by a teammate to join the Athletes' Council at U.S. Soccer. It was a minor obligation, just one meeting a year, but one of the council's goals was to find ways for athletes to have more of a voice in the federation. When the role of vice president opened up in 2019, Cindy and others thought players should fill some leadership positions. She tried to recruit two. "We need an athlete's voice in the room when important decisions are being made in our sport," she said. But both players turned the opportunity down.

"Fine, I'll do it," Cindy said. She was soon elected vice president of U.S. Soccer, an unpaid position that she juggled with being the mother of a young child and coaching a local girls' club team.

"Cindy really took one for the team," Julie Foudy said. "She clearly wanted to get the federation to a place where it was better culturally, better inclusively, better equally—all the things we'd been wanting and working toward for so long."

Cindy had long been dismayed about the treatment of the women's team. As vice president, Cindy wasn't part of many of the important conversations and didn't have much power. When U.S. Soccer filed its offensive brief, she tweeted, "I am hurt and saddened by the brief USSF filed. This issue means so much to me, but more broadly to all men and women and, more importantly, to little girls and boys who are our future. I disavow the troubling statements and will continue to work to forge a better path forward."

She was on a conference call with U.S. Soccer's board of directors the night of March 12 when someone noticed that Carlos Cordeiro had announced his resignation on Twitter. As vice president, Cindy was expected to take over immediately. That night she became the first female president of U.S. Soccer, and the first who had played for a senior U.S. national team.

Cindy felt "thrown into the deep end." The pandemic had just hit. Sports events had shut down, and no one had any idea when those games, and the revenue they generated, would return. She inherited a toxic environment and an expensive and disheartening dispute. U.S. Soccer had already spent millions in legal fees and had alienated fans and perhaps their most valuable team. Sponsors were threatening to abandon the federation and its teams.

But Cindy had been part of the equal pay fight for several decades. She knew that something had to be done.

How could she be the one to do it? Her initial reaction was to list all the ways she was inadequate for the job. She hadn't gone to an Ivy League business school. She had never been the CEO of a Fortune 500 company. How could she lead this massive organization through so many crises? Who was she to think she could change the direction of U.S. Soccer in any meaningful way?

Cindy's former teammate Mia Hamm contacted her to offer help.

"I'm sure your head is spinning right now, but we're going to support you in every way we can," Mia said. Mia also tweeted support: "I have known Cindy Parlow Cone for over two decades as both a teammate and friend. She has always led with integrity and a commitment to others. I have no doubt that she will dedicate herself to making our game better for all."

Still, Steven Goff of the *Washington Post* reported that "there is some skepticism about whether someone already working in the federation can change things." Teammate Julie Foudy understood that "her challenge, as I'm sure Cindy would say, is making people understand that what was in those 2,600 pages is not something that she or many people at U.S. Soccer believe."

But the key challenge for Cindy was overcoming her own insecurities.

She took a deep breath. "Okay," she thought, "what do I bring to this team?"

She cared about equal pay, so that was a top priority. To make equal pay happen, it *had* to be a top priority. She was a former player, so many of the women knew her and knew her level of integrity. Over the years she had become a team builder, and U.S. Soccer needed that. She loved the U.S. Soccer motto: "One nation. One team." She was excited for U.S. Soccer to really embody it.

How could she make that happen?

Postponed

March 2020

The U.S. women's soccer team still hoped to do something that no team had ever done before: win gold at the 2020 Olympics in Tokyo just a year after winning the World Cup. Former player Julie Foudy completely understood that mentality. "We want to be on top of that podium so we could shout out about how we wanted to make the world a better place," she said.

That hope was dashed on March 24 when, in response to the pandemic gripping the globe, the International Olympic Committee announced that the games would "be rescheduled to a date beyond 2020 but not later than summer 2021."

It was a scary prospect for some of the veteran players. Carli Lloyd, Megan Rapinoe, Becky Sauerbrunn, all in their mid- to late thirties, had played in Olympic qualifying games and expected to be on the roster for the Olympics. With the tournament now at least a year off, all the players' spots would be up for grabs again. Would these senior players, these leaders on and off the field, miss their last hurrah?

No matter how the decision impacted them personally, the players supported it. "I do believe this is the right thing to do to ensure the health of spectators, workers, health-care systems and athletes around the world," Carli told the press.

"Absolutely the right decision," Megan said. "There's just no way that I can imagine that a convening of that many people—even if you did only athletes—that that would be safe."

Everyone went their separate ways and into lockdown. The players felt cooped up, only venturing out to empty fields or parking garages to do some training.

Courts and legal offices closed. The women worried their case could stall out too.

"We had no idea what was going to happen," lawyer Jeffrey Kessler said, "whether and when the case would move forward."

Soccer America commentator Beau Dure urged serious settlement talks between the women and U.S. Soccer. "If Covid-19 forces a delay in the proceedings," he wrote, "it's incumbent on both sides to take advantage of that extra time and get this resolved." He pointed out that U.S. Soccer had "plenty of incentive to settle for nearly any sum that won't force them to cut programs" and that the players also had "plenty of incentive to settle because they'll have a tougher time persuading a judge and jury than they've had persuading people in the media and social media." But until the two sides settled, the women and their lawyers had to get ready for trial.

Trial Preparations

April 2020

In April, Judge R. Gary Klausner, who was still considering the motions on summary judgment, postponed the trial until June 16. He would start with jury selection then, and the whole trial could take two to four weeks. Both sides filed motions to exclude any evidence or testimony that they argued was inaccurate or could be distracting or misleading to the jury. The two sides also began drawing up witness lists that could add to up nearly a hundred hours of testimony.

Preparing a case for trial is a matter of telling a compelling story with the facts. The story the team wanted to tell was that they were the best female soccer players in the world, that they had won multiple World Cups and Olympic medals, and that they had outperformed the men's team by every metric. They had the same job as the male players, playing on the same size fields, for the same length of time, by the same rules. They were more popular and brought in more revenue. And yet, by every measure, they were paid less in terms of base pay and bonuses. The only thing that could explain the difference in compensation was discrimination. They were paid less because they were women. That was wrong, and it was illegal.

The lawsuit put former player and U.S. Soccer president Cindy Parlow Cone in a tricky position. She appreciated where the players were coming from. She had walked in their shoes. "I understood their anger, their frustration, their passion," she said. "And on the other side,

I understood the limitations of U.S. Soccer." U.S. Soccer had responsibilities beyond the senior national teams. They ran twenty-five other national teams, including youth national teams, beach and futsal (indoor soccer) teams, and teams for players with hearing loss and cerebral palsy, and for players who used power chairs. They also oversaw training for coaches and referees.

And even as president, Cindy didn't have the power to make any final decisions. She wanted to pursue settlement discussions, but the board of directors had authority over the legal strategy.

U.S. Soccer's new legal team dropped its claims that there was "indisputable science" that female players lacked the "skill" of male players and that they faced a lower level of "responsibility." Instead, they worked to show that the women's total compensation was higher than the men's.

The lawyers began figuring out what witnesses to call, in what order, and what evidence to share at trial. They drafted, tweaked, and practiced opening arguments to the jury. They even made plans for hotel rooms, office space, and lunch for lawyers, players, and witnesses.

Then Judge Klausner dropped a legal bomb.

A Surprise Ruling

May 2020

On May 1, 2020, defender Becky Sauerbrunn was passing the time in lockdown playing a video game when her cell phone dinged. It was a text message from the team's leadership group chat. Midfielder Sam Mewis had written, "So what does this mean we fucking lost?"

Kelley O'Hara had just returned from a workout when she got the text. She was confused and wondered if Sam had meant to text something else or someone else.

"What are you talking about?" she texted back.

The judge had ruled. He dismissed the part of the women's case focused on pay discrimination. "It was a horrible decision," Jeffrey Kessler said. "A horrible day."

Sports Illustrated deemed the ruling "a stunning legal development." The *Wall Street Journal*'s headline called it "a severe blow." *ESPN* described it as "a potentially fatal setback."

As news spread to the U.S. National Team players around the country and globe, they dialed into a conference call.

"This just doesn't fundamentally make sense," someone said.

"I don't understand it at all."

Everyone wanted to know: Why? How could Judge Klausner do that? On what basis?

Jeffrey tried to explain what felt unexplainable. "So what the judge said was, first of all, that we agreed to the deal."

No one had to point out that the federation had never once offered them equal pay. The team had felt bullied into their current contract.

Jeffrey went on. The judge had also accepted an "erroneous argument." He said that the women's side had not proved unequal pay, because the women's team made more than the men's team.

As the players listened, they looked grimly at their screens. They rubbed their foreheads in disbelief, stared out the window, pressed their fists to their mouths.

They had heard this argument before and wanted to scream. "But we won the World Cup! And they didn't even qualify! Of course we made more!"

Everyone was shocked, upset, and deeply frustrated. They struggled to wrap their heads around the ruling. What it basically said was to be paid equally in the future, the women had to continue to win more and win at the highest levels. Jeffrey was disturbed by the implication. "The kind of pressure that puts on them," he thought, "isn't remotely lawful."

Here they were in the middle of the Covid pandemic, separated by many miles and not playing the game that gave them so much joy, so much purpose. And it felt like they had lost everything. Many on the call shed tears.

The battle was "exhausting," according to Megan Rapinoe, who envied the simplicity of the male players' lives. "From age fourteen or fifteen, these guys are not thinking about, nor do they have to think about, anything other than being an amazing soccer player," she said. "That's their job; that's their sole focus." And that's how it should be for her and her teammates, how it should have been for the women who preceded them, and how it should be for all the girls good enough to make it to the top in the future.

Everything seemed bleak.

"I'm confident this decision was wrong, and it will be reversed on appeal," Jeffrey told the women.

"We can't give up, right?" one of the players said.

"Yes, it's a setback. Yes, it's a disappointment," said midfielder Sam Mewis. "But we did this for a reason. It's gonna take a lot more than this to stop us."

DANESHA ADAMS • MICHELLE AKERS • KORBIN ALBERT • HEATHER ALDAMA • AMY ALLMA
YAEL AVERBUCH • SAMANTHA BAGGETT • BETHANY BALCER • NICOLE BARNHART • TRACEY BA
TAMI BATISTA • JUSTI BAUMGARDT • LAKEYSIA BEENE • DEBBIE BELKIN • KEISHA BELL • D
BENDER • JENNY BENSON • ANGELA BERRY • JACKIE BILLETT • KYLIE BIVENS • DANIELLE BORGM
SHANNON BOXX • DENISE BOYER-MURDOCH • JEN BRANAM • AMBER BROOKS • THORI (STA
BRYAN • TARA BUCKLEY • SHERI BUETER • SUSAN BUSH • LORI BYLIN • JANE CAMPBELL •
CASSELLA • LORI CHALUPNY • BRANDI CHASTAIN • MANDY CLEMENS • SAM COFFEY • DAN
COLAPRICO • LISA COLE • ROBIN CONFER • KERRY CONNORS • KIM CONWAY • ALANA COOK • ANN
• PAM (BAUGHMAN) CORNELL • STEPHANIE (LOPEZ) COX • ALEISHA CRAMER • AMANDA CROM
• COLETTE CUNNINGHAM • ABBY DAHLKEMPER • MARIAN DALMY • TIERNA DAVIDSON • CINDY
• SAVANNAH DEMELO • MICHELLE DEMKO • KRISTI DEVERT • TINA DIMARTINO • IMANI DORS
BETSY DRAMBOUR • TRACY (NOONAN) DUCAR • JOAN DUNLAP-SEIVOLD • CRYSTAL DUNN • DAN
EGAN • TINA (FRIMPONG) ELLERTSON • WHITNEY ENGEN • STACEY ENOS • JULIE (JOHNSTON)
• RONNIE FAIR • LORRIE FAIR • JOY (BIEFELD) FAWCETT • KAREN FERGUSON • JESSICA FISCH
MIA FISHEL • KENDALL FLETCHER • MEREDITH FLORANCE • DANIELLE (GARRETT) FOTOPOUL
JULIE FOUDY • EMILY FOX • ADRIANNA FRANCH • MICHELLE FRENCH • CARIN (JENNINGS) GAB
• LINDA GANCITANO • MORGAN (BRIAN) GAUTRAT • WENDY GEBAUER • GRETCHEN GEGG • N
GIRMA • LISA GMITTER • CINDY GORDON • SANDI GORDON • JEN GRUBB • SARAH HAGEN • KR
HAMILTON • LINDA HAMILTON • MIA HAMM • HALEY HANSON • RUTH HARKER • ASHLYN HAR
MARY HARVEY • ASHLEY HATCH • DEVVYN HAWKINS • TUCKA HEALY • TOBIN HEATH • APRIL HEINR
• HOLLY HELLMUTH • LORI HENRY • SHANNON HIGGINS • JAELENE HINKLE • LAUREN (CH
HOLIDAY • LINDSEY HORAN • JAELIN HOWELL • ANGELA HUCLES • SOFIA HUERTA • SARAH HUF
• LINDSEY HUIE • PATTY IRIZARRY • MARCI (MILLER) JOBSON • LAURA JONES • NATASHA
CHRISTINA KAUFMAN • BETH KELLER • DEBBIE KELLER • SHERRILL KESTER • AUBREY KINGS
• MEGHAN KLINGENBERG • JENA KLUEGEL • TAYLOR KORNIECK • NANCY KRAMARZ • ANNA K
• ALI KRIEGER • CASEY (SHORT) KRUEGER • JENNIFER LALOR • ROSE LAVELLE • AMY LEPE

PART III
Overtime

We've begun to raise daughters more like sons . . .
but few have the courage to raise our sons
more like our daughters.
—Gloria Steinem

DNEY LEROUX • GINA LEWANDOWSKI • KRISTINE LILLY • KELLY LINDSEY • LORI LINDSEY •
LLOYD • JOANNA LOHMAN • ALLIE LONG • JILL LOYDEN • KRISTIN LUCKENBILL • CATARINA
ARIO • HAILIE MACE • SHANNON MACMILLAN • HOLLY MANTHEI • KATE (SOBRERO) MARKGRAF
Y MARQUAND • ELLA MASAR • JEN (STREIFFER) MASCARO • KIM MASLIN-KAMMERDEINER
RRITT MATHIAS • STEPHANIE MCCAFFREY • MEGAN MCCARTHY • SAVANNAH MCCASKILL •
IA MCDERMOTT • JESSICA MCDONALD • TEGAN MCGRADY • JEN MEAD • KRISTIE MEWIS •
NTHA MEWIS • TIFFENY MILBRETT • [illegible] ARY-FRANCES MONROE • ALEX MORGAN
IA MOULTRIE • SIRI MULLINIX • CASEY MURPHY • ALYSSA NAEHER • CHRISTINE NAIRN • NATALIE
N • JENNA NIGHSWONGER • CAS [illegible] KES • KEALIA OHAI • KELLEY O'HARA •
OLEKSIUK • HEATHER O'REILLY • LAUREN ORLANDOS • ANN ORRISON • LESLIE OSBORNE • CARLA
DEN) OVERBECK • MEGAN OYSTER • JAIME PAGLIARULO • CINDY PARLOW CONE • TAMMY PEARMAN
LY PICKERING • CARSON PICKETT • LOUELLEN POORE • CHRISTEN PRESS • NANDI PRYCE
DGE PURCE • CAROLINE PUTZ • SARAH RAFANELLI • CHRISTIE (PEARCE) RAMPONE •
A RAMSEY • SARA RANDOLPH • MEGAN RAPINOE • KERI (SANCHEZ) RAYGOR • SHARON
URTRY) REMER • KATHY RIDGEWELL • STEPHANIE RIGAMAT • TIFFANY ROBERTS • LEIGH
ROBINSON • TRINITY RODMAN • AMY RODRIGUEZ • SHAUNA ROHBOCK • CHRISTY ROWE •
UTTEN • ASHLEY SANCHEZ • BECKY SAUERBRUNN • KELLY (WILSON) SCHMEDES • MEGHAN
UR • LAURA SCHOTT • LAURIE SCHWOY • BRIANA SCURRY • NIKKI SERLENGA • JAEDYN
• DANIELLE SLATON • GAYLE SMITH • SOPHIA SMITH • TAYLOR SMITH • HOPE SOLO •
SONNETT • ZOLA SPRINGER • AMY STEADMAN • JILL STEWART • JENNIFER STRONG •
SULLIVAN • MALLORY PUGH SWANSON • JANINE SZPARA • LINDSAY TARPLEY • BRITTANY
R • ALYSSA THOMPSON • CHRIS TOMEK • RITA TOWER • INDIA TROTTER • ERIKA TYMRAK
HEL (BUEHLER) VAN HOLLEBEKE • TISHA VENTURINI • M.A. VIGNOLA • ALY WAGNER • KELLY
ERT • ABBY WAMBACH • MARCIE WARD • MORGAN WEAVER • SASKIA WEBBER • KRISTEN
S • CHRISTIE WELSH • SARA WHALEN • KACEY WHITE • CAT (REDDICK) WHITEHILL • LYNN
AMS • STACI WILSON • ANGIE WOZNUK • KIM WYANT • VERONICA ZEPEDA • MCCALL ZERBONI

Picking Apart the Ruling

May 2020

"If you know this team at all you know we have a lot of fight left in us," Becky Sauerbrunn posted on Twitter. "We knew this wasn't going to be easy, change never is."

Before deciding next steps, the women and their lawyers had to understand what the judge had said and why. In the ruling, District Court Judge R. Gary Klausner explained that any discrimination lawsuit must first establish that wage discrimination has happened. "To do this, Plaintiffs must show that (1) they performed substantially equal work as MNT players, (2) under similar working conditions, and (3) MNT players were paid more."

The opinion focused on number three, whether the women's team earned more or less than the men's team. The judge had leaned on U.S. Soccer's expert report by Carlyn Irwin, which showed that "WNT players received *more* money than MNT players on both a cumulative and an average per-game basis." (Emphasis by the judge.)

He continued, writing, "In response, Plaintiffs have offered evidence that (1) WNT players are paid lower bonuses for friendlies, World Cup-related games, and other tournaments; (2) WNT players would have made more under the MNT CBA than they did under their own CBA, and; (3) USSF agents made statements to the effect that the WNT players are paid less than MNT players."

Judge Klausner pointed out that the women were offered and rejected a pay-to-play model similar to the men's contract, while acknowledging that the women's offer had lower bonuses than the men's contract. To the judge, it didn't matter that the women's bonuses were lower because they were part of a broader package that the women negotiated and agreed to as a union. It also didn't matter to him that the women would have made much more money if they were paid under the men's agreement. "This method of comparison not only fails to account for the choices made during collective bargaining, it also ignores the economic value of the [security] that WNT players receive. . . ."

Finally, it didn't matter to him than U.S. Soccer officials had admitted under oath that the women were paid less than the men, if, as the Irwin report showed, they actually made more. Thus, his opinion discounted the women's expert analysis on differing rates and instead was based heavily on the numbers and analysis from U.S. Soccer's expert.

Because Judge Klausner believed that the women had failed to prove they were paid less, he did not have to address whether the women performed substantially equal work as male players. He simply dismissed the equal pay part of the case.

The *Washington Post* called the ruling "a crushing blow." *New York Times* reporter Andrew Das called it "a devastating rejection of the core argument of the women's case." The women were, he pointed out, beaten by their own success. They had received so much performance pay for their global dominance that it overshadowed the huge inequities in their rates of pay. Andrew noted that if the men had qualified for their World Cup, their earnings would have "swelled their paydays from U.S. Soccer far beyond what the women could ever earn."

Columnist Sally Jenkins's heart went out to the team. "They can beat sexism," she wrote. "And they can beat the world. But they can't beat sexism, a global pandemic, and a bad referee all at the same time."

By bad referee, she meant Judge Klausner. His decision, she contended, was "nonsensical." Without even getting into the math, she said, "Even I can see that the women had to win more games, with higher stakes—in fact, they had to win everything in sight—just to get within $8,000 of a men's team that couldn't win a preliminary."

"To repeat," she emphasized, "U.S. Soccer essentially paid a woman the same for winning two championships as it paid a man for a preliminary round loss."

"Worse, and most offensively," she pointed out, the judge said that "the women chose this."

The general counsel of the National Women's Law Center was also critical of the "they bargained for it" part of the ruling. "It's not a defense under the law to say that [an employee] agreed to discrimination," she told the *Washington Post*. "It's not a defense legally, and I don't think it's a defense morally."

The whole ruling was worrisome to the law center, which was fighting for pay equity in Congress, the states, and the courts. Judges in future cases would look to the ruling for guidance—and that could be damaging to discrimination claims. "No one is happy here when courts make bad decisions about equal pay cases," the law center wrote in a blog. "And the mistake that was made in this case definitely drew our attention. U.S. Soccer is violating the law—namely the Equal Pay Act—and they need to be held accountable just like anyone else who isn't paying their employees equally."

This case, the center recognized, was about more than just soccer. "The women's soccer team's fight for equal pay isn't just about one team, or one group of players. It's setting a precedent for athletes and women everywhere."

A Minor Victory

May 2020

Judge Klausner's ruling also included the Title VII part of the lawsuit, which focused on working conditions. Most compelling to the judge was the fact that from 2015 to 2020, U.S. Soccer spent $9 million on airfare for the men's team while spending only $5 million on the women's team even though the women had more games.

He was not persuaded by the federation's argument that they booked charter flights for the men but not the women because the men needed the "competitive advantage" that came from charter flights. "For one, this rationale does not fully explain the gross disparity in money spent on airfare and hotels for the teams," he wrote. "Additionally, it compels the implausible conclusions that the WNT never faced a similar situation during the relevant time period when it too would have benefited from the 'competitive advantage' that comes from charter flights."

The judge ruled that the women had a legitimate claim for discriminatory working conditions, for differences in charter flights and hotels and support such as medical professionals and trainers. The ruling did not mean that the women had won on those claims, just that they would be allowed to try to make their case in front of a jury at trial.

Overall, the victory for U.S. Soccer was far from unequivocal. Sponsors continued to voice outrage at the situation. The fight had tarnished the federation's reputation with elite players, youth players, and fans. "It's like if they win," Megan Rapinoe said, "no one wins."

Congress Holds a Hearing

March 2021

Not much happened with the lawsuit, the equal pay battle, or on soccer pitches as the world struggled through the pandemic.

On March 24, 2021, U.S. Representative Carolyn Mahoney of New York presided over a Congressional hearing on the gender pay gap. "Today is Equal Pay Day. But it's not a celebration," she said. "Today marks the extra days and weeks it takes American women to earn the same pay that their male counterparts made in the previous year." Her outrage was palpable. "Three. Extra. Months. Of work!" she exclaimed. "Just to earn the same amount."

Representative Mahoney presided over the hearing from her central podium in a vast, nearly empty hearing room. She sat on a large black leather chair with many chairs on each side of her. But they were all empty. Large tables where witnesses would normally testify were also empty. So were the seats for spectators. A lone tech person managed screens in the room.

Though the Covid pandemic had shut down the ordinary operations of Congress, Representative Mahoney and other members of Congress thought the ongoing problem of the gender pay gap was too important and too persistent to ignore. So they held the hearing with members, witnesses, and spectators tuning in by videoconference.

"Today in 2021, on average, women are still paid only eighty-two cents to every dollar paid to a man." Representative Mahoney pointed out that the gender pay gap is even worse for women of color, with Black women earning sixty-three cents to the dollar, Native American women earning sixty cents, and Latina women making just fifty-five cents. "This is a disgrace, and it has long-term consequences."

Pay Gap

All men: $1.00

All women: 82 cents

Black women: 63 cents

Native American women: 60 cents

Latina women: 55 cents

Representative Mahoney's first witness was Megan Rapinoe, who videoconferenced in from Seattle.

"Do you swear to tell the truth, the whole truth, and nothing but the truth?" Representative Mahoney asked.

"Yes," Megan replied. She sat in a beige room with long curtains, a table lamp, and two small framed prints. She wore a blue-and-white striped shirt buttoned to the top, a simple string of pearls, and a navy blazer.

She began her testimony. "Thank you everyone for having me here today. It is an honor to be here in front of you. It's probably no surprise, but equal pay and equality in general is a deep and personal passion of mine. And what we've learned and what we continue to learn is that there's no level of status and there's no accomplishment or power that will protect you from the clutches of inequality," she said.

"One cannot simply outperform inequality or be excellent enough to escape discrimination of any kind. And I'm here today because I know firsthand that this is true. We're so often told in this country that if you just work hard and continue to achieve, you will be rewarded and rewarded fairly. It's the promise of the American dream. But that promise has not been for everyone." Megan's pinkish-lavender hair was brushed up in a neat, almost playful pompadour. But she seemed sad and deadly serious.

"The United States Women's National team has won four World Cup championships. We've won four Olympic gold medals on behalf of this great country. We've filled stadiums, we've broken viewing records, we've sold out of our jerseys—all the popular metrics by which we are judged. And yet despite all of this, we're still paid less than our male counterparts for each trophy, of which there are many, for each win, for each tie, for each time we play—less.

"In fact, instead of lobbying with the women's team in our efforts for equal pay and equality in general, the U.S. Soccer Federation has continually lobbied against our efforts and the efforts of millions of people marginalized by gender in the United States. And if it can happen to us and can happen to me—with the brightest light shining on us at all times—it can and it does happen to everyone who is marginalized by gender."

One of Representative Mahoney's colleagues in the U.S. Senate, Kirsten Gillibrand, knew from experience how true this statement was. Before being elected to Congress, she was a lawyer working in a big firm in New York. Early in her career, she learned that a male colleague who had graduated from law school the same year, had a similar background and experience, and worked on the same kinds of cases had an hourly rate higher than hers.

"I really don't think this is fair," she told the managing partners of the firm.

They agreed and upped her rate.

The next year, she noticed the same problem with another colleague.

Again she approached the managing partners, and again they adjusted her rate.

The third year it happened again.

"The story is the same everywhere, whether you're an executive, whether you're a domestic worker, whether you're a soccer player," the National Women's Law Center noted.

But the U.S. Women's National Team had not given up, and Megan Rapinoe did not want Congress to give up either. She finished her testimony on a rousing note. "We don't have to wait. We don't have to continue to be patient for decades on end. We can change that today. We can change that right now. We just have to want to."

Two Women in Charge

Spring 2021

Cindy Parlow Cone desperately wanted change. She had been on both sides of the table, as a player and as a volunteer at U.S. Soccer. Now her goal was to change the shape of the table to a circle so there would be no sides. "How do we bring everyone together to figure out how we solve this?" she wondered.

For Cindy, the first order of business was building trust. She remembered as a player that no one trusted the federation. They called them "the feds" and "the suits." But the team trusted Cindy. "The players knew that I was never going to say anything that I couldn't do," she realized. Even more, the players also had a sense that "this was *my* fight that I wanted to solve." She would be careful not to violate that trust.

Union leader Becca Roux was hopeful at the prospect of working with Cindy. "Cindy didn't crave power," Becca said. "She actually just craved helping make change and making things better, which is a rarity in this world."

Cindy and Becca thought they might be able to resolve the working conditions part of the lawsuit out of court. They both knew two things: one, going to trial on the narrow issue of working conditions would be expensive for both sides. Two, settlement of the working conditions part of the lawsuit could create some positive momentum toward bigger changes.

U.S. Soccer had cleaned house, and there were many new faces around the table. The federation had new lawyers negotiating the CBA and new lawyers working on the lawsuit. The tone had shifted too. The two sides began talking and sharing data about stadiums, playing surfaces, staffing, hotels, and transportation. Instead of fighting over whether women and men had a right to equal working conditions, they focused on what equal really meant and what language in a settlement and an updated contract might spell out.

Both sides came to agreement relatively quickly. On April 12, 2021, Judge R. Gary Klausner approved the settlement on working conditions. Though thirty-five pages long, the agreement's tenets were simple: U.S. Soccer would provide equal resources to the USMNT and USWNT with the respect to charter air travel and specialized professional support services, and would also provide "equally acceptable venues and playing surfaces" and comparable hotel accommodations.

But on one important point, U.S. Soccer wouldn't budge. The final document stated that "nothing contained herein . . . is to be construed or deemed an admission of liability, culpability, negligence, or wrongdoing on the part of USSF." In other words, U.S. Soccer denied that it had done anything wrong.

That was a disappointment. "For huge societal change to happen, there first has to be acknowledgment that there was wrongdoing in the past," Becca Roux said.

The two sides also remained far apart on compensation. Cindy went on the radio to tout U.S. Soccer's open offer to talk with the team about equal pay for games the federation controlled, such as international friendlies, a men's tournament called the U.S. Open Cup, and the women's SheBelieves Cup. That left out other major tournaments, including the World Cup. The women's team released a statement: "USSF has not offered to meet with the players to resolve equal pay. In truth, USSF's last settlement offer, which was over a year ago, offered far less than equal pay to the players." Still, U.S. Soccer continued to declare an intention to "come to resolution outside of the court system."

"To be clear," said Jeffrey Kessler, attorney for the players, "this was not a case of new leadership coming in and immediately saying, 'Oh, you're getting equal pay.' No. The women had to continue to fight."

The Appeal

April 2021

With U.S. Soccer still not agreeing to equal pay, the women forged ahead with their legal battle. On April 14, 2021, they filed their appeal with the U.S. Court of Appeals for the Ninth Circuit. It powerfully countered the federation's argument that there was no discrimination because the women's team earned more than the men's team. The women earned slightly more, but they won *a third* more games than the men's team. When pay is linked to performance, as it is in soccer, pay should be equal for equal performances and notably different for notably different levels of performance.

"In effect, the court held that pay is equal if a woman can obtain the same amount of pay as a man by working more and performing better. That is not the law," the appeal said. "Under the court's approach, the women had to be the best in the world to achieve the same per-game pay as the much less successful men. That is not an equal rate of pay."

Again, the women had to wait to see what U.S. Soccer—and ultimately a three-judge appeals panel—would do next.

U.S. Soccer vs. the Men's National Team

Spring 2021

Meanwhile, the men's national team had been playing under an expired contract since 2018. Their negotiations were also contentious. When Cindy Parlow Cone accepted the presidency, she got a call from Mark Levinstein, the acting executive director of the men's players' union. "I just wanted to say hi and touch base before we have to get more adversarial."

She appreciated that.

"You know, Cindy, there's one thing that every single player who has ever played for a men's team or a women's team has in common," he said.

"What's that?"

"They all hate the federation."

She laughed. "I know, I was one of those players."

"Okay, I just want you not to forget that, because that's the world we're in and that's what we're trying to change."

"I know," she replied.

Mark hoped she really could work from the inside to turn things around.

Though their plight wasn't as dire as the women's situation, the men's team had also felt mistreated and underpaid by U.S. Soccer for decades. Before they had a union, U.S. Soccer told them, "Pick a player rep and we'll negotiate with them."

"We're not doing that," the players replied.

"Why not?"

"We've had three player reps in the last six years. Each one was forceful, the kind of guy we wanted to represent us, and each went and met with you. And each time, they never got called up to the team again."

"Well, maybe they weren't that good," U.S. Soccer said.

"And maybe they were," the team replied.

Even after they unionized, the male players still felt at a disadvantage when negotiating with their employer. U.S. Soccer controlled every U.S. player's access to international soccer. National team players, whether male or female, had nowhere to turn if they wanted to play for their country. A monopoly employer like that has enormous power and can pay their employees as little as they want and do as little for them as they want.

Employers also have an incentive to delay updating an expired contract. The longer they pay the lower rates of the old contract, the more money they save. That was why the men's players' union insisted throughout their negotiations in 2019 and 2020 that any final deal had to include retroactive pay.

While negotiating, the men's team also tried to keep an eye on the issue of equal pay for the women's team. "We were totally on board with the idea that they're a national team like we are," Mark told U.S. Soccer. But his priority, his job, was looking out for the men's team. Mark worried about the short careers of top-level soccer players, particularly what would happen to the ones without college degrees once forced off the field by age or injury. So he fought hard for them.

By June 2021, the men's team thought they finally had a reasonable deal. Key components were generous revenue sharing and $11 million to cover the pay the men would have earned if this agreement had been in place, as it should have been, by 2018. But before final confirmation, U.S. Soccer went silent. And while the men were playing in the Gold Cup tournament, they got a letter from U.S. Soccer. The board did not approve the deal. There was still no new contract.

The men were furious. Even worse, they had lost the leverage they could have had by threatening to strike. Sixteen of the next seventeen games were World Cup qualifiers. If they called a strike and missed a qualifying game, they would forgo any chance of playing in the most important tournament in the world. They couldn't even think of striking until qualifiers were over in March 2022.

In the meantime, the men found another way to make their voices heard.

Friends of the Court

July 2021

"Noteworthy" and "the strongest backing they have offered yet," is how soccer journalist Meg Linehan of *The Athletic* characterized the next move by the men's national team. On July 30, 2021, with settlement discussions ongoing and the women's team continuing to pursue their appeal, the U.S. men's national team filed an amicus, or friend of the court, brief.

Amicus briefs tell the court how some people not in a lawsuit view the legal arguments and possible implications of various rulings. Courts welcome these briefs because interested parties offer expertise and perspectives that might be missing from the two opposing sides.

The amicus brief from the U.S. men's national team stated, "The men stand with the women in their fight to secure the equal pay they deserve." They wanted to share their view from the inner circle of U.S. Soccer: the women's deals were not as good as the men's deals, U.S. Soccer had been intentionally trying to give less to the women, and the discrimination had been ongoing since 1996.

The men's decades working for the same employer as the women gave them valuable perspective, they explained. "The United States Soccer Federation markets the United States Men's and Women's National Teams under the slogan, 'One Nation. One Team.' But for more than thirty years, the federation has treated the Women's National Team players as second-class citizens, discriminating against the women in their wages and working conditions and paying them less than the Men's National Team players, even as U.S. Soccer has enjoyed a period of extraordinary financial growth. The federation has never offered or provided equal pay to the women, and the district court's holding to the contrary cannot be squared with the facts." They argued that the discrimination was clear and obvious just by looking at the contracts: "The federation pays the women lower performance bonuses and lower per-game appearance fees than the men."

They pointed out that the district court used "oversimplified math" by "improperly adding" the men's and women's pay and then dividing by the total number of games. The calculation did not consider whether those games were wins, draws, or losses, or whether they were low-stakes friendly games or high-stakes tournament games. Since U.S. Soccer regularly paid differently according to those metrics, they should have been part of the calculation.

"A woman's rate of pay is not equal to a man's if the woman must consistently achieve better outcomes merely to get to the same place," the brief explained. If the women had won fewer games and fewer important games and if the men had won more, "the per-game disparity would have been obvious, glaring, and undeniable."

The men's team also took on U.S. Soccer's claim that the men's and women's contract structures were too different to compare. They broke this down for the judge. Players on both teams were paid for two main tasks: playing games regardless of the outcome (appearance fees) and bonuses for wins and ties, especially against high-ranked teams and in important tournaments (pay for performance).

They detailed for the court how this worked. In the women's contract, some appearance fees came in the form of a salary that ranged from $36,000 to $100,000. Players' per-game appearance fees were easily found by dividing the salary by the number of games they played. For the salaried female players, the per-game fees were $3,600 to $4,250. The women who were not salaried earned $3,240 to $4,000 per game. Notably, both were paid less than men, who all earned roughly $5,000 per game.

Per-Game Appearance Fees:

Unsalaried female players: $3,240 to $4,000

Salaried female players: $3,600 to $4,250

All male players: $5,000

Performance bonuses, based solely on the outcome of a match, were also skewed. In 2019, for example, if the men's team won a friendly match against a team ranked third in the world, each man would earn an additional $12,675. For a similar win, the women's performance bonus was only $8,500.

Performance Bonus for Beating a Team Ranked Third Internationally:

Women: $8,500

Men: $12,675

If there was any doubt that the men's and women's national team players did equal work, the men's brief cleared that up. "The women have dedicated their minds and bodies to competing and succeeding at the highest level. They have spent long hours in practice and trained relentlessly to stay in peak physical condition. They have risked injury and played through pain for the benefit of their team. They have sacrificed time with their family and friends to train and travel across the globe. Representing the United States on the international soccer stage is an honor and a privilege for every athlete, male or female—and it is also an incredibly demanding job, mentally and physically, that warrants fair and appropriate pay and working conditions." They addressed the women's high level of responsibility, noting that the USWNT "held off their toughest challengers in hostile stadiums, and succeeded even while carrying the burden and stress of sky-high expectations."

The men were also concerned about how damaging the district court's ruling was to women everywhere. "The federation's discrimination also sends a corrosive public message to women and girls that, even at the highest level, no matter how hard they work or how much they succeed, they can and will be diminished and undervalued by their employers. That is as dispiriting as it is unlawful."

More Friends of the Court

July 2021

The Equal Employment Opportunity Commission (EEOC), where the players had first registered a complaint, also filed an amicus brief, which delved into the pertinent legal issues in the case. The brief highlighted a ruling in an earlier equal pay case that dictated that comparisons of pay rates should consider "*quantity or quality of output*." (Emphasis theirs.) The lower court's analysis, they wrote, "ignored the quality of the women's output—i.e., their significantly larger number of high-profile games played and won, including two World Cup championships." In fact, the EEOC pointedly criticized the district court, which "generally credited the defendant's evidence over the plaintiffs'.

"Simply put, the WNT offered sufficient evidence to support a finding that they received a lower rate of pay to perform the same job as the MNT," the EEOC wrote.

The EEOC also took issue with U.S. Soccer's claim that the women got exactly what they wanted and bargained for. "As to the notion that the women 'traded' higher bonuses for more salaries, the record reflects that the WNT was never offered the same bonus structure as the MNT in the first place—one cannot trade away what one does not have to bargain with."

A third brief was filed by sixty-five equal-rights organizations led by the National Women's Law Center and the Women's Sports Foundation, founded by tennis pioneer Billie Jean King. These organizations offered the court a broader context for the case. "The gender wage gap harms hundreds of millions of women in the United States and is persistent across every segment of the labor market," they wrote. "The district court's erroneous interpretation of the EPA and Title VII—and its endorsement of blatant pay disparities here—threatens to perpetuate unequal pay and thus, gender discrimination." The brief shared the latest data on the gender pay gap.

- Women make up nearly half of the workforce.
- Women are typically primary or co-breadwinner in their households.
- They receive more than fifty percent of bachelor's, master's, and doctorate degrees awarded each year.
- To close lifetime pay gaps, white women would have to work twelve years longer, Black women twenty-six years longer, Native American women thirty years longer, and Latina women thirty-five years longer than an average man.
- The gender pay gap has not changed significantly over the last decade.
- The wage gap hits women as soon as they enter the workforce and increases over their careers.
- Pay parity would cut the poverty rate for working women in half.

They also shared some sports-specific data:

- Boys have over one million more opportunities to play sports in high school than girls.
- Female athletes have "substantially fewer" sports opportunities in college than men and receive $240 million less in athletic scholarship funding.
- Men's sports receive "overwhelmingly more media coverage" than women's sports.

Further, the brief pointed out that U.S. Soccer controlled the size of venues where the teams played, the ticket pricing, and how much marketing was done, and that U.S. Soccer had "chosen to underinvest in the women's team, hamstringing the team's ability to generate revenue.

"USSF cannot limit the ways in which the women's team brings in revenue, and then point to lower revenues to justify unequal pay," they wrote.

They too reminded the court that the text of the EPA requires courts to evaluate rates of pay. "Employers cannot require women to be more successful in their jobs to make up for the difference in their rate of pay." And they quoted the EPA regulation that stated, "The inclusion in a collective bargaining agreement of unequal rates of pay does not constitute a defense."

All three amicus briefs were unanimous in their recommendation to the court of appeals: the judges should reverse the district court's decision and put the women's case back on track for trial.

Pressure to Settle

2021

No one knew how the persuasive amicus briefs would affect the appeal. But other developments were also putting pressure on U.S. Soccer to settle. *Northeastern University Law Review* published a scathing critique of U.S. Soccer's position in the lawsuit. It wasn't so much that the three professors who wrote the article thought U.S. Soccer should lose the lawsuit. Rather, they pointed out that U.S. Soccer, as a nonprofit organization with a stated commitment to gender equity, needed to "set a standard of equal pay for male and female players." On its website, U.S. Soccer described its mission as "promoting and governing soccer in the U.S. to achieve recognition for excellence in, among other things, gender equality." Whether or not U.S. Soccer could win the appeal, the law review authors urged the federation to do the right thing and settle the case.

A journalist for *Sportico* also raised some important questions about U.S. Soccer's resistance to equal pay. Delving into the federation's financials, he noted that U.S. Soccer had spent nearly $19 million for outside legal help from spring 2019 to spring 2020. In fact, U.S. Soccer's legal fees added up to more than $100 million since August 2016. While there were other lawsuits, the primary fight was the battle for equal pay. Was the money better spent fighting the women, or equalizing their pay?

U.S. Soccer also found themselves on the defensive after HBO Max released a sports documentary called *LFG*, named after the USWNT's rallying cry "Let's Fucking Go!" The dramatic, emotional film followed several key players behind the scenes in the equal pay battle, with their lawyer Jeffrey Kessler explaining the legal issues. U.S. Soccer declined to be involved, but a series of tweets defending the federation from their portrayal in the film ended with this: "We're confident that working together we can reach an agreement that benefits everyone moving forward."

Cindy Parlow Cone knew that U.S. Soccer was continuing to wallow in the mud with this conflict. She was desperate to pull the players and the federation back onto a firm field. "We're not on opposite sides," she said in an interview in the fall of 2021. "It may seem that way at times, but we're on the same team, we all have the same goal. It's just how we get there."

She didn't have a clear path forward. The current men's and women's contracts were very different and very complex. Different unions represented the men and the women. Any national team pay deal had to be approved by U.S. Soccer's leadership and board of directors, which also had to manage the organization's total budget, with all its competing priorities.

But Cindy did see an opening. The men's national team was still playing on an expired contract. The women's contract was soon to expire. It would be the first time U.S. Soccer could negotiate both contracts at the same time. Could she bring both teams together to negotiate one contract? What could be more equal than that?

She sent letters to the players' unions and released one to the public. It said, "As a former player, I want to once again make it clear that I, along with all of U.S. Soccer, am 100 percent committed to equal pay for our national team players." She promised that U.S. Soccer would offer the Men's National Team and the Women's National Team the exact same contract. For this to work, she wrote, "We need our men's and women's national teams to come together and rethink how we've done things in the past." The biggest challenge: the vast difference in prize money awarded by FIFA for the World Cup tournaments. She proposed a new round of negotiations between the federation and both teams.

When should this happen? a reporter asked.

"Tomorrow? Yesterday?" Cindy joked. "As soon as possible?"

A Challenge to Her Leadership

January 2020

The lawyers on both sides were scheduled to give oral arguments on the women's appeal before a panel of three judges of the Ninth Circuit on March 7, 2022. Meanwhile, backroom negotiations continued. One of Cindy Parlow Cone's former coaches observed, "I'm actually convinced she's going to work herself to death."

In early January 2022, strangely to some, former U.S. Soccer president Carlos Cordeiro, who resigned under pressure over the offensive legal filing, decided to run for reelection against Cindy. Carlos's platform listed four priorities: invest in all members; men's and women's World Cups in the U.S. within a decade; inclusive governance; and ensuring equal pay.

On his platform, he complained that "after nearly two years, the current U.S. Soccer leadership has not resolved the various lawsuits facing the federation," and he promised that he would "make it a top priority to reach a settlement with our Women's National Team players . . . who deserve equal pay."

But almost immediately, he backpedaled, adding that "our women's players continue to seek the difference in prize money between past FIFA men's and women's World Cups. Yet if U.S. Soccer paid the full difference in past FIFA prize money, it would be harder for the federation to meet its obligations to its other teams, players, coaches, and referees."

Concern about his candidacy was widespread. Beau Dure in the *Guardian* said, "Imagine if, two years after resigning amid the Watergate scandal, Richard Nixon had run for president again."

Adnan Ilyas wrote for *Stars and Stripes FC*, "I frankly think this move represents a stunning degree of arrogance and lack of self-awareness that itself should disqualify him from office." He asked, "Why is it okay to assume that the man who allowed USSF's name to be thrown into the mud, who let sponsors publicly question their support, who fundamentally alienated the most successful program in American soccer history, why assume that man is fit to rule and restore that man to power? Are there really no other, less toxic, options?"

Julie Foudy and the current national team players backed Cindy. "So much happened under your watch, buddy," she said of Carlos's candidacy. "She's actually trying to clean up your mess."

Ticking Clock

February 2022

Lawyer Jeffrey Kessler and the women's team thought they had a good chance of winning the appeal. Whether U.S. Soccer thought they would win or lose the appeal, they knew that the case was not going away. The women had vowed to take their case to the U.S. Supreme Court if need be. And Cindy wanted to reset the relationship between the women and the federation and make things right. The two sides made a last-ditch effort before oral arguments to try to settle the case and end the fight.

Any settlement had to include a commitment to equal pay going forward. For the women, that was nonnegotiable. The other main question was: what would U.S. Soccer pay the women for the years they had suffered discrimination? That came down to a simple number. U.S. Soccer had once offered $9 million to settle. The women's expert calculated that the women would have earned $64 million if they had been paid as much as the men. They had to find a number in between.

Separate from the lawsuit, the women were also in active contract negotiations with U.S. Soccer. The women's and men's union leaders were wary of U.S. Soccer trying to "pit players against players," Becca Roux said. "So we as labor needed to make sure we were working together and not doing things that one of us was going to disagree with at the table."

The two unions worked hard behind the scenes to find a common approach. The women's team wanted equal rates of pay for equal work. The men's team was more focused on equal sharing of revenue. For months they tried to fashion an agreement that would give them both. But how would revenue get divided among players? Would they be paid by number of games? Would performance matter? Becca Roux likened it to trying to fit a round peg in a square hole.

Finally they realized they couldn't do it. They had to return to what mattered most to each team. The women wanted, once and for all, equal rates of pay with the men. If men were offered $8,000 to play a match, they wanted $8,000 to play a match. If the men were offered $20,000 for winning a game, the women wanted $20,000 for winning a similar game. The men realized that they ultimately wanted total annual payments similar to what they thought they had negotiated in 2021. So the question now was: what rates of pay, when added up, would get both teams close to the 2021 total that the men wanted?

U.S. Soccer weighed in, making an offer. The negotiating teams and the players hopped on the phone to discuss it in a flurry of calls. For periods of time they seemed close to agreement. Other times it seemed they would never be able to resolve the conflict.

The clock was ticking. Oral arguments on the appeal were just weeks away.

Settlement talks accelerated, the two sides struggling to agree on what equal pay included and how much back pay U.S. Soccer would cough up. Meanwhile, soccer players on both teams also faced battles on the field. At the end of January, the men played World Cup qualifying matches, beating El Salvador and losing to Canada. On February 2, they prevailed over Honduras.

Toward the middle of February, the women faced the Czech Republic, New Zealand, and Iceland in the SheBelieves Cup. During the tournament, contract talks advanced, with both teams and the federation battling over details. The women juggled matches, trainings, recovery, Zoom calls about their contract, and discussions about the potential lawsuit settlement. On February 23, the women won their third straight SheBelieves title.

Time was running out. On March 7, the women's appeal was due to be heard before the appeals court. No one knew how the three-judge panel would rule. It seemed safer to come to an agreement that both sides could abide by.

But Cindy's position was in jeopardy, with U.S. Soccer's election for president scheduled for March 5. Most who wanted the lawsuit settled realized that having Cindy in charge might be their last best chance to get this done. "If she loses," Becca Roux worried, "who knows what will happen."

The federation suggested that they might be willing to agree to equal pay for the friendly games. The sticking point continued to be the World Cup bonuses. The women held strong to their simple and clear demand for equal pay. They didn't care where U.S. Soccer got their money. U.S. Soccer had to pay national team players equally. The women would settle for nothing less.

The sides went back and forth. They all felt that resolution was near. But the players were so accustomed to the endless back and forth that they continued to wonder—"How do we get this done?"

It had been such a roller coaster, with equal pay once so clearly off the table, with days and weeks and months of being told that they were not good enough to be treated equally, with offensive messages tucked into legal briefs. The players had endured hundreds of hours of negotiations, hundreds of hours of reviewing proposals, Google docs, and legal briefs. There were the brutal depositions, when their entire lives were scrutinized, their personal phones copied and reviewed by strangers, leaving them feeling vulnerable and violated. "It was all just fucking terrible," Becca said.

"You just keep going because you believe in something," the union leader pointed out. The team knew that equality was right, equality was the only way forward, and that real change would not happen until there was a substantial acknowledgment of wrongdoing. Players in the past deserved more. Current players, now at the table, deserved more. And girls and women of the future deserved more. "You have to believe and hold on to hope that despite how dark the day is, you will get there," Becca said.

Then, at long last, both sides seemed on the verge of agreement on the settlement.

But they got hung up on how to present it to the public. Everyone was on edge. Cindy knew she had to tread carefully. She got everyone together on a phone call. She reminded everyone how close they were and what was at stake.

And she did one more thing. "Cindy apologized to us," Megan Rapinoe said, "and it's the first time anyone has done that."

Finally the negotiating teams for U.S. Soccer and the women came to settlement. The leaders called every player, sharing the terms.

We asked for more than $60 million in the lawsuit, some said. Why should we settle for less?

Team leaders explained that though the chances of winning the appeal seemed good, they could lose. And even if they did win, they still faced a costly trial. This compromise would offer some reparations. And it would mean a big change in pay in the future.

All they had to do was to vote to accept the settlement.

It Was All True

February 22, 2022

On February 22, 2022, exactly 2,154 days after filing the lawsuit, the women's team announced an historic settlement with U.S. Soccer.

A "landmark win for fairness," read *CNN*'s headline, which called the settlement "groundbreaking." "An unexpected victory," crowed the *New York Times*. The *Washington Post* heralded it as "a remarkable achievement," that would have "reverberations across the sport—and beyond."

In the settlement, U.S. Soccer promised the women's team equal pay and support and offered $22 million in back pay to players with an additional $2 million fund to support their retirement and charitable endeavors.

Andrew Das of the *New York Times* called the millions in back pay "a tacit admission that compensation for the men's and women's teams had been unequal for years."

"Nearly two years after losing in court," he wrote, "they were able to extract not only an eight-figure settlement but also a commitment from the federation to enact the very reforms the judge had rejected."

"The governing body led by Cindy Parlow Cone essentially made an admission: it was all true," *Washington Post* columnist Sally Jenkins wrote. "The members of the women's team had been wronged. For years, they had to play more, and win bigger, to be paid anything close to their male counterparts. They got less pay for better work."

When first asked about the settlement, Megan Rapinoe seemed dazed. "It's honestly kind of surreal," she told *The Athletic*. "I feel like I need to take a step back. We've all been in the trenches of it for so long. I honestly don't even understand how monumental this is."

But the next day, on *Good Morning America*, Megan glowed. "It's a really amazing day," she said. She was so proud of what they'd accomplished, especially that the next generation wouldn't have to deal with what they'd endured.

In fact, this was "one of those incredible moments that we look back on and say the game changed forever, U.S. Soccer changed forever, and the landscape of soccer in this country and in the world changed forever," she told the press.

Even though they did not win the full $64 million in back pay they had sought, to the women, the settlement felt like nothing short of a complete victory. "What we set out to do was to have acknowledgement of discrimination from U.S. Soccer, and we received that through back pay," Alex Morgan said. "We set out to have fair and equal treatment in working conditions, and we got that through the working conditions settlement. And we set out to have equal pay moving forward for us and the men's team though U.S. Soccer, and we achieved that."

In a joint statement between the women's team and U.S. Soccer, they said they "proudly stand together in a shared commitment to advancing equality in soccer." They dedicated this moment to "the past USWNT leaders who helped make this day possible, as well as all of the women and girls who will follow."

Not a Done Deal

March 2022

Still, the settlement wasn't a rah-rah moment for Cindy Parlow Cone. "Yes, I wanted to resolve the litigation," she said. "Yes, I wanted to reset the relationship between U.S. Soccer and our women's national team. But I didn't want to just do it with a lump sum. That doesn't solve systemic issues. That doesn't solve the problem going forward. I wanted to solve equal pay forever."

Indeed, UCLA law professor Steven Bank writing about the agreement for *ESPN* cautioned against celebrating too soon. "Lost amid this collective back-patting, however, was a big catch." Both teams were still playing under expired agreements. The details of the equal pay contracts still had to be negotiated and ratified.

Former player Julie Foudy thought the settlement was "monumental not just for us, but for giving women in other industries the courage to ask for what they deserve." But Julie was also holding her breath. "The team needed the [collective bargaining agreement] to get equal pay locked in."

While the legal settlement captured the spirit of equal pay, the question remained—what exactly would equal pay look like in the contract? How would base pay and performance bonuses be truly equalized? And would the men's and women's contracts be exactly the same, or would there be room for different priorities, such as childcare offered when the players were in training camps? And, until FIFA equalized prize money, U.S. Soccer, the women's team, and the men's team had to find a way to do it themselves. It still remained to be seen: would the men's and women's teams and their employer really be able to hash out equal pay contracts?

This was a huge concern for powerhouse goalkeeper Hope Solo. Long ago, she had recruited for the women's team the lawyer Rich Nichols, who first spearheaded the EEOC complaint. She was also one of the five players who had filed with the EEOC. Ultimately, the players' union parted ways with Rich, but in August 2018, Hope Solo worked with him to file her own gender discrimination lawsuit against U.S. Soccer, six months *before* the other players filed their class action.

The two lawsuits were similar but filed in different courts. Hope Solo's was put on hold until *Alex Morgan v. U.S. Soccer* could be resolved. But as someone who played on the team during the class period, Hope was a member of the class in the suit brought by the women's team.

When the settlement was announced, Hope had deep concerns about the "promise of equal pay from the federation." In a long Instagram post, she wrote, "Read the fine print. 'Contingent upon the negotiation of a new collective bargaining agreement.' It doesn't exist and is not guaranteed."

And she pointed out, "If the players had ever been successful in negotiating an equal CBA, there would've been no reason to sue the federation in the first place."

Cindy Parlow Cone updated the media by saying, "Are we close? It depends on your definition of close. Are we going in the right direction? Yes."

But Hope Solo continued to believe that finalizing an equal pay contract with U.S. Soccer would be "very, very, very difficult, if not impossible." Even though U.S. Soccer and fans and players around the world had begun pressuring FIFA to equalize prize money, Hope's lawyer told the press that equalization is "never going to happen."

How would the women, men, and U.S. Soccer overcome the FIFA prize money stumbling block?

A Vital Election

March 2022

On March 5, 2022, U.S. Soccer's election day for president, union leader Becca Roux woke with a pit in her stomach. Yes, they had an equal pay settlement, but the collective bargaining agreement was far from finished. The settlement would collapse without it. Becca had real doubts about whether they could work out the details of the actual contract without Cindy Parlow Cone as U.S. Soccer president.

Becca turned on her computer and logged into Zoom to watch the election tally. There were technical difficulties, and Becca couldn't even tell what was going on. In moments when the video conference worked, she could tell that Carlos Cordeiro had a surprising amount of support. She felt increasingly tense, stressed, then upset that the election was taking so long and that it was even close.

At last, toward the end of the day, the results came in.

Cindy Parlow Cone had won by a slim margin.

Still, Cindy seemed buoyed by the win. "The moment of division is now in the past. We are one federation. We are one team," she said. "Now is the time for all of us to work together."

Two Teams, Together

Spring 2022

Everyone involved was well aware that commentators and observers said that equal pay was not possible. But as world-class athletes who had risen to the highest heights of their sport, these female and male soccer players also knew what it felt like to defy expectations and do the impossible. They doubled down, working separately and together to see if they could get it done.

Both teams continued to struggle to address the elephant in the room: how would they equalize the wildly different prize money that FIFA awarded the men's and women's teams? The women wanted equal rates of pay extended throughout all tournaments. They imagined male and female players getting a set amount for each World Cup qualifying game, each early round match, and each stage of the elimination rounds. In this equal pay scenario, regardless of FIFA award amounts, U.S. Soccer would pay both teams the same amount for third-, second-, and first-place finishes. As their team had been historically more successful, the women would likely go further in their tournament and take home more pay. For their part, the men's team was used to bonuses linked to FIFA prize amounts, which kept their World Cup earnings higher than the women's even if they didn't go as far in the tournament.

One key player on the men's side who could help bridge this gap was defender Walker Zimmerman. Tall with long dirty-blond hair often twisted in a Thor-like bun, the center defender was known for winning aerial duels and for precise passing. Honest, straightforward, and thoughtful, Walker was also known for his ability to see things from other people's point of view and to discern how to best motivate others. A leader on the pitch, guiding players during games, Zimmerman often played the role of the conscience of the team.

Walker brought all this to bear when he got on video calls with teammates during these contract negotiations. Equalizing pay was a big deal, and they had a chance "to do something no other team had done before," he told them. Let's be on the front foot of change, he urged his teammates. That's who we are as a team, who we want to be as a team.

Walker knew the most difficult question was: were the men willing to share World Cup prize money should they do well in the tournament? "There was a potential chance of making less money, no doubt about it," Walker acknowledged. But the team had to look at things differently and get excited about creating an everybody-wins solution.

The male players considered. Okay, what would a loss look like? A loss would be a contract much like their old CBA, or one that was less lucrative.

And they explored what a win could look like, World Cup award money aside. They decided that a win might be more pay overall for a greater number of players. Usually, fewer than two dozen men made the roster for a World Cup, and hence won prize money. But more than twice that many—fifty-seven—played in at least one national team game in 2021. What if the team could earn more for non-World Cup games, which would better compensate more players, especially those earlier in their careers? Consistent distribution of higher income to more players might make it palatable for the team to share their riskier potential World Cup winnings.

The men were also excited about getting a portion of the revenue they generated for U.S. Soccer. And the team had been playing on an expired contract for more than two years. Retroactive pay would also sweeten the deal.

Similar but different discussions happened on the women's side as they considered concessions too. In the spirit of looking out for the interests of the many over the few, they talked about giving up guaranteed salaries. After all, only sixteen players had been securing salaries. Many more players would benefit from the huge boosts in pay the team could get for matches in an equal-pay scenario.

The negotiations had so many moving parts. All three groups had to consider each group's wants and needs. Communicating within and between the men's and women's players' unions, attempting negotiations with U.S. Soccer, and writing and sharing documents filled hours of everyone's time. Becca Roux continued to be amazed at how the female players dug into the details and documents, that they were so willing to get into the weeds. Still, she wished for a time when they didn't have to do this tedious, unpaid work, when they would get to just be soccer players.

Cindy Parlow Cone lost hours of sleep every night trying to find a formula that would work for everyone. Often she felt "the weight of the world on my shoulders" and feared she was failing. "No one believed we could get there," Cindy said. "My family didn't believe it. My staff didn't believe it. I don't even think the players really believed it."

At times Cindy felt daggers thrown her way from all sides. She felt jostled in different directions. "I knew that any little thing could throw it off and bring down the house of cards," Cindy said. But she held strong to her own values, her own moral compass. She would not be pushed off the path.

One day Cindy thought they had had a particularly constructive meeting. "We were progressing and moving forward in a really positive direction," she said. She went home with high hopes. "We may really be able to do this," she told her husband. "This might actually happen!"

The phone rang. The U.S. Soccer leadership had balked. "And it literally felt like everything was falling apart again," she said. "We had the darkest of moments, when all three sides didn't think it was ever going to work." But they had one thing going for them. The parties kept coming back. They kept talking.

Cindy did everything in her power to keep the conversation respectful. "I'm a true believer in treating people as well as you possibly can," she said. "And that has to be true in difficult times and with people you oppose as well."

At times Cindy had to throw her weight around for the players. When the players asked for something related to how things ran at camp, such as access to ice baths, physical therapy, or massage, and U.S. Soccer said, "No, we can't do that," Cindy stepped in. "Guys, we have to really listen when the players are telling us something is important," she said. "If you haven't played the sport and you haven't played at this level and you haven't been in those environments, you might not understand that the smallest difference in something in camp can make a big impact on your performance. Though it might cost a bit more, it is the right thing to do."

Other times Cindy had to share hard truths with the players. There were things the players wanted, such as pay based only on revenue sharing, that Cindy knew she couldn't deliver, that the board would never approve. So she tried to think creatively, asking the players or U.S. Soccer, "Okay, I know I can't do that, but would you be willing to do something like this?"

As the negotiations unfolded, the union leaders noticed an

interesting dynamic. When the men asked U.S. Soccer to keep group licensing rights like the women had, the negotiators had said, "Absolutely not!" But when the women brought up discussions about group likeness rights in the room with everyone there, it went much more smoothly. The two teams realized that they could get better outcomes if the women advocated for issues they had already won, and the men advocated for others where they had a stronger history.

Each side took the lead with their priorities. The men bargained hard to reach the 2021 total, to include a revenue-sharing component, and for retroactive pay to cover the years they went without a contract. The women were sticklers on equal rates of pay and keeping and improving all the provisions on player safety, schedule, team licensing rights, and childcare support during camps and tournaments. With both unions negotiating together, one plus one really did seem to equal more than two.

As discussion between the two teams and U.S. Soccer unfolded, player leaders took the temperature on different proposals and messaged their team when they needed to make decisions. There were "difficult conversations, a lot of listening, a lot of learning," Walker Zimmerman said.

As the parties got closer to agreement, the men's union checked in with the players. The deal included equal payment for wins, losses, and ties for both teams. The union wanted to make sure that the men understood that if the women played more games, played more top twenty-five teams, or won more, they would earn more money in total than the men.

"Why do you keep telling us this?" the men asked.

"Because if we do this deal, it's gonna happen."

"We don't care," one said.

"As long as we get a deal that works for us, it's all good," said another.

"If the women win more and do better, more power to them," said a third.

As the parties got near to finalizing the deal, U.S. Soccer negotiators made one more move. They tried to take away most of the men's retroactive pay, which amounted to more than $11 million. It was a provision the men's union held tightly in each negotiation and had been agreed to in June 2021.

"The June deal clearly had all this money paid to my guys," the union negotiator said.

"Well, things have changed since June," the U.S. Soccer negotiator said.

"Yeah? What has changed?"

"You shouldn't have filed that amicus brief."

The $11 million in retroactive pay could have driven a wedge between the women's and men's teams. It benefited the men only. But Becca Roux of the women's union would not allow U.S. Soccer to drive that wedge. She told U.S. Soccer, "You have to give them what they were promised."

Equal Means Equal

Fall 2022

On Women's Equality Day, September 6, 2022, after cheering on the U.S. Women's National Team as they won a friendly match against Nigeria, the capacity crowd of 15,000 did not pour out of the stadium. Instead, they waited expectantly while the U.S. players gathered at center field with U.S. Soccer president Cindy Parlow Cone, representatives of the men's players' association, members of Congress, and the U.S. Secretary of Labor to officially sign the first truly equal pay agreement for women's and men's soccer teams in the world. "It's a dawn of a new era," Megan Rapinoe said.

MCing the event was former U.S. Women's National team captain, ESPN commentator, two-time World Cup winner, and two-time Olympic champion Julie Foudy, whose smile seemed to reach from goal to goal and who could hardly contain her excitement. She introduced Cindy, who took the mic and called out, "Wow! We're here. We finally got here!"

As the crowd cheered, Cindy thought about how making the women's national team had changed the trajectory of her life, how she had transformed as a person and a leader on that team. She looked down for a moment and drew in a deep breath. "Today, I stand on many people's shoulders," she said. "I could not have achieved this without the people who came before me." When she handed the mic back to Julie, one of the leaders she so admired, she felt humble and thankful.

Julie turned to the many generations of players gathered for the signing ceremony with a full heart. Beside her stood national team members past and present: steely goalkeeper Briana Scurry and fireball Kelley O'Hara; veteran forward Alex Morgan and newer scoring phenoms Sophia Smith and Mallory Pugh Swanson; team reps and stalwart defenders Meghan Klingenberg and Crystal Dunn.

"Many of us have been in this equal pay fight for over two decades," Julie said. She made eye contact with the younger players, the ones who had negotiated the deal. "When we passed that baton on, we wanted to make sure [you] understood the fight," she said. "You guys sprinted like hell and got it over the line. And for that we are very grateful."

She smiled warmly as she handed the mic over to captain and union president Becky Sauerbrunn. Becky stood on the field still sweaty from the game, with her long light-colored braid and signature pink headband. She gazed at the players clustered around the signing table and the thousands of joyful fans who had stayed after the game to witness this historic moment. She hadn't been sure that equal pay would happen in her career—or her lifetime.

To the athletes on the field, she said, "I want to thank the players past and present for [your] persistence, and basically never shying away from asking the question 'Why not?'" The crowd burst into applause. She thanked all the player reps, the labor lawyers, and staff. "This is a huge win for the labor movement and for workers' rights." The clapping grew louder.

Then she turned toward the fans, "Last but not least, I want to thank all of you guys for all the support . . ." Stomping and cheering filled the stadium as if a goal has been scored. Becky Sauerbrunn's eyes brightened with emotion. She smiled broadly at the crowd, her voice rising.

"All the social media posts, the messages of support, the chants for equal pay at really funny times," she said. "You guys made the difference, and you are truly, truly the best fans in the world." The crowd applauded with pleasure and pride.

"And now let's sign this thing!"

Sitting at a long table covered with a bold blue tablecloth, representatives of U.S. Soccer and the men's and women's players' associations passed along a black folder with the contract signature page inside. The agreement, which would last through 2028, had the word "identical" written all over it: identical roster fees, identical appearance fees, identical performance payments. It talked of fifty-fifty splits and comparable budgets. "Equal" was another repeating beat: equal support, equal quality of venues and fields, equal hotel accommodations, equal number of charter flights. In case it was not obvious, the agreement made clear that this is what equality looks like.

The linchpin of the contracts, the element that overcame FIFA's vastly different prizes, was that both teams agreed to pool and share equally in the World Cup prize money from their respective tournaments. Specifically, U.S. Soccer would get 10 percent of all World Cup awards from 2022 and 2023, and 20 percent of the 2026 and 2027 award payout. The remaining money would be split evenly between the men's and women's teams. The only caveat was that players would only receive the pooled World Cup prize money if their team qualified for the tournament. If not, the other team, if they qualified, would get the full chunk remaining after U.S. Soccer took its cut.

The per-game bonuses were generous and equal: players would receive $8,000 per game minimum. Against a top-ranked team, players would get $12,000 for a draw and $18,000 for a win. The teams would take in more than $5 per ticket sold to their games. For the first time, the players would also get a cut of commercial revenue from broadcasting deals and the like.

Many, many players on both teams stood to benefit from the new contracts. In all, national team players, women and men, rostered for all games outside the World Cup could make close to a half-million dollars in a year. Their pay during a World Cup year could potentially be double that.

But what really changed for the women was that they didn't have to fight anymore—at least for themselves. "I feel a lot of pride for the girls who are going to see this growing up and recognize their value rather than having to fight for it," U.S. forward Midge Purce said. "However, my dad always told me that you don't get rewarded for doing what you're supposed to do—and paying men and women equally is what you're supposed to do."

As the men and women sitting side by side at the table opened the folder and signed and dated the agreement, a faint chanting of young voices from the stands grew slowly louder.

USA! EQUAL PAY! USA! EQUAL PAY!

When the last person signed the agreement, Julie yelled, "It's official!"

The women threw their fists into the air and pounded on the table.

The crowd roared.

Equality in Action

Fall 2022

Midfielder Sam Coffey was relatively new to the national team when she played the full ninety minutes of the Nigeria game. She stood shoulder to shoulder with greats such as Julie Foudy, Briana Scurry, Megan Rapinoe, and Becky Sauerbrunn during the signing and was in the photos with them. She had heard horror stories about national team players barely getting by, struggling to cover expenses, and working multiple jobs. She was grateful to face a different future. Her national team paychecks, she told a reporter, would be "literally life changing."

Life changed for the men's team too. In the fall of 2022, the U.S. men's national team headed off to Qatar for their World Cup. Goalkeeper Matt Turner's partner had given birth to their first child just four months prior. Instead of leaving the baby at home for the long stretch, the couple brought him with them. The new equal pay agreement included a feature never before available to the men's team. It paid for childcare during training camps and tournaments, including care provided by a parent.

The men's team performed respectably, making it to the first stage of the knockout round, where they ultimately lost to the Netherlands. But competing in the round of sixteen won U.S. Soccer $13 million in prize money. The federation's cut was $1.3 million. The men's and women's teams split the rest, to the tune of more than $5.8 million for each team. "That's right," a *USA Today* columnist wrote. "The USWNT got more in prize money because men reached the knockout rounds in Qatar than they did for their last two World Cup titles. Combined."

Women's World Cup

Summer 2023

In July 2023, the U.S. Women's National Team headed to their World Cup in Australia and New Zealand with high hopes. They were ranked number one and favored to win. But in the group stage, while they beat Vietnam 3–0, the Americans only managed ties against the Netherlands (1–1) and Portugal (0–0). Squeaking into the round of sixteen, they faced a tough battle against powerhouse Sweden.

The USWNT met the moment with the strength, skill, and joy that had been lacking earlier in the tournament. They outshot Sweden twenty-two to nine. Only one of Sweden's shots was on target, compared with eleven by the Americans. But Swedish goalkeeper Zecira Musovic was on fire, and the U.S. was unable to score.

Regulation time ended in a 0–0 tie. Overtime ended in a 0–0 tie. To move on to the semifinals, the U.S. women had to win the penalty kick shoot-out.

The first four shots, two by Americans and two by Swedes, went in, putting the penalty shot score at 2–2.

U.S. player Kristie Mewis, Sam Mewis's sister, stepped up and smashed the ball high and left and also scored. But then the Swedish player Nathalie Björn skyed the ball over the goal. The U.S. pulled ahead, 3–2.

Veteran star Megan Rapinoe stepped to the line and took a deep breath. She trotted up, struck the ball, and it also soared over the goal. She was due to retire from the national team later in the month. In what was her last shot ever in a World Cup, she missed. Surprise, disbelief, and a painful, nervous grin flashed across her face. After all she had done for the team, she'd failed to clinch this win.

The next Swedish player, Rebecka Blomqvist, rocketed a shot to the right. But U.S. goalkeeper Alyssa Naeher guessed correctly. Leaping in the same direction, she blocked the shot, keeping the Americans' hope alive.

The U.S. players cheered and squeezed each other tight. Victory was within reach. With the score at 3–2, each team had only one shot left. If the U.S. nailed their last kick, the tally would be 4–2, and there would be nothing the Swedes could do to catch up. The U.S. women would head to the semifinals.

Young U.S. scoring star Sophia Smith lined up, jogged lightly forward, and took a strong shot. But the ball whipped out to the right of the goal. Sophia briefly covered her eyes with her hands, raised her face to the sky, and blinked back tears. It was still 3–2, and Sweden could tie it up.

Sweden's Hanna Bennison stepped to the line. Leaning hard into her shot, she nailed it high and just left of center. Score! The teams were tied, 3–3.

Though both teams had taken five shots each, they would continue to shoot in pairs until one team prevailed. Alyssa, the American goalie, already under tremendous pressure defending the penalty kicks, walked out of the goal to the line to take a shot. She nailed the ball high and to the center as the Swedish goalie guessed wrong and leapt away. Alyssa's shot put the U.S. ahead once more.

She returned to the goal to face Swedish player Magdalena Eriksson, who rifled the shot into the upper right-hand corner. The score stood at 4–4. It felt like the battle would never end.

Veteran U.S. defender Kelley O'Hara, who had subbed in late in the game specifically to take a penalty shot, approached the line. She pressed her lips together and swallowed. She jogged forward and chipped the ball toward the upper right corner.

It ricocheted off the post.

With the miss, Sweden could win on their next kick. Twenty-year-old Lina Hurtig strode to the line and struck hard, high and toward the center of the goal. Alyssa palmed the shot, falling backward as the ball popped straight up into the air. The ball dropped toward the goal line, and Alyssa swatted it away.

"Did it go in?" the commentator yelled. Everyone on the field and in the stands waited, tension palpable as the referee checked the video to see if the ball had, at any time, completely crossed the line.

After a few moments, the ref blew her whistle. The ball had made it into the goal by a hair.

Sweden won.

The women in bright yellow and blue dashed across the field toward their bench and piled on top of each other. The U.S. women stood on the field stunned. They slowly fell into each other's arms for long hugs, wiping tear-stained cheeks. It was the earliest the U.S. Women's National Team had ever departed a World Cup.

The game of soccer can be beautiful but also brutal, especially when a hard-fought game is lost in penalty kicks. After the game, midfielder and captain Lindsey Horan said she was proud of her team. "We came out and controlled the entire game," she said. "We played like ourselves, with freedom, patience, and confidence."

As with the battle for equal pay, the women knew they would just have to continue to stick together and keep fighting. The summer Olympics in Paris in 2024 would give them their next chance to regain their spot at the top.

World Cup payday for the U.S. Women's National Team players was bittersweet. For this women's World Cup, FIFA offered a total of $110 million, compared to $440 million for the men's World Cup the previous summer. The Spanish women who ultimately won the cup took home $10.5 million. The winning Argentinian men's team had walked away with $42 million.

But as a result of decades of work by scores of female U.S. soccer players, World Cup payments from now on would be equal for the U.S. men's and women's national teams. The women's World Cup performance contributed $1.87 million in team prize money to the pot, plus $60,000 allocated to each of the twenty-three rostered players. From the $3.25 million, U.S. Soccer would take 10 percent, or $325,000. The men's and women's teams would split the rest, with $1.46 million for each team to be distributed to players as dictated by union contracts.

When added to the men's World Cup winnings, both teams ended up with an equal total of $7.31 million in World Cup winnings.

2022–2023 WORLD CUP PRIZE PAYMENTS

MEN'S NATIONAL TEAM

2022 World Cup

Reached: Round of 16

Prize allocated by FIFA: $13 million

Amount awarded to each team by U.S. Soccer: $5.85 million

Total USNT World Cup winnings: $7.31 million

WOMEN'S NATIONAL TEAM

2023 World Cup

Reached: Round of 16

Prize allocated by FIFA: $3.25 million

Amount awarded to each team by U.S. Soccer: $1.46 million

Total USWNT World Cup winnings: $7.31 million

During the men's World Cup, the women gathered to cheer loudly for the men's team. When the women played their tournament, the men's team watched and supported them too. "We're actually all on the same boat, rowing together," Julie Foudy said, "which is a nice change."

And it's a change that could spread worldwide.

The Domino Effect

2023 and into the future

This equalization of prize money has grabbed the world's attention and spurred important conversations. "How often do we talk about what equal pay means in different areas in the world? In our own country?" USMNT captain Tyler Adams asked. "We can be the milestone for other people to look at and say, 'Is this a possibility?'"

Some players on the men's team felt guilty about how hard and how long the women had been fighting for equal pay, how long it took to get the job done. "It's not easy to look back and think about this whole journey and where it started for them and how we ended," Walker Zimmerman acknowledged. The men's team, he admitted, came to the fight "a little late." But he learned that "it's never too late to get involved." And, he said, "we hope this will awaken others to the need for this type of change."

The pioneering work of the U.S. Women's National Team has awakened a drive for change in individuals, teams, and whole nations. Women across the country have told players that the soccer team's success empowered them to ask for a raise. One woman said she could imagine the women's national team standing behind her, giving her strength.

As a direct result of the work of the women's soccer team, President Joe Biden signed into the law the Equal Pay for Team USA Act in January 2023. The law requires that regardless of gender, all athletes representing the United States in international competitions must receive equal pay and benefits. It applies to fifty different sports, including swimming, figure skating, gymnastics, wrestling, squash, and curling.

Inspired by the U.S. team, female soccer players have made strides all across the globe. Between 2017 and 2022, Ireland, Spain, England, Brazil, and New Zealand equalized appearance fees for players on their two national teams. Brazil and New Zealand also offered their women's and men's teams an equal percentage of their World Cup prizes. The Netherlands began paying equal salaries and licensing fees, while Australia pioneered revenue sharing with both teams.

Though these agreements are not perfect, they send the ball in the right direction. "What's hugely significant and important," union leader Becca Roux said, "is that they are trying to achieve equality, that they will not agree to something unless all sides can say it is equal."

These days Cindy Parlow Cone fields calls regularly from leaders in other sports, other soccer federations, and other industries interested in what the U.S. women's team accomplished. "How did you do this?" they ask. "How do we go about doing this?"

These agreements, these discussions, this movement has made the women's epic battle even more worthwhile for the players. "It's been incredible to see that for us it's like, yes, we're in our own fight, but it's really not our own fight," Crystal Dunn said. "It's a fight for women everywhere to be recognized and paid what they are deserving of being paid. I'm seeing the effect all across the world and I think that's what we are hopeful we can continue doing."

"The domino effect that we helped kick-start," said Alex Morgan, "we're really proud of it."

You're Next: The Ongoing Fight for Equal Pay

The fight for gender equality has only begun. In the United States today, girls have 1.3 million fewer opportunities to play high school sports than boys. Colleges spend only 33 percent of sports scholarship money, 25 percent of athletic budgets, and 16 percent of recruitment budgets on female athletes. Though 40 percent of all sports participants are female, women make up less than 10 percent of the highest-level coaches and less than a quarter of the governing bodies of national sports federations and Olympic committees. Transgender athletes are also struggling for equal access to sports.

FIFA still pays countries wildly different prizes for men's and women's World Cup wins. FIFA allocated $440 million in prize money for the 2022 men's World Cup. It boosted the women's World Cup prize money from $60 million to $110 million in 2023, but that was still just a quarter of the men's pot.

"You know what? You're next," Megan Rapinoe said to FIFA.

U.S. Soccer president Cindy Parlow Cone promised to "go hand in hand" with the players to push FIFA to equalize World Cup prize money. Their efforts, coupled with pressure worldwide, seem to be having an impact. FIFA President Gianni Infantino has promised, "Our ambition is to have equality in payments for the 2026 men's and 2027 women's World Cup."

Salaries in the women's professional soccer league, the NWSL, are dwarfed by salaries in the men's league, called Major League Soccer. In 2020, the *minimum* MSL salary—roughly $64,000—was higher than the *maximum* NWSL salary of $50,000. The male players' top salary that year was twelve times higher—$612,500. Lionel Messi now earns more than $20 million a year on his U.S. pro team.

And that is just soccer.

In basketball, the average WNBA salary is just over $120,000. That is dwarfed by the average NBA salary of $8.2 million. Female golfers make under $50,000 on average, while male golfers bring home more than $1.2 million on average.

And that is just sports.

Women in finance earn seventy-seven cents to every dollar made by men. Female lawyers make eighty-three cents on the dollar. It's eighty-eight cents for retail and eighty-nine cents for hospitality and manufacturing.

Indeed, unequal pay remains the norm in most countries and in most fields. Though Congress passed the Equal Pay Act in 1963, in the United States the situation is still bleak. On average, women earn just eighty-two cents for every dollar men in the U.S. earn, for the same work. Black women earn just sixty-three cents on the dollar, and Latina women earn a mere fifty-five cents compared to the average man's dollar. This gap has barely budged in two decades.

Genderqueer people also face significant disparities in wages. New research shows that trans men, nonbinary, and gender-nonconforming people earn seventy cents for every dollar cisgender men earn. Trans women earn just sixty cents on the dollar.

The gender wage gap is a problem that continues to plague working people of every race and background, at every level, in every industry, at the beginning, middle, and end of their careers.

It affects people's well-being, the well-being of their families, their access to medical care, education, and retirement. Low wages, and unequal wages, keep 15 million women in the United States in poverty. That's more than one in nine women aged eighteen and older.

But the soccer fight can signal—and inspire—a shift. This battle, wrote Amy Bass, an author and professor of sports studies, "should be seen as much more than a win on the pitch or an attempt to change policy. Rather, it's a move to change the culture that surrounds not just women's sports, but women writ large."

Indeed, "this lawsuit has put the fight for equal pay on maybe the biggest stage that it's ever been on in this country," NPR's Ailsa Chang said.

To make real change is going to require a huge shift in mindset from people of all genders. "For so long, women have been brainwashed into just feeling gratitude for what they have," said star defender and union president Becky Sauerbrunn. "It's something that will be very difficult to break universally." The key, she said, is having other women, mentors, who model a new way of viewing the world.

For pioneering player Julie Foudy, it was the people she fought alongside that made the battle worth it. "When you're in it, you're like, 'God, this is really hard,'" she said. "Equal pay didn't happen in a year, and it didn't happen in a decade. But we've seen throughout history that as hard as it gets, when you get the collective fighting together, good things happen. If you keep working together and stay unified, you can change the world."

DANESHA ADAMS • MICHELLE AKERS • KORBIN ALBERT • HEATHER ALDAMA • AMY ALLMAN
YAEL AVERBUCH • SAMANTHA BAGGETT • BETHANY BALCER • NICOLE BARNHART • TRACEY BAT
TAMI BATISTA • JUSTI BAUMGARDT • LAKEYSIA BEENE • DEBBIE BELKIN • KEISHA BELL • DE
BENDER • JENNY BENSON • ANGELA BERRY • JACKIE BILLETT • KYLIE BIVENS • DANIELLE BORGM
SHANNON BOXX • DENISE BOYER-MURDOCH • JEN BRANAM • AMBER BROOKS • THORI (STAP
BRYAN • TARA BUCKLEY • SHERI BUETER • SUSAN BUSH • LORI BYLIN • JANE CAMPBELL •
CASSELLA • LORI CHALUPNY • BRANDI CHASTAIN • MANDY CLEMENS • SAM COFFEY • DAN
COLAPRICO • LISA COLE • ROBIN CONFER • KERRY CONNORS • KIM CONWAY • ALANA COOK • ANN C
• PAM (BAUGHMAN) CORNELL • STEPHANIE (LOPEZ) COX • ALEISHA CRAMER • AMANDA CROMW
• COLETTE CUNNINGHAM • ABBY DAHLKEMPER • MARIAN DALMY • TIERNA DAVIDSON • CINDY D
• SAVANNAH DEMELO • MICHELLE DEMKO • KRISTI DEVERT • TINA DIMARTINO • IMANI DORS
BETSY DRAMBOUR • TRACY (NOONAN) DUCAR • JOAN DUNLAP-SEIVOLD • CRYSTAL DUNN • DAN
EGAN • TINA (FRIMPONG) ELLERTSON • WHITNEY ENGEN • STACEY ENOS • JULIE (JOHNSTON)
• RONNIE FAIR • LORRIE FAIR • JOY (BIEFELD) FAWCETT • KAREN FERGUSON • JESSICA FISCH
MIA FISHEL • KENDALL FLETCHER • MEREDITH FLORANCE • DANIELLE (GARRETT) FOTOPOUL
JULIE FOUDY • EMILY FOX • ADRIANNA FRANCH • MICHELLE FRENCH • CARIN (JENNINGS) GABA
• LINDA GANCITANO • MORGAN (BRIAN) GAUTRAT • WENDY GEBAUER • GRETCHEN GEGG • NA
GIRMA • LISA GMITTER • CINDY GORDON • SANDI GORDON • JEN GRUBB • SARAH HAGEN • KRIS
HAMILTON • LINDA HAMILTON • MIA HAMM • HALEY HANSON • RUTH HARKER • ASHLYN HARR
MARY HARVEY • ASHLEY HATCH • DEVVYN HAWKINS • TUCKA HEALY • TOBIN HEATH • APRIL HEINR
• HOLLY HELLMUTH • LORI HENRY • SHANNON HIGGINS • JAELENE HINKLE • LAUREN (CHE
HOLIDAY • LINDSEY HORAN • JAELIN HOWELL • ANGELA HUCLES • SOFIA HUERTA • SARAH HUFF
• LINDSEY HUIE • PATTY IRIZARRY • MARCI (MILLER) JOBSON • LAURA JONES • NATASHA K
CHRISTINA KAUFMAN • BETH KELLER • DEBBIE KELLER • SHERRILL KESTER • AUBREY KINGSB
• MEGHAN KLINGENBERG • JENA KLUEGEL • TAYLOR KORNIECK • NANCY KRAMARZ • ANNA KR
• ALI KRIEGER • CASEY (SHORT) KRUEGER • JENNIFER LALOR • ROSE LAVELLE • AMY LEPEI

PART IV
Penalty Kicks

Give me the effing ball.

Give me the effing job.

Give me the same pay that the guy next to me gets.

Give me the promotion.

Give me the microphone.

Give me the Oval Office.

Give me the respect I deserve—

And give it to my wolfpack, too.

—from *Wolfpack*

by U.S. Women's National Team star Abby Wambach

Be an Equal Pay Warrior

At the current rate of change, the gender pay gap is not expected to close until 2111. And there is no guarantee it will even happen by then. In the meantime, women will make an average of $10,434 less a year than men. This lost pay could have covered:

Eleven months of groceries (at $914 a month), or

Nine and a half months' rent (at $1,097), or

More than three years of student loan payments (at $272 a month).

Real change will require people of all genders and races to speak up about the problem and advocate for change for themselves and others in their workplaces and in state and federal laws. Here's how to stand up for yourself and to advocate for equal pay for everyone.

Consider Higher-Paying Fields

Part of the wage gap problem is that society undervalues work traditionally done by women. Pay is lower in fields dominated by women, such as teaching and health care, while pay tends to be higher in male-dominated fields such as construction and engineering, even when the jobs require the same level of skill, education, and training. In fact, occupational segregation accounts for about half of the wage gap. If you are female, trans, or nonbinary, consider a career in a male-dominated field. Also support efforts to increase pay in traditionally female-dominated fields. But remember, the wage gap persists within every occupation, so work to close it no matter where you land.

Learn Key Negotiation Tactics

Before negotiating pay for any job, do some research to find out average salaries for the position you want. Websites like payscale.com and glassdoor.com can offer insight.

If a potential employer asks for your salary history, explain why this is problematic—it tends to reinforce past salary discrimination—and ask to see the salary range for the position.

Do not accept the first offer. Ask for time to consider the offer. Always ask for more money. You have to ask for it to get it. Prepare to make a case for higher pay. Will your request raise your pay to the industry standard? Do you bring particular skills, training, or experience to the job?

"You are not powerless," said union leader and experienced negotiator Becca Roux. "If you get informed and get educated and get good advice, you can make informed decisions on what to ask for and how to approach negotiations."

It helps to create a vision for yourself and your future, Becca suggests. What strengths do you bring to any job? What are you willing to do to learn and grow? How do you see yourself in the future? Keep that vision in mind as you negotiate, and don't be afraid to share that vision with your potential employer.

Take a Free Class on Negotiation

The American Association of University Women (AAUW) offers a free online seminar and online tool that shows you how to research a target salary, highlight accomplishments, and find the right words to negotiate for better pay and benefits. The class takes less than two hours but can help boost your earnings your whole life. Find it online at www.aauw.org/resources/programs/salary/.

Know Your Rights

Two federal laws protect you from gender discrimination at work. The Equal Pay Act states, "No employer . . . shall discriminate . . . between employees on the basis of sex by paying wages to employees . . . at a rate less than the rate at which he pays wages to employees of the opposite sex . . . for equal work on jobs the performance of which requires equal skill, effort, and responsibility, and which are performed under similar working conditions. . . ."

Title VII of the Civil Rights Act of 1964 states, "It shall be an unlawful employment practice for an employer . . . to discriminate against any individual with respect to his compensation, terms, conditions, or privileges of employment, because of such individual's race, color, religion, sex, or national origin. . . ."

In other words, it is illegal to underpay someone because of their gender. Not only is unequal pay illegal, but it is also illegal to offer unequal working conditions.

If you or someone you know is suffering from illegal wage discrimination, let your employer know that these laws make their behavior illegal.

Contact the EEOC

The Equal Employment Opportunity Commission (EEOC) is the agency that enforces federal laws against discrimination at work because of gender, sexual orientation, race, color, religion, national origin, disability, or age. It is free to file a complaint. Full-time, part-time, seasonal, and temporary workers can file, regardless of citizenship or immigration status. If you are afraid that your employer will punish you for speaking up, another person or organization can file for you to protect your identity.

The EEOC will ask your employer to file a written answer to your complaint. The agency will then investigate, interviewing people and reviewing documents.

The EEOC will try to determine whether discrimination happened and what to do about it. They may ask you and your employer to try to solve the problem with mediation. If they cannot resolve your complaint, the EEOC will issue a notice of right to sue. That gives you ninety days to file a lawsuit at your own expense.

File a complaint online at www.publicportal.eeoc.gov/Porta/Login.aspx. If you would like to learn more, you can call an EEOC office near you. Find the nearest office at www.eeoc.gov/field-office or call 1-800-669-4000.

Be an Equal Pay Advocate at Your Workplace

No matter your gender, you can push for pay fairness. Ask your employer whether the compensation for your job is the same for all similar jobs regardless of gender. Gather with your colleagues to request that the company share a list of wages and salaries by gender. Even better, ask for the list by gender and race to identify whether women of color face larger gaps.

If your employer refuses, ask your co-workers to share their pay rates and post your own list. Talk to your employer if you notice a gender or gender and race gap. Many states have laws on pay transparency that can help with this effort. Search the internet using your state's name and "pay equity laws" or "pay transparency laws" to learn more.

Advocate for Equal Pay Laws

The federal Equal Pay Act and Title VII of the Civil Rights Acts offer some pay equity protections. But judging from how slowly the pay gap is narrowing, we need stronger protections. Consider supporting:

- The Paycheck Fairness Act, which would strengthen the Equal Pay Act. Find out more about this legislation on the website of the American Bar Association: www.americanbar.org/advocacy/governmental_legislative_work/priorities_policy/discrimination/the-paycheck-fairness-act/.
- The Pay Equity for All Act, which would prohibit employers from asking for and using salary history to set pay. Read the text of H.R. 1600 and track the legislation at www.govtrack.us/congress/bills/118/hr1600.
- The Fair Pay Act, which would require employers to offer pay for jobs of equivalent value, even if they are different occupations. Read the text of H.R. 1598 and track the legislation at www.govtrack.us/congress/bills/118/hr1598.

You can voice your support in Congress by contacting your representatives and senators. To find their contact information, type your address into www.congress.gov/members/find-your-member.

Be an Employer Who Equalizes Pay

At some point in your career, you may become an employer or the manager who makes hiring and pay decisions. If so, you can equalize pay in your workplace. You can do this by:

- Posting salary ranges for jobs. Studies show providing pay ranges narrows the wage gap.
- Eliminating the use of salary histories in setting pay.

- Telling all applicants clearly if pay is negotiable.
- Allowing workers to share information about wages without retaliation.
- Regularly reviewing your company's pay by gender and race.
- Correcting any differences in pay for the same work that are not attributable to relevant differences in tenure, education, or experience.

Former player and U.S. Soccer president Cindy Parlow Cone also offered this advice: "Invite women to the table. Scoot your chair over and make room. Promote women, invest in women, pay women well." To young women she suggested, "Be proud of the space you take up. You have earned it. Don't apologize. Pull up a chair to that table and throw some elbows if you need to." And if you make it to the top, "Lower the ladder. Make it easier for the next person, the next woman, coming up behind you."

Pushing for equal pay for yourself and others can be tough. Union leader Becca Roux suggests that you ask yourself: How could this have ripple effects on other women and disenfranchised or underrepresented groups in the future? "The hope is that by fighting a battle today," she said, "somebody else doesn't have to fight it in the future."

DANESHA ADAMS • MICHELLE AKERS • KORBIN ALBERT • HEATHER ALDAMA • AMY ALLMAN
YAEL AVERBUCH • SAMANTHA BAGGETT • BETHANY BALCER • NICOLE BARNHART • TRACEY BAT
TAMI BATISTA • JUSTI BAUMGARDT • LAKEYSIA BEENE • DEBBIE BELKIN • KEISHA BELL • DE
BENDER • JENNY BENSON • ANGELA BERRY • JACKIE BILLETT • KYLIE BIVENS • DANIELLE BORGM
SHANNON BOXX • DENISE BOYER-MURDOCH • JEN BRANAM • AMBER BROOKS • THORI (STAP
BRYAN • TARA BUCKLEY • SHERI BUETER • SUSAN BUSH • LORI BYLIN • JANE CAMPBELL •
CASSELLA • LORI CHALUPNY • BRANDI CHASTAIN • MANDY CLEMENS • SAM COFFEY • DAN
COLAPRICO • LISA COLE • ROBIN CONFER • KERRY CONNORS • KIM CONWAY • ALANA COOK • ANN C
• PAM (BAUGHMAN) CORNELL • STEPHANIE (LOPEZ) COX • ALEISHA CRAMER • AMANDA CROMV
• COLETTE CUNNINGHAM • ABBY DAHLKEMPER • MARIAN DALMY • TIERNA DAVIDSON • CINDY D
• SAVANNAH DEMELO • MICHELLE DEMKO • KRISTI DEVERT • TINA DIMARTINO • IMANI DORS
BETSY DRAMBOUR • TRACY (NOONAN) DUCAR • JOAN DUNLAP-SEIVOLD • CRYSTAL DUNN • DAN
EGAN • TINA (FRIMPONG) ELLERTSON • WHITNEY ENGEN • STACEY ENOS • JULIE (JOHNSTON)
• RONNIE FAIR • LORRIE FAIR • JOY (BIEFELD) FAWCETT • KAREN FERGUSON • JESSICA FISCH
MIA FISHEL • KENDALL FLETCHER • MEREDITH FLORANCE • DANIELLE (GARRETT) FOTOPOUL
JULIE FOUDY • EMILY FOX • ADRIANNA FRANCH • MICHELLE FRENCH • CARIN (JENNINGS) GABA
• LINDA GANCITANO • MORGAN (BRIAN) GAUTRAT • WENDY GEBAUER • GRETCHEN GEGG • NA
GIRMA • LISA GMITTER • CINDY GORDON • SANDI GORDON • JEN GRUBB • SARAH HAGEN • KRIS
HAMILTON • LINDA HAMILTON • MIA HAMM • HALEY HANSON • RUTH HARKER • ASHLYN HARR
MARY HARVEY • ASHLEY HATCH • DEVVYN HAWKINS • TUCKA HEALY • TOBIN HEATH • APRIL HEINR
• HOLLY HELLMUTH • LORI HENRY • SHANNON HIGGINS • JAELENE HINKLE • LAUREN (CHE
HOLIDAY • LINDSEY HORAN • JAELIN HOWELL • ANGELA HUCLES • SOFIA HUERTA • SARAH HUFF
• LINDSEY HUIE • PATTY IRIZARRY • MARCI (MILLER) JOBSON • LAURA JONES • NATASHA K
CHRISTINA KAUFMAN • BETH KELLER • DEBBIE KELLER • SHERRILL KESTER • AUBREY KINGSB
• MEGHAN KLINGENBERG • JENA KLUEGEL • TAYLOR KORNIECK • NANCY KRAMARZ • ANNA KF
• ALI KRIEGER • CASEY (SHORT) KRUEGER • JENNIFER LALOR • ROSE LAVELLE • AMY LEPEI

Postgame

Fútbol is life!

—Dani Rojas on *Ted Lasso*

YDNEY LEROUX • GINA LEWANDOWSKI • KRISTINE LILLY • KELLY LINDSEY • LORI LINDSEY •
LI LLOYD • JOANNA LOHMAN • ALLIE LONG • JILL LOYDEN • KRISTIN LUCKENBILL • CATARINA
ARIO • HAILIE MACE • SHANNON MACMILLAN • HOLLY MANTHEI • KATE (SOBRERO) MARKGRAF
LY MARQUAND • ELLA MASAR • JEN (STREIFFER) MASCARO • KIM MASLIN-KAMMERDEINER
ERRITT MATHIAS • STEPHANIE MCCAFFREY • MEGAN MCCARTHY • SAVANNAH MCCASKILL •
CIA MCDERMOTT • JESSICA MCDONALD • TEGAN MCGRADY • JEN MEAD • KRISTIE MEWIS •
ANTHA MEWIS • TIFFENY MILBRETT • HEATHER MITTS • MARY-FRANCES MONROE • ALEX MORGAN
VIA MOULTRIE • SIRI MULLINIX • CASEY MURPHY • ALYSSA NAEHER • CHRISTINE NAIRN • NATALIE
TON • JENNA NIGHSWONGER • CAS[illegible]KES • KEALIA OHAI • KELLEY O'HARA •
YOLEKSIUK • HEATHER O'REILLY • LAUREN ORLANDOS • ANN ORRISON • LESLIE OSBORNE • CARLA
RDEN) OVERBECK • MEGAN OYSTER • JAIME PAGLIARULO • CINDY PARLOW CONE • TAMMY PEARMAN
ILY PICKERING • CARSON PICKETT • LOUELLEN POORE • CHRISTEN PRESS • NANDI PRYCE
IDGE PURCE • CAROLINE PUTZ • SARAH RAFANELLI • CHRISTIE (PEARCE) RAMPONE •
SA RAMSEY • SARA RANDOLPH • MEGAN RAPINOE • KERI (SANCHEZ) RAYGOR • SHARON
MURTRY) REMER • KATHY RIDGEWELL • STEPHANIE RIGAMAT • TIFFANY ROBERTS • LEIGH
ROBINSON • TRINITY RODMAN • AMY RODRIGUEZ • SHAUNA ROHBOCK • CHRISTY ROWE •
RUTTEN • ASHLEY SANCHEZ • BECKY SAUERBRUNN • KELLY (WILSON) SCHMEDES • MEGHAN
NUR • LAURA SCHOTT • LAURIE SCHWOY • BRIANA SCURRY • NIKKI SERLENGA • JAEDYN
V • DANIELLE SLATON • GAYLE SMITH • SOPHIA SMITH • TAYLOR SMITH • HOPE SOLO •
Y SONNETT • ZOLA SPRINGER • AMY STEADMAN • JILL STEWART • JENNIFER STRONG •
SULLIVAN • MALLORY PUGH SWANSON • JANINE SZPARA • LINDSAY TARPLEY • BRITTANY
OR • ALYSSA THOMPSON • CHRIS TOMEK • RITA TOWER • INDIA TROTTER • ERIKA TYMRAK
CHEL (BUEHLER) VAN HOLLEBEKE • TISHA VENTURINI • M.A. VIGNOLA • ALY WAGNER • KELLY
BERT • ABBY WAMBACH • MARCIE WARD • MORGAN WEAVER • SASKIA WEBBER • KRISTEN
S • CHRISTIE WELSH • SARA WHALEN • KACEY WHITE • CAT (REDDICK) WHITEHILL • LYNN
IAMS • STACI WILSON • ANGIE WOZNUK • KIM WYANT • VERONICA ZEPEDA • MCCALL ZERBONI

Huddle Up to Learn More

Amazing Autobiographies

The following titles offered important insights and anecdotes that informed this book. Read these excellent autobiographies for even more inspiration.

Howard, Tim. *The Keeper: A Life of Saving Goals and Achieving Them*. New York: HarperCollins, 2014.

Lloyd, Carli, with Wayne Coffey. *When Nobody Was Watching: My Hard-Fought Journey to the Top of the Soccer World*. Boston: Houghton Mifflin Harcourt, 2016.

Rapinoe, Megan. *One Life*. New York: Penguin Books, 2020.

Scurry, Briana, with Wayne Coffey. *My Greatest Save: The Brave, Barrier-Breaking Journey of a World-Champion Goalkeeper*. New York: Harry N. Abrams, 2022.

Wambach, Abby. *Forward: A Memoir*. New York: William Morrow, 2016.

Wambach, Abby. *Wolfpack: How to Come Together, Unleash Our Power, and Change the Game*. New York: Celadon, 2019.

Interesting Histories of the U.S. Women's National Team

Goldman, Rob. *The Sisterhood: The 99ers and the Rise of U.S. Women's Soccer*. Lincoln, Nebraska: University of Nebraska Press, 2021.

Murray, Caitlin. *The National Team: The Inside Story of the Women Who Changed Soccer.* New York: Abrams Press, 2019.

Lisi, Clemente A. *The U.S. Women's Soccer Team: An American Success Story.* Lanham, Maryland: Scarecrow Press, 2010.

Another Perspective on the Equal Pay Fight

Nichols, Rich, with Sam Yip. *All Things Being Equal: The Genesis, Costs and Aftermath of the USWNT's Equal Pay Battle.* Foreword by Hope Solo. New York: Skyhorse, expected in 2024.

Gripping Films

These excellent films brought this story to life for me and will for you too.

Cortese, Anthony J. *The Only.* Paramount+, 2022.

Fine, Sean, and Andrea Nix. *LFG/Let's F*cking Go!* Change Content, 2021.

Entertaining and Informative Podcasts

Foudy, Julie. *Laughter Permitted with Julie Foudy.* ESPN podcast. www.espn.com/espnradio/podcast/archive/_/id/26092845

O'Hara, Kelley, host. *The Players' Pod.* Just Women's Sports podcast. www.justwomenssports.com/podcast/the-players-pod/

Williams, Lynn, and Sam Mewis, hosts. *Snacks.* Just Women's Sports podcast. www.justwomenssports.com/podcast/snacks/#all-episodes

Great Coverage of Women's Sports

The Equalizer, year-round and daily coverage of USWNT and NWSL. www.equalizersoccer.com/

Just Women's Sports. www.justwomenssports.com

U.S. National Teams

United States Soccer Federation. www.ussoccer.com

U.S. Women's National Team Players Association. www.uswntplayers.com

U.S. (Men's) National Soccer Team Players Association. www.ussoccerplayers.com

Equal Pay Organizations

American Association of University Women (AAUW). www.aauw.org/issues/equity/pay-gap

Equal Pay International Coalition (EPIC). www.equalpayinternationalcoalition.org

Equal Pay Today. Find out about, and participate in, Equal Pay days. www.equalpaytoday.org

Institute for Women's Policy Research. www.iwpr.org

National Women's Law Center. www.nwlc.org

It Takes a Team

While I played a bit of soccer in elementary and middle school and watched my two children play in hundreds of matches, I don't consider myself a soccer expert. Luckily, I have two players/coaches built into my family. I have been watching my sister, Danielle Swope, who played for the United States before there was a national team, play soccer my whole life. I also married a soccer nut. Craig has played on many soccer teams, served as volunteer president of our local soccer club, and coached both our children, from kindergarten on, including several seasons juggling four teams. It's a wonder he got any work done.

He also manages and tries to never miss Sunday Soccer, an all-ages pick-up game every weekend in our neighborhood in Portland. Craig's pregame, postgame, and in-game commentary—along with hours of soccer talks while hiking with Dani and her husband, Mike—have definitely deepened my love and understanding of the game. My two "soccer coaches," Dani and Craig, also reviewed the manuscript.

I want to extend my thanks to the talented sports journalists and authors—especially Caitlin Murray, Sally Jenkins, Andrew Das, Clemente A. Lisi, Liz Clarke, and Rob Goldman—who have covered the women's game and this controversy so beautifully. I found their work information packed, entertaining, and insightful.

I deeply appreciate the following people for their willingness to participate in extensive interviews: Julie Foudy, Cindy Parlow Cone, Jeffrey Kessler, Becca Roux, Molly Levinson, and Mark Levinstein. Thank you so much for taking the time to share your experiences. This book—and the equal pay deal—would not have been possible without your work. Thank you for your contributions to both.

The national team players often thank a whole staff of people who support them and make their work possible. I too am blessed with a vital support team. Five young interns, who are also talented and dedicated budding writers, assisted with background research and offered essential feedback on drafts. Look for these names in print in the years to come: Claire Alongi, Ailie Coffey, Angelina Conklin, Yomari Lobo, and Isabel Zerr. Thanks to my lovely and powerful agent Fiona Kenshole for cheering on my diverse interests and landing me contracts that allow me to focus on what I do best—writing. Thanks also to my enormously talented editor, Virginia Duncan, who saw the worth in the book despite not being a huge soccer fan and who helped whip it into shape in time for the Olympics. I'm deeply grateful to the whole Greenwillow/HarperCollins team, including Tim Smith, Paul Zakris, and Anna Ravenelle, who rallied around the book to get it done—and done beautifully—before the final whistle. For reading and commenting on so many draft pages and for cheering me on, I'm grateful to the Lits (Chloe Ackerman, Eileen Bobek, Heidi Kaufman, Deb Miller Landau, and Kaarin Smith) and the Viva Scrivas (Addie Boswell, Cathy Camper, Ruth Feldman, Robin Herrera, and Sara Ryan).

My final thanks go to all the women of the U.S. Women's National Team past and present.

You are an inspiration to us all.

Source Notes

Events in this book involved many hundreds of players and countless lawyers, staff, and other people and took place over more than forty years. Each person's experiences and memories of these events may have differed. To write this book, I relied on details gathered from the sources I had access to that were closest to the events at hand, including newspaper and magazine articles and blogs; videos, documentaries, and podcasts; memoirs by players; books by sports journalists who covered the time and the teams; research reports and other materials by government agencies and equal pay advocates; and court filings.

Essential behind-the-scenes stories were described and confirmed through interviews with former USWNT players Julie Foudy (also a commentator for ESPN) and Cindy Parlow Cone (also the current U.S. Soccer president); women players' attorney Jeffrey Kessler, union leader Becca Roux, and public relations executive Molly Levinson; and men's players' attorney Mark Levinstein. I thank all these sources for their important contributions.

When accounts differed, I went with the source closest to the action. Any mistakes are mine. Section by section, sources are:

Part I: The First Half

No country can ever: Michelle Obama, "Remarks by the First Lady at the Summit of the Mandela Washington Fellowship for Young African Leaders," The White House, Office of the First Lady, July 30, 2014.

Kickoff: The Chant

"Everyone is ready": Kevin Baxter, "A Forward-Facing Morgan; U.S. Soccer's Cover Girl Eager to Get This Women's World Cup Started," *Los Angeles Times*, June 11, 2019.

"I don't think": Joshua Robinson, "U.S. Wins Women's World Cup," *Wall Street Journal*, July 7, 2019.

1 The Beginning: Pay to Play

Unless otherwise noted, material in this section comes from author interviews with Julie Foudy; Caitlin Murray, *The National Team, The Inside Story of the Women Who Changed Soccer*; Clemente A. Lisi, *The U.S. Women's Soccer Team: An American Success Story*; and Rob Goldman, *The Sisterhood: The 99ers and the Rise of U.S. Women's Soccer.*

"Oh my gosh" and *"That sounds pretty"*: Foudy, interview.

"I don't want you": Murray, *National Team*, 6.

"[When] you get into": Liz Clarke, "USWNT Fights for Equal Pay as It Fights to Defend World Cup Title," *Washington Post*, June 6, 2019.

From *Julie tried working* to *"That doesn't seem"*: Foudy, interview.

"Come on, sweetie": Sally Jenkins, "What Pay Means to U.S. Women's Soccer Players: R-E-S-P-E-C-T," *Washington Post*, March 31, 2016.

"You should just be": Andrea Nix Fine and Sean Fine, *LFG, HBO Max*, June 17, 2021.

U.S. Soccer bought to *spread out in a hotel:* Ken Shulman, "'Let's Move on This': The '99 U.S. Women's National Team's Fight for Equality," *WBUR*, June 07, 2019, and Foudy, interview.

Shuttle bus story: Murray, *National Team,* p. 17.

"It was just one": Fine and Fine, *LFG.*

"Why are the men": Clarke, "USWNT fights."

2 Gender Bias and the Pay Gap

In the 1980s: Mary Leisenring, "Women Still Have to Work Three Months Longer to Equal What Men Earned in a Year," U.S. Census Bureau, March 31, 2020.

"If you don't have": Chabeli Carrazana, "On LGBTQ+ Equal Pay Day, the U.S. Still Doesn't Know the Size of the Wage Gap," *The 19th,* June 16, 2021.

"not physiologically able to": Ailsa Rose, "The Woman Who Crashed the Boston Marathon," *JSTOR Daily,* March 18, 2018.

In the 1970s: Maya Salam, "The Long Fight for Pay Equality in Sports," *New York Times,* March 11, 2019.

In 1988: Staff, "The History of Gender Inequality in Sports," *Goal Five.com,* February 23, 2022.

3 The M&M's World Cup

In 1991: Murray, *National Team,* 8.

"make things easier": Glenn Crooks, "The Silent Trigger: The '91ers," *Our Game,* June 7, 2015.

Team captain April Heinrichs: Nakul Karnik, "1991 Women's World Cup in China," *Duke WordPress, Duke University,* 2015.

No one knew: Michael Lewis, "World Cup Qualifying Memories from 1991," *U.S. Soccer,* April 28, 2021.

The Americans played five: Lewis, "World Cup Qualifying Memories from 1991."

When the men's: Scurry, *Greatest Save,* 102.

Still, the U.S.: Goldman, *The Sisterhood.*

The tournament proved: Barbara Basler, "SOCCER: U.S. Women Beat Norway to Capture World Cup," *New York Times,* December 1, 1991, and Glenn Crooks, "The Silent Trigger: The '91ers," *Our Game,* June 7, 2015.

The men had: Clemente A. Lisi, *The U.S. Women's Soccer Team: An American Success Story.* Lanham, Maryland: Scarecrow Press, 2010.

Though the men's: Lisi, *The U.S. Women's Soccer Team.*

When Julie Foudy: Glenn Crooks, "The Silent Trigger: The '91ers," *Our Game,* June 7, 2015.

"We came home": Crooks, "The Silent Trigger."

A few weeks and *At the time:* Murray, *National Team,* 12.

A book written: Lisi, *The U.S. Women's Soccer Team.*

Shannon Higgins: Murray, *National Team,* 19.

"I gotta go" and *"That's not right"* and *"Why do we"*: Foudy interview.

4 I Have a Dream

This section is from Scurry, *Greatest Save,* 46, 80, 86, 168.

"You've been invited": Scurry, *Greatest Save,* 78.

OLYMPICS 1996: Scurry, *Greatest Save,* 27.

"The place itself": Scurry, *Greatest Save,* 79.

5 Lockout

Unless otherwise noted, this section is from Scurry, *Greatest Save,* 93, 102–105, 135; author interview with Julie Foudy; Goldman, *The Sisterhood*; Murray, *National Team;* and Shulman, "'Let's Move on This.'"

"We're facing" to *"what you want it to be for them"* and *"How dare you?"* to *"not moving on it"* and *"We're good"*: Foudy, interview.

"I was extremely": Scurry, *Greatest Save,* 104.

"Well, I am too" and *One day at 6* to *"just hold out"*: Shulman, "'Let's Move on This.'"

6 Playing for Olympic Gold

The waiting paid off: Joshua Robinson and Matthew Futterman, "U.S. Women's Soccer Team Stars Allege Pay Discrimination," *Wall Street Journal,* April 1, 2016.

At age sixteen: Tim Nash, "Cindy Parlow Cone: "Like a Kid in a Candy Store,"" *US Soccer,* October 16, 2018.

Indeed, she soon: "CLASS OF 2018: Cindy Parlow Cone," *National Soccer Hall of Fame,* YouTube video, October 20, 2018, www.youtube.com/watch?v=tVI63KNK5Jg.

Like a growing number: Nash, "Cindy."

Mia, Carla, and: "National Soccer Hall of Fame, "2018 Induction Speech: Cindy Parlow Cone," YouTube video, October 21, 2018.

As she continued: Cone, interview.

The whole team: Goldman, *The Sisterhood.*

On the day of: Scurry, *Greatest Save,* 111.

All that calm went: Lisi, *The U.S. Women's Soccer Team.*

In an exhausting: Lewis, "Golden Memories."

More than 75,000: 1996 U.S. Olympic Women's Soccer Team," *Team USA*.org.

Then the U.S. players: William Gildea, "U.S. Women's Soccer Team Wins Gold," *Washington Post,* August 2, 1996; and Ben Smith III, "On This Day: U.S. Women Capitalize on Golden Opportunity | 1996 Atlanta Olympics," *The Atlanta Journal-Constitution,* August 1, 2021.

The stadium erupted: Lisi, *The U.S. Women's Soccer Team.*

Julie was swept up: Conan O'Brien, "Julie Foudy's Strange Soccer Superstition," *Late Night with Conan O'Brien,* YouTube video, November 20, 1997.

When it was time: "1996 Women's Soccer Team," *United States Olympic & Paralympic Museum*, USOPM.org.

As Briana bent down: Scurry, *Greatest Save,* p 124.

7 Finding Fans

Unless otherwise noted, this material comes from author interviews with Julie Foudy and Murray, *National Team.*

U.S. participation in soccer: Alexandra E. Petri, "Once an 'Easy Way Out' for Equality, Women's Soccer Is Now a U.S. Force," *New York Times,* June 27, 2022.

And excitement was: Dave Litterer, "An Overview of American Women's Soccer History," Rec. Sport.Soccer Statistics Foundation, September 2010.

"It was all hands," "What's going on?," and *"Oh my god!"*: Foudy interview

They didn't seem and *At the same time*: Goldman, *The Sisterhood*

While doing this second and *"Why would they"* and *Before the game*: Scurry, *Greatest Save,* 30, 131–132.

"What the heck": Murray, *National Team,* vii.

8 The Whole World Watching

The group stage: Julie Foudy, "SOCCER: A Dream Becomes Tangible," *New York Times,* July 18, 1999.

In front of and *A tight win*: Foudy, interview.

For the 1999: Scurry, *Greatest Save,* 142.

Record-breaking crowds: Foudy, "SOCCER."

Usually an agile: Goldman, *The Sisterhood.*

In the final: Scurry, *Greatest Save,* 143.

Regulation time ended: Goldman, *The Sisterhood.*

But "Title IX" baby: FOX Soccer, "8th Most Memorable Women's World Cup Moment: Lilly Off the Line," YouTube Video, May 30, 2019.

American goalie Briana: Scurry, *Greatest Save,* 146.

But the reality: Sally Jenkins, "What Pay Means to U.S. Women's Soccer Players: R-E-S-P-E-C-T," *Washington Post,* March 31, 2016.

Winning the 1999 World Cup: Fine and Fine, *LFG.*

9 Soccer Is Sexy

The 1999 World Cup: Murray, *National Team,* 51.

10 Players in the Making

In the small town: Fine and Fine, *LFG.*

Born into an: Megan Rapinoe, *One Life,* 26.

11 The B Team

Unless otherwise noted, material from this section comes from author interviews with Julie Foudy and Cindy Parlow Cone; Caitlin Murray, *National Team;* Kayla Patrick and Sarah David Heydemann, "Union Membership Is Critical for Equal Pay," National Women's Law Center, Fact Sheet, March 2018.

"You signed a": Jenkins, "What Pay Means."

"They're currently unemployed": Sally Jenkins, "It Took a Revolution, but the U.S. Women's Soccer Team Got What It Deserved," *Washington Post,* May 18, 2022.

"We're doing this": Murray, *National Team,* 65.

"You can't": Murray, *National Team,* 66.

"Who's driving the bus?": Goldman, *The Sisterhood.*

12 Saving Her Brain

Unless otherwise noted, material in this section comes from Samantha Bresnahan, "U.S. Soccer Star's Career Ended by Concussion," *CNN,* November 12, 2015.

"She never ever": Foudy, interview.

If Mia said: Grant Wahl, "Who U.S. Soccer President Cindy Parlow Cone Is, From the Ex-Teammates Who Know Her Best," *Sports Illustrated,* March 26, 2020.

"I was just": Bresnahan, "U.S. Soccer Star's Career."

13 Blood and Guts on the Field

Unless otherwise noted, material in this section comes from Abby Wambach, *Forward: A Memoir.*

"Abby Wambach would": Julie Foudy, "Ultimate XI: The Ladies," Goal, *New York Times Soccer Blog,* April 22, 2009.

"She['s] so strong": Scurry, *Greatest Save,* p. 178

"a cocked gun": Wambach, *Forward,* 56.

14 Life-Altering Injury

Material in this section is from Briana Scurry, *My Greatest Save.*

"My goal was": Scurry, *Greatest Save,* 210.

15 A Losing Battle for Gold

Unless otherwise noted, material from this section comes from Abby Wambach, *Forward: A Memoir,* and Megan Rapinoe, *One Life,* 6, 26.

Megan signed to "And I didn't": Rapinoe, *One Life,* 81.

"We train to": Rapinoe, *One Life,* 95.

"You need to": Carli Lloyd, *When Nobody Was Watching,* 44.

"We're fucked": Rapinoe, *One Life,* 95.

"detach my leg": Wambach, *Forward,* 109.

"Bitch, you'd better": Rapinoe, *One Life,* 95.

"OH, CAN YOU": Commentary from TheresBeautyInSoccer, "Abby Wambach Goal vs. Brazil in the 122' - 2011 FIFA Women's World Cup," YouTube video, July 10, 2012.

"I know!": Rapinoe, *One Life,* 95.

"The Japanese earthquake": Neil Johnson, "Women's World Cup 2023: Japan in 'unstoppable' form before Sweden quarter-final," BBC Sport, August 10, 2023.

"But we didn't win": Murray, *National Team,* 170.

16 Playing for More Than Gold

Unless otherwise noted, material in this section comes from Department of the Treasury/Internal Revenue Service Form 990, Return of Organization Exempt from Income Tax, U.S. Soccer Federation, April 1, 2010–March 31, 2011; Andrew Das, "U.S. Soccer Sponsor Enters Equal Pay Fight on Women's Side," July 14, 2019.

"With each passing game": Rapinoe, *One Life,* 109.

"Even if the younger players" to *"to take the baton"*: Foudy, interview.

"one of the": Rapinoe, *One Life,* 115.

"apply pressure, tackle": Lloyd, *When Nobody,* 151.

17 Locked In to Low Wages

"browbeaten into submission": Rapinoe, *One Life,* 129.

"These are things": "Illegal in Massachusetts: Asking Your Salary in a Job Interview," Stacy Cowley, *New York Times,* August 2, 2016.

"save the money" to *"the difference between"*: "Black Women's (Un)Equal Pay Day is another Reminder of the Discrimination Black Women Experience Every Day," *NWLC blog,* July 31, 2017.

18 Pawning Gold

The material in this section comes from Briana Scurry, *My Greatest Save.*

"a butcher's knife": Scurry, *Greatest Save,* 211–221.

"I could get": Scurry, *Greatest Save,* 223.

"You take them" to *"You won them"*: Scurry, *Greatest Save,* 227.

"Wow, it's heavy": Scurry, *Greatest Save,* p. 229.

19 Turf Battle

Unless otherwise noted, material in this section comes from Juliet Macur, "With Turf, Women See Unequal Footing," *New York Times,* Aug 12, 2014; Wambach, *Forward*; Laken Litman, "Alex Morgan on Why Artificial Turf Is Tough for Players," *USA Today,* October 15, 2014; Kevin Baxter, "Top Women's Soccer Players Sue Over Artificial Turf Plans for World Cup," *Los Angeles Times,* October 25, 2014; Laken Litman, "Abby Wambach, Players Drop Turf Lawsuit Against FIFA," *USA TODAY Sports,* January 14, 2015.

"takes the skin": Rapinoe, *One Life,* 134.

"I'm not going": Macur, "With Turf."

"Forget our mounting success" to *"women themselves are inferior"* and *"We have to make sure"*: Wambach, *Forward*, 146–147.

"Every person has a right to": Section One of Ontario Human Rights Code, www.ohrc.on.ca.

"nonsense": Bill Chappell, "Soccer Players End Lawsuit Over Artificial Turf at Women's World Cup," *NPR*, January 21, 2015.

20 Watching and Hoping

"make it even harder": Rapinoe, *One Life*, 134.

21 The World Watches

"The artificial turf is a metaphor": Laurent Dubois, "Artificial Turf Controversy a Constant in Backdrop of Women's World Cup," *Sports Illustrated*, June 23, 2015.

The night before to *the 5 p.m. kickoff*: Lloyd, *When Nobody*, 205.

"Are you even human?": Lloyd, *When Nobody*, 211.

Teammate Ali Krieger joked to *"the entire field?"*: Murray, *National Team*, 237.

A record-breaking forty-three million: Murray, *National Team*, 238.

"When I'm eighty": Abigail Johnson Hess, "Former USWNT Player Briana Scurry on the Decades-Long Soccer Pay Gap: 'They Didn't Want Us to Be Equal,'" *CNBC Make It*, October 5, 2021.

22 Victory?

Sixteen-year-old Addie to *she told a reporter*: Lauren Gambino, "Historic Ticker-Tape Parade Enshrines US Women's Soccer Team in Sports Lore," *The Guardian*, July 10, 2015.

median annual income: Joint Economic Committee of U.S. Congress, "The Consequences of Gender Pay Inequality," July 2016.

"How will I support": Wambach, *Forward*, 130.

Aloha Stadium: "U.S. Players Say Field 'Looked like It Hadn't Been Replaced in Years,'" *ESPN.com*, December 6, 2015.

In fact, in 2015 to *grass for the men*: Jeff Kassouf, "Leveling the Playing Field," *NBC Sports*, December 14, 2015, Caitlin Murray, "Were the U.S. Women's Soccer Team Right To Boycott Their Own Victory Tour?," *The Guardian*, December 7, 2015, and Ryan Rosenblatt, "U.S. Soccer Continues to Treat the USWNT Worse than They Do the USMNT," *Stars and Stripes FC (SBNation)*, December 6, 2015.

"argue all you want": Rosenblatt, "U.S. Soccer Continues."

The women left the field: Nina Mandell, "USWNT Players Explain Decision to Cancel Game over Poor Field Conditions in Players' Tribune Post," *For the Win (USA Today Sports)*, December 6, 2015.

"We have become": USWNT, "Equal Footing," *The Players' Tribune*, December 7, 2015.

Abby's last: U.S. Soccer, "WNT Sends Off Abby Wambach in Front of Record Crowd in New Orleans," December 17, 2015.

At the various venues: Murray, *National Team*, 244.

23 A More Perfect Union

Material in this section comes from interviews with Becca Roux, February and March 2023.

24 Stepping Up Their Game

"The women's game": Rapinoe, *One Life,* 139.

On January 4: Stephen J. Kimmerling, "Winston & Strawn Files Action with EEOC on Behalf of United States Women's National Soccer Team," press release, March 31, 2016.

"the various bonus": Order Re: Plaintiff's Motion for Partial Summary Judgment; Defendant's Motion for Summary Judgment, *Alex Morgan v. U.S. Soccer,* May 1, 2020, 7.

equal pay off the table: Levinson, interview.

"irrational": Jenkins, "What Pay."

"Now that might be": Scott Stump, "U.S. Women's Soccer Stars on Filing Equal Pay Complaint: 'We've Proven Our Worth,'" *TODAY,* March 31, 2016.

Poverty presentation: Murray, *National Team,* 250; and Kessler, interview.

"You can't go into": Rapinoe, *One Life,* p. 140.

Memorandum to *union refused*: Sam Borden and Andrew Das, "U.S. Soccer Lawsuit Disclosed Players' Personal Information," *New York Times,* February 4, 2016.

25 U.S. Soccer Sues

"there were no": Andrew Das, "U.S. Soccer Sues Union Representing the Women's National Team," *New York Times,* February 3, 2016.

National Girls: Grant Wahl, "U.S. Soccer Sues USWNT Players Union over Labor Agreement Dispute," *Sports Illustrated,* February 3, 2016.

"The players are": SI Staff, "USWNT Players Livid, Have Personal Info Redacted from Lawsuit," *Sports Illustrated,* February 4, 2016.

U.S Soccer apologized: Borden and Das, "U.S. Soccer Lawsuit Disclosed Players' Personal Information."

galvanizing: Liz Mullen and Ian Thomas, "USSF Files Suit in Dispute with Players Union," *Sports Business Journal,* February 8, 2016.

26 An Audacious Idea

Material in this section comes from Murray, *National Team,* 250–251, 253–254 and Jonathan Tannenwald, "Details of U.S. Soccer's Budget for National Teams, *Philadelphia Inquirer,* March 7, 2016.

27 The Players Meet

Material in this section comes from interviews with Jeffrey Kessler, along with Kevin Baxter, "Playing Catch-Up; U.S. Women Soccer Players Challenge the National Federation over Pay, Reflecting an Effort to Move the Game Ahead, Not Just Here But Globally," *Los Angeles Times,* May 8, 2016.

28 The Five

Material in this section comes from EEOC Form 5, Charge of Discrimination, Case 440-2026-03570, April 19, 2016.

"the strongest case": Grant Wahl and Ted Keith, "The Case for . . . Taking a Stand," *Sports*

Illustrated, April 11, 2016.

Part II: The Second Half

29 The Media React

"If they don't": Garson O'Toole, "If They Don't Give You a Seat at the Table, Bring a Folding Chair," Quote Investigator, December 2, 2022.

In a press release to *"equal treatment"*: Stephen J. Kimmerling, "Winston & Strawn Files Action with EEOC on Behalf of United States Women's National Soccer Team," Press release, March 31, 2016.

"Every single day": "U.S. Women's Team Files Wage-Discrimination Action vs. U.S. Soccer," ESPN, March 31, 2016.

The EEOC office: Murray, *National Team,* 256.

"bombshell": Wahl and Keith, "The Case for . . . Taking a Stand."

"turning point" to *Hispanic women*: Sally Jenkins, "What Pay Means to U.S. Women's Soccer Players: R-E-S-P-E-C-T," *Washington Post,* March 31, 2016.

"chasm" to *"grow its game"*: Christine Brennan, "In Soccer, Men Get $17K Bonus in Win, Women $1K," *USA TODAY Sports,* April 1, 2016.

"whatever victories": Baxter, "Playing Catch-Up."

"the world's most popular": Brennan, "In Soccer."

30 Male Players React

"None of us" and *"Any time, no matter"* and *"As we all know""*: Victor Mather, "Tim Howard Says Women's Team Should Fight for Rights," *New York Times,* March 31, 2016.

Tim had a long and winding to *swept the internet, including "were what I had"* and *"Touch the ground"* and *"I could see"*: Tim Howard, "Tim Howard: Growing Up with Tourette Syndrome and My Love of Football," *The Guardian,* December 6, 2014.

"I'm not sure if those": "Howard Supports Fight for Equal Pay Rights," YouTube video, original interview from *Sports Illustrated,* posted by "coconut juice x," April 4, 2016, 1:16. www.youtu.be/6BY6M-Rd_is.

"We understand": SI WIRE, "Hillary Clinton Tweets Support for USWNT Wage Complaint," *Sports Illustrated,* March 31, 2016.

Landon Donovan to *"support the U.S. women's team"*: Joe Prince-Wright, "USMNT's Howard: We Support USWNT's Concerns in Equal Pay Fight," *NBC Sports,* March 31, 2016.

"no comment": Kelsey McKinney, "Here's What Every Member of the USMNT Has to Say About U.S. Soccer's Wage Inequality," *Deadspin,* June 24, 2019.

31 Best Paid in The World

Material in this section comes from ESPN.com news services, "U.S. Women's Team Files Wage-Discrimination Action vs. U.S. Soccer," ESPN, March 31, 2016.

32 To Strike or Not to Strike?

Sitting out: Baxter, "Playing Catch-Up."

"This is not something": Elise Craig, "Game Changers," *Marie Claire*, July 2016.

Description of negotiations: Order Re: Plaintiffs' Motion for Partial Summary Judgment [DE170]; Defendant's Motion for Summary Judgment [DE 171], *Alex Morgan v. U.S. Soccer*, May 1, 2020.

33 An Angry Icon

Icon award anecdote and *"why do I feel"* and *"My biggest concern"*: Dawn Porter, *37 Words*, Trilogy Films, June 21, 2022.

"We made the same": Abby Wambach, Barnard College Commencement Speech, May 18, 2018.

Kobe earnings: Weston Blasi, "Kobe Bryant Made Over $300 Million Playing Basketball—Here's How He Invested His Money," Morningstar, August 16, 2022.

Peyton earnings: Fanbuzz staff, "Peyton Manning's Net Worth: Being 'The Sheriff' Pays Really, Really Well," Fanbuzz, February 7, 2022.

Popularity of soccer: Jim Norman, "Football Still Americans' Favorite Sport to Watch," *Gallup*, January 4, 2018.

"we want the same": BRIEF OF THE EQUAL EMPLOYMENT OPPORTUNITY COMMISSION AS AMICUS CURIAE IN SUPPORT OF PLAINTIFFS/APPELLANTS AND IN FAVOR OF REVERSAL, *Alex Morgan v. U.S. Soccer*, July 30, 2021, p. 11.

"We would prefer": Andrew Das, "Fight for Equal Pay Returns to Public Eye," *New York Times*, July 8, 2016.

"If you are feeling": Megan Rapinoe, "Dear Megan: A Letter to My 13-Year-Old Self," *Bleacher Report*, August 5, 2016.

34 Brazil Olympics

"just burns": ESPN2, "Team USA Women's Soccer Falls to Sweden at Rio Olympics," YouTube: *Breaking Sports*, August 12, 2016.

"break" the organization: EEOC Amicus Brief.

"The only settlement": Kessler interview.

In December 2016: Andrew Das, "U.S. Women's National Team Fires Its Union's Leader," *New York Times*, December 28, 2016.

35 Waking to the Problem

Michelle Ngwafon to *"needs to do better"*: Michelle Ngwafon, "A Lifetime of the Wage Gap: A College Student's Perspective," NWLC blog, April 6, 2016.

State initiatives: "Progress in the States for Equal Pay," NWLC report, September 2016.

More than two dozen companies to *men for the same work*: "Over 100 Employers Sign White House Equal Pay Pledge," NWLC blog, December 13, 2016.

36 Worldwide Protests

Why I march to *into the streets*: The Women's March, 2017, National Museum of American History, March 2017.

Women's march: Anemona Hartocollis and Yamiche Alcindor, "Women's March Highlights as

Huge Crowds Protest Trump: 'We're Not Going Away,'" *New York Times*, January 21, 2017.

The platform for: "Guiding Vision and Definition of Principles," WomensMarch.com from Way Back Machine archive: web.archive.org/web/20170224032539/https://www.womensmarch.com/principles/ February 2017.

On March 8 to *half of their menus:* Perry Stein, Michael Alison Chandler and Sandhya Somashekhar, "The Strike Is On: Women Protest as Part of 'Day Without a Woman,'" *Washington Post*, March 8, 2017.

"Women power": Eric Westervelt, "Female Workers Asked to Join In 'A Day Without a Woman' Protests," *NPR News*, March 8, 2017.

37 Fighting for a Fair Contract

Much of the material on player negotiations in this section come from author interviews with Rebecca Roux, February and March 2023.

"Part of the problem": Rapinoe, *One Life*, 189.

Revenue sharing proposal: Order Re: Plaintiffs' Motion, *Alex Morgan v. U.S. Soccer*, May 1, 2020.

"I think so many": Sally Jenkins, "U.S. Soccer Team Could Settle to Help Itself—or Fight On for All Women," *Washington Post*, May 12, 2020.

Wrangled over each word: Andrew Das, "Long Days, Google Docs and Anonymous Surveys: How the U.S. Soccer Team Forged a Deal," *New York Times*, April 5, 2017.

38 Hardball

"It was a shitty": Roux, interview.

Camp negotiations: Murray, *National Team*, 284–288.

"You are getting abused": Roux, interview.

Tournament bonuses: Rapinoe, *One Life*, 178.

Progress on side issues: Andrew Das, "U.S. Women's Team Restructures Union in Effort to Revive C.B.A. Talks," *New York Times*, February 3, 2017.

"He physically stood": Roux, interview.

"Sometimes the suggestions": Das, "Team Restructures."

Accept it: Kessler, interview.

39 Concede or Strike?

"In my perception": Kessler, interview.

April 4 negotiations: Daniel Roberts, "What Critics Get Wrong About the U.S. Women's Soccer Pay Debate," *Yahoo! finance*, July 9, 2019.

"Maybe we have done" to *"All twenty-two"*: Roux and Kessler interviews.

"When we settled": Rapinoe, *One Life*, 178.

"We've always had": Das, "Long Days."

40 Time's Up on the Men's Contract

"This is horrendous": author interview with Mark Levinstein and fact-checking.

"He makes everyone's": Joshua Robinson, "The Captain Driving the U.S. in Qatar—Tyler Adams Doesn't Ring Up a Lot of Goals or Assists. But His European Experience as a Midfielder Is Anchoring the Squad," *Wall Street Journal,* December 1, 2022.

Tyler felt shock to *"the bottom line"*: Response to author's question, *Washington Post* Live, "NEXT: Tyler Adams, U.S. Men's National Soccer Team Captain, and Midfielder, Leeds United Football Club," *Washington Post,* January 24, 2023.

41 "I'm Going to Make a Change"

Around the same time to *companies around the globe*: Anita Olsen, "Gender Pay Gap Video—1 Year Later, an Interview with Ann-Helen Hopland," *LinkedIn,* March 4, 2019, and Ann-Helen Hopland, "Equal Pay: What Do These Kids Understand That Your Boss Doesn't," YouTube, Finansforbundet, August 23, 2019.

A similar video to *"If I don't forget"*: Celeste Geer, "Pocket Money," YouTube, ANZ, March 7th, 2016.

Iceland had been: Sarah David Heydemann, "Iceland's New Equal Pay Law Is a Huge Deal – But Let's Be Clear Why," *NWLC,* January 18, 2018.

"In Iceland": Tanya Tarr, "How Icelandic Women Really Feel About the New Equal Pay Law," *Forbes,* January 8, 2018.

42 A New Leader for U.S. Soccer

A columnist: Parker Cleveland, "Carlos Cordeiro Deserves a Chance," *Stars and Stripes FC,* February 12, 2018.

an institution guilty: Roux, interview.

43 A Tale of Two World Cups

Material in this section comes from Rapinoe, *One Life,* 188, plus author's calculations.

44 Freaking Out

Unless otherwise noted, the material for this section comes from Fine and Fine, *LFG,* and Ailsa Chang, "The U.S. Women's Soccer Team Struggle for Equal Pay Featured in New 'LFG' Documentary," *NPR All Things Considered,* June 29, 2021.

"We're running out": Author interview with Molly Levinson.

"Lawsuit?" and *"freaking out"*: Chang,"Struggle."

"Let's pump" and *"Okay, we're gonna"* to *"Let's do it"*: Fine and Fine, *LFG.*

45 Preparing a Lawsuit

Unless otherwise noted, material from this section is drawn from author interviews with Molly Levinson and Jeffrey Kessler.

"It was like, dang": Sarah Hashemi and Tom LeGro, "USWNT's March to the 2019 World Cup Title: An Oral History," *Washington Post* video, June 11, 2020.

46 Lawsuit Filed

Quotation from lawsuit complaint come from PLAINTIFFS COLLECTIVE ACTION COMPLAINT FOR VIOLATIONS OF THE EQUAL PAY ACT AND CLASS ACTION COMPLAINT FOR VIOLATIONS OF TITLE VII OF THE CIVIL RIGHTS ACTS OF 1964, DEMAND FOR JURY TRIAL, *Alex Morgan v. U.S. Soccer*, U.S. District Court Central District of California Western Division, March 8, 2019.

"No employer": The Equal Pay Act of 1963, SEC. 206. [Section 6] (d) Prohibition of sex discrimination, www.eeoc.gov/statutes/equal-pay-act-1963.

"It shall be": Title VII of the Civil Rights Act of 1964, UNLAWFUL EMPLOYMENT PRACTICES SEC. 2000e-2. [Section 703], www.eeoc.gov/statutes/title-vii-civil-rights-act-1964.

"Wow, that was" to *"bold and brave"*: Foudy, interview.

"It just shows" to *"DNA of this team"*: Roux, interview.

"Always believe": Liz Clarke, "U.S. National Soccer Team Hopes to Send a Message to Girls Everywhere," *Washington Post*, March 8, 2019.

47 The Response

Unless otherwise noted, this section is from DEFENDANT UNITED STATES SOCCER FEDERATION'S ANSWER AND AFFIRMATIVE DEFENSES TO PLAINTIFF'S COMPLAINT, *Alex Morgan v. U.S. Soccer*, April 6, 2019. P. 1, 9, 10.

"The United States National Soccer": United States National Soccer Team Players Association, "Statement of Support," March 8, 2019.

"The answer was kind of": Kessler, interview.

"They refused to pay": Fine and Fine, *LFG*.

48 Four-Star World Cup

"For what felt like": Rapinoe, *One Life*, 196.

"It was important": Grant Wahl, "USWNT's Historic Rout of Thailand and the Question of Sportsmanship," *SI.com*, June 11, 2019.

"I don't want to hear": Sally Jenkins, "The U.S. Women's National Team Is an American Treasure. Pay Them a Bounty," *Washington Post*, June 12, 2019.

"the confidence": Fine and Fine, *LFG*.

"Purple-Haired": Lauren Theisen, "Purple-Haired Lesbian Goddess Flattens France Like a Crêpe," *Deadspin*, June 28, 2019.

49 A Greater Goal

"take the noise": Rapinoe, *One Life*, 200.

"A little public": Andrew Das, "The U.S. Women Won, the Men Lost, and the Equal Pay Fight Tied Them Together Again," *New York Times*, July 8, 2019.

"The way I like": Kelley O'Hara, "The Player's Pod Mallory Pugh," *Just Women's Sports* podcast, Episode 6, December 1, 2020.

50 Sponsors Step Up

"We—all the players": Andrew Das, "The U.S. Women Won."

In the wake of to *"about values"*: Andrew Das, "U.S. Soccer Sponsor Enters Equal Pay Fight on Women's Side," *New York Times*, July 14, 2019.

Nike released to *"equally compensated"*: Kevin Draper, "Pushed by Consumers, Some Sponsors Join Soccer's Fight Over Equal Pay," *New York Times*, August 5, 2019.

51 Invested More Than Any Country in the World

The team returned to *"Equal pay!"*: NBC New York, "World Cup Parade 2019: USWNT's Crystal Dunn Shouts 'Equal Pay' at Ticker-Tape Parade," YouTube video, July 10, 2019.

Cordiero and Rapinoe speech excerpts: Fine and Fine, *LFG*.

"Caring is cool" to *"get your money"*: Rapinoe, *One Life*, 4, 208.

52 Settlement?

Unless otherwise noted, material in this section comes from Fine and Fine, *LFG*, and Carlos Cordeiro, OPEN LETTER TO OUR MEMBERSHIP FROM U.S. SOCCER PRESIDENT CARLOS CORDEIRO, USSoccer.com, July 29, 2019.

"Stop assuming": Roux, interview.

53 Support and Derision

Unless otherwise noted, material in this section comes from "USNSTPA statement in response to 7/29/2019 Carlos Cordeiro letter," US Soccer Players, United States National Soccer Team Players Association, July 30, 2019.

"There's a big difference": Christopher Bumbaca, "Former USMNT Player Jermaine Jones Questions Equal Pay in Soccer, Criticizes Alex Morgan," *USA Today (Online)*, August 1, 2019.

54 Mediation

Material in this section comes from Fine and Fine, *LFG*, and Kessler, interview.

55 Class Action?

Material in this section comes from National Women's Law Center, "Equal Employment Opportunity Restoration Action of 2016: What it Means for Women," Fact Sheet, July 12, 2016; Nina Martin, "The Impact and Echoes of the Wal-Mart Discrimination Case," *ProPublica*, September 27, 2013, and Kessler, interview.

56 Can Four Players Represent the Class?

This material comes from DEFENDANT UNITED STATE SOCCER FEDERATION, INC.'S OPPOSITION TO PLAINTIFFS' MOTION FOR CLASS CERTIFICATION, *Alex Morgan v. U.S. Soccer*, September 30, 2019; REPLY IN SUPPORT OF MOTION FOR CLASS CERTIFICATION, *Alex Morgan v. U.S. Soccer*, October 10, 2019; and *Ebbert v. Nassau County*, cited in REPLY IN SUPPORT OF MOTION FOR CLASS CERTIFICATION, *Alex Morgan v. U.S. Soccer*, October 10, 2019.

57 A Ruling

All material from R. Gary Klausner, U.S. District Court Judge, United States District Court Central District of California, *Alex Morgan v. U.S. Soccer*, Order Re: Plaintiffs' Motion for Class Certification, November 8, 2019, p. 5-6, 14-15.

58 The Search for Evidence

Material in this section comes from the author's interview with Jeffery Kessler, along with Fine and Fine, *LFG*.

"Our female" and *"We clearly,"* Videotaped Deposition of Carlos Cordeiro, Miami, Florida, January 29, 2020.

59 Questioning the Media

Speech: "Megan Rapinoe Accepts the 2019 SI Sportsperson of the Year Award," YouTube, SI.com September 9, 2019.

Media research: Melissa Jacobs, "Summer of Gold: How the 1996 Olympics Inspired a Generation of Female Athletes," *The Guardian*, August 16, 2021; Tucker Center, "Media Coverage and Female Athletes," YouTube video, April 22, 2022; and Ed Dixon, "Study: 88% of People Want to Watch More Women's Soccer," SportsProMedia.com, October 21, 2021.

60 A Dangerous Virus

Covid history comes from Scott LaFee, "Novel Coronavirus Circulated Undetected Months Before First Covid-19 Cases in Wuhan, China," UC San Diego Health Newsroom, March 18, 2021; Carl Zimmer, Benjamin Mueller, and Chris Buckley, "First Known Covid Case Was Vendor at Wuhan Market, Scientist Says," *Washington Post*, November 18, 2021; Amy Qin and Javier C. Hernández, "China Reports First Death from New Virus," *New York Times*, January 10, 2020; and CDC Museum Covid-19 Timeline, www.cdc.gov/museum/timeline/covid19.html.

Olympic discussions: Andrew Keh and Ben Dooley, "Grappling with Coronavirus, Tokyo Olympic Leaders Have No Good Options," *New York Times*, February 26, 2020.

61 A Word from the Men's Team

This material is from U.S. Soccer Players, "Statement about USWNT 2017-2018 CBA," *USSoccerplayers.com*, February 12, 2020.

62 Asking for Judgment

Material from PLAINTIFFS' NOTICE OF MOTION AND MOTION FOR PARTIAL SUMMARY JUDGMENT; MEMORANDUM OF POINTS & AUTHORITIES IN SUPPORT, *Alex Morgan v. U.S. Soccer*, February 20, 2020; and DEFENDANT'S MEMORANDUM OF POINTS AND AUTHORITIES IN SUPPORT OF ITS MOTION FOR SUMMARY JUDGMENT, *Alex Morgan v. U.S. Soccer*, February 20, 2020.

63 Dueling Experts

"USSF paid more": as quoted in EEOC amicus brief, p. 8.

"Particularly since": Michael McCann, "U.S. Soccer-USWNT Trial Date Postponed, Belittling Comments Removed from Record," *Sports Illustrated*, April 8, 2020.

"Both the players": Andrew Das, "U.S. Women's Soccer Team Sets Price for Ending Lawsuit: $67 Million," *New York Times*, February 21, 2020.

64 A Pandemic Brewing

"neither the word": Victor Mather, "How the Coronavirus Has Disrupted Sports Events," *New York Times*, March 2, 2020.

"an actual": Andrew Das, "United States 1, Spain 0: For U.S. Women, a Narrow Victory and a Growing Divide," *New York Times,* March 8, 2020.

65 What He Believes

"update" to *"controlled by U.S. Soccer"*: Carlos Cordeiro, "Our proposal for equal pay for women and men national team players—March 7, 2020," attachment to tweet @CACSoccer, March 7, 2020.

no commitment to match: Rachel Bachman, "U.S. Soccer Offers Women Equal Pay in Some Matches—and They Reply, Do Better," *Wall Street Journal,* March 8, 2020.

"misleading" and *"dishonest"*: Andrew Das, "United States 1, Spain 0: For U.S. Women, a Narrow Victory and a Growing Divide," *New York Times,* March 8, 2020.

"distracting": Meredith Cash, "US Soccer Wrote an Open Letter Critical of the USWNT's Equal Pay Lawsuit on the Eve of International Women's Day, and the Team Was Not Happy About It," *Insider,* March 9, 2020.

Spain game: Das, "United States 1, Spain 0."

"It was an honor" to *"#Equal Pay"*: Carlos Cordeiro, @CACSoccer, tweet, 10:17 AM, March 9, 2020. Comments posted March 9-12.

"that the job" to *"more prestige"*: Defendant's Memorandum of Points and Authorities in Opposition to Plaintiffs' Motion for Partial Summary Judgment, *Alex Morgan v. U.S. Soccer,* March 9, 2020.

"My god" to *"misogyny"*: Rapinoe, *One Life,* 216–217.

"sounds as if": Associated Press, "Sponsor Coca-Cola Rips U.S. Soccer for 'Offensive' Legal Arguments vs. USWNT," *Sports Illustrated,* March 11, 2020.

"How are we ever": Roux, interview.

"sadly": Jerry Brewer, "Words Matter, and U.S. Soccer Exposed Its Sexism in Its Latest Legal Filing," *Washington Post,* March 11, 2020.

"you shouldn't make" to *"loves a winner"*: Foudy, interview.

"Using biological": "Taylor Twellman RIPS U.S. Soccer Over USWNT Equal Pay," YouTube, *Banter,* posted by ESPN FC, March 11, 2020.

"unacceptable": "'Blatant Misogyny': U.S. Women Protest, and U.S. Soccer President Resigns," *New York Times,* March 12, 2020.

"one which": Staff, "U.S. Soccer Faces Backlash from Top Sponsors After Latest Comments," *Sports Business Journal,* March 12, 2020.

"deeply offended": Molly Hensley-Clancy, "Sponsors Are Blasting US Soccer For 'Offensive' Comments That Women Players Aren't as Skilled as Men," *Buzzfeed.com,* March 11, 2020.

"did you happen" to *"shameful"*: Carlos Cordeiro, @CACSoccer, tweet comments.

"Words matter": Brewer, "Words Matter."

"It's so dangerous": Fine and Fine, *LFG.*

66 What She Believes

Pandemic details: CDC timeline.

Earlier that week: Andrew Keh, “Postpone the Olympics? Tokyo Official Backtracks After Causing Confusion,” *New York Times*, March 11, 2020.

“We were so ready” and *“I noticed something different”* to *“honor you”*: Fine and Fine, *LFG*.

Midway through the game to *“mind on this”*: Foudy, interview

“it was surreal”: Tom Rimback, “With Olympics Postponement Coming, USA Women’s Soccer Star Carli Lloyd Adapting to New World,” *Burlington County Times*, March 23, 2020.

“blatant misogyny” to *“line completely”*: Kevin Draper and Andrew Das, “‘Blatant Misogyny’: U.S. Women Protest, and U.S. Soccer President Resigns,” *New York Times*, March 15, 2020.

“It’s false”: Fine and Fine, *LFG*.

67 Pressure Builds

“They didn’t give up”: Kessler, interview.

“We stand by”: Kevin Draper and Andrew Das, “‘Blatant Misogyny.’”

“you’re ridiculous” to *“please resign”*: Carlos Cordeiro, @CACSoccer, tweet comments.

“The arguments” to *“an organization”*: Katie Whyatt, “Carlos Cordeiro Resigns as US Soccer Federation President over Women’s National Team Equal Pay Row,” *The Telegraph*, March 12, 2020, and Carlos Cordeiro, Open Letter to Friends, Colleagues, and Supporters of U.S. Soccer, March 12, 2020.

“What do you mean”: Fine and Fine, *LFG*.

“it struck me as”: Kessler, interview.

“it’s undoubtedly” to *“sexism itself”*: Meredith Cash, “US Soccer Federation President Carlos Cordeiro Resigned over USWNT Equal Pay Lawsuit Backlash—but He’s Just a Symptom of a Larger Problem,” *Insider*, March 13, 2020.

68 March Madness

imploded to *“outlandish thing”*: Victor Mather, “How the Coronavirus Is Disrupting Sports,” *New York Times*, March 12, 2020.

“Our basic stance” to *“throughout the globe”*: Andrew Keh, “Postpone the Olympics? Tokyo Official Backtracks After Causing Confusion,” *New York Times*, March 11, 2020.

“all Americans”: Knvul Sheikh, “No More Than 10 People in One Place, Trump Said. But Why?” *New York Times*, March 16, 2020.

March 17: Steven Goff, “U.S. Soccer monitoring USWNT Players Who Shared Stadium with Coronavirus-Infected Official,” *Washington Post*, March 18, 2020.

athletes polled: Juliet Macur, Karen Crouse, Andrew Keh, and Matthew Futterman, “Olympians Have Another Year to Prepare for Tokyo. It’s a Blessing and a Curse,” *New York Times*, March 24, 2020.

69 A Teammate Takes the Helm

Unless otherwise noted, material in this section comes from author interviews with Cindy Parlow Cone and Julie Foudy, as well as "2022 WICC Best XI Winner: Cindy Parlow Cone, International Champions Cup," YouTube video, November 9, 2022, and Sam Carp, "'It's Quite Literally a New Day': US Soccer President Cindy Parlow Cone on Equal Pay, the 2026 World Cup, and Being a Team Player," *Sports Pro Media*, June 17, 2022.

"I am hurt": Steven Goff, "Carlos Cordeiro Resigns as President of U.S. Soccer," *Washington Post*, March 17, 2020.

resignation on Twitter: Ronald Blum, "Cordeiro Tries to Oust Cone, Regain US Soccer presidency," *AP News*, February 17, 2022.

"I'm sure your" and *"her challenge"*: Grant Wahl, "Who U.S. Soccer President Cindy Parlow Cone Is, From the Ex-Teammates Who Know Her Best," *Sports Illustrated*, March 26, 2020.

"I have known" and *"there is some"*: Steven Goff, "A Woman Unfamiliar with Defeat as a Player or Coach Takes Reins of Troubled U.S. Soccer," *Washington Post*, March 13, 2020.

70 Postponed

"We want to be": Katie Couric, "Trailblazing Soccer Star Julie Foudy Is Teaching Girls to Lead Both On and Off the Field," *Glamour* video, March 15, 2022.

"be rescheduled": ZK Goh and Shintaro Kano, "Tokyo 2020 Olympic and Paralympic Games postponed to 2021," Olympics.com, March 24, 2020.

On senior players: Avi Creditormar, "What Olympic Postponement Means for the USWNT," *SI.com*, March 24, 2020.

"I do believe": Rimback, "With Olympics postponement."

"absolutely the right": Ben Pickman, "USWNT's Megan Rapinoe Hopes to Play in Tokyo Games, Fears Olympics Are 'In Doubt,'" *Sports Illustrated*, May 5, 2020.

"We had no idea": Kessler, interview.

"If Covid-19" to *"social media"*: Beau Dure, "Will Covid-19 Push U.S. Women's Lawsuit to Settlement or Catastrophe?" *Soccer America*, April 2, 2020.

71 Trial Preparations

Trial schedule: Michael McCann, "U.S. Soccer-USWNT Trial Date Postponed, Belittling Comments Removed from Record," *Sports Illustrated*, April 8, 2020.

The story the team wanted to tell: Kessler, interview.

"I understood their" to *legal strategy*: Cone, interview.

dropped its claims: Nancy Armour, "US Soccer Backs Off Sexist, Demeaning Characterizations of USWNT in Latest Legal Filing," *USA Today*, March 17, 2020.

72 A Surprise Ruling

Unless otherwise noted, material in this section comes from Fine and Fine, *LFG*, and the author's interview with Jeffrey Kessler.

"a stunning": Michael McCann, "Why U.S. Soccer Prevailed in USWNT's Gender Discrimination Lawsuit," *Sports Illustrated,* May 1, 2020.

"a severe": Rachel Bachman, "Judge Rejects U.S. Women's Soccer Players' Pay-Discrimination Claim," *Wall Street Journal,* May 2, 2020.

"a potentially": Graham Hays, "Judge Sides with U.S. Soccer in USWNT's Equal Pay Lawsuit," ESPN, May 1, 2020.

"From age fourteen": Liz Clarke, "USWNT Fights for Equal Pay as It Fights to Defend World Cup Title," *Washington Post,* June 3, 2019.

Part III: Overtime

73 Picking Apart the Ruling

"If you know this team": Andrew Das, "U.S. Women's Soccer Team's Equal Pay Demands Are Dismissed by Judge," *New York Times,* May 1, 2020.

"To do this, Plaintiffs must show" and *"WNT players received more money"* and *"In response, Plaintiffs have offered evidence"* and *Judge Klausner pointed out* and *"This method of comparison"* and *Finally, it didn't matter*: Order Re: Plaintiffs' Motion for Partial Summary Judgment [DE170]; Defendant's Motion for Summary Judgment [DE 171], *Alex Morgan v. U.S. Soccer,* May 1, 2020.

"a crushing blow": Molly Hensley-Clancy, "U.S. Soccer, Women's Team Members Settle Equal Pay Lawsuit for $24 Million," *Washington Post,* February 22, 2022.

"a devastating rejection" and *"swelled their paydays"*: Andrew Das, "Can U.S. Soccer and Its Women's Team Make Peace on Equal Pay?" *New York Times,* May 2, 2020.

"They can beat sexism" and *"even I can see that the women had to win more games"* to *"the women chose this"*: Sally Jenkins, "U.S. Soccer Team Could Settle to Help Itself—or Fight On for All Women," *Washington Post,* May 12, 2020.

"It's not a defense": Liz Clarke, "Settlement Talks in Pay Dispute May Be the Best Play for U.S. Women's Soccer Team," *Washington Post,* May 9, 2020.

"No one is happy" to *"athletes and women everywhere"*: Erin Longbottom and Lark Lewis, "LFG: Why We're Joining the Women's Soccer Team's Fight for Equal Pay," National Women's Law Center blog, July 30, 2021.

74 A Minor Victory

"competitive advantage" to *"comes from charter flights"*: Order Re: Plaintiffs' Motion for Partial Summary Judgment.

"It's like if they win": Longbottom and Lewis, "LFG: Why We're Joining."

75 Congress Holds a Hearing

"Today is Equal Pay Day" to *"marginalized by gender"*: Oversight Committee Democrats, "Equal Pay Day 2021," Congressional Oversight and Reform Committee hearing, YouTube, March 24, 2021.

Rapinoe's testimony: Oversight Committee Democrats, "Equal Pay Day 2021," Congressional Oversight and Reform Committee hearing, YouTube, March 24, 2021.

"I really don't think" to *"it happened again"*: Macarena Carrizosa, "If Women Still Earn Less, Can Laws Even Fix the Pay Gap?" Bloomberg Law video, February 17, 2022.

"The story is the same everywhere": Katie Wiese, "Connecticut, Nevada, and Rhode Island Enact Salary Range Transparency Laws to Help Close the Wage Gap," NWLC blog, July 19, 2021.

"We don't have to wait": Oversight Committee Democrats, "Equal Pay Day 2021."

76 Two Women in Charge

"How do we bring everyone together" and *"the feds"* to *"wanted to solve"*: Cone, interview.

"Cindy didn't crave power" and *Cindy and Becca thought* to *updated contract might say*: Roux, interview.

"charter air travel" and *"Nothing contained herein"*: CLASS ACTION SETTLEMENT AND RELEASE OF WORKING CONDITIONS CLAIMS, Alex Morgan et al. v U.S. Soccer Federation, December 1, 2020.

"For huge societal change": Roux, interview.

The two sides to *SheBelieves Cup*: "USWNT, U.S. Soccer Settlement Concerning Unequal Working Conditions Approved," *The Athletic*, April 12, 2021.

"USSF has not offered": Jeff Carlisle, "Judge Grants USWNT Unequal Working Conditions Settlement," ESPN, April 12, 2021.

"come to resolution": Rebecca Falconer, "U.S. Women's Soccer Team Wins Partial Deal on Equality," *Axios*, April 12, 2021.

"To be clear": Kessler, interview.

77 The Appeal

"In effect": "U.S. Women's Soccer Team Asks Ninth Circuit to Reinstate Equal Pay Claim," *Lexology*, September 8, 2021.

78 U.S. Soccer vs. The Men's National Team

This section comes from recollections shared in author interviews with men's players union lawyer Mark Levinstein.

79 Friends of the Court

"Noteworthy": Meg Linehan, "U.S. Women's Soccer Players Get Support from Men's Team in Equal Pay Lawsuit," *The Athletic*, July 30, 2021.

"The men stand with the women": Brief for the United States National Soccer Team Players Association as Amicus Curiae in Support of Plaintiffs-Appellants," *Alex Morgan v. U.S. Soccer*, July 30, 2021.

They wanted to share: Author interviews with Mark Levinstein.

"The United States Soccer Federation" and *"The federation"* to *"glaring and undeniable"*: Brief for the United States National Soccer Team Players.

The women who were not salaried: Brief of the Equal Employment Opportunity Commission as Amicus Curiae in Support of Plaintiff/Appellants and in Favor of Reversal, *Alex Morgan v. U.S. Soccer*, July 30, 2021.

"The women have dedicated" and *"held off their toughest challengers"*: Brief for the United States National Soccer Team Players.

"The federation's discrimination": Brief for the United States National Soccer Team Players.

80 More Friends of the Court

"quantity or quality of output" and *"ignored the quality"* and *"generally credited"* and *"Simply put, the WNT offered"* and *"As to the notion"*: EEOC brief.

"The gender wage gap harms": Brief for the National Women's Law Center, Women's Sports Foundation, and 63 Additional Organizations as Amici Curiae in Support of Plaintiff-Appellants," *Alex Morgan v. U.S. Soccer*, July 30, 2021.

Women make up to *working women in half* and *Boys have more* to *less in scholarship funding* and *Men's sports receive* and *"chosen to underinvest"* and *"Employers cannot require women"* and *"the inclusion"*: Brief for the National Women's Law Center.

All three amicus briefs were unanimous: USMNT brief, 4; EEOC brief, 38: "Judgment of the district court should be vacated, and the case remanded for further proceedings." NWLC brief, 35: "this court should reverse the district court's decision and allow Plaintiff's claims for equal pay to proceed."

81 Pressure to Settle

"set a standard" and *"promoting and governing soccer"*: Sarah Pack, Thomas A. Baker III, and Bob Heere, "One Nation, Two Teams: The U.S. Women's National Team's Fight for Equal Pay," *Northeastern University Law Review*, May 13, 2021.

Delving into the federation's financials to *equalizing pay*: Daniel Libit, "Going for Gold: Team USA Eyes $100M+ in Legal Fees Since Rio Games," *Sportico*, May 10, 2021.

"We're confident that working together": U.S. Soccer Comms, @ussoccer-comms, tweets June 24, 2021.

"We're not on opposite sides": Andrew Das, "U.S. Soccer Ties World Cup Prize Money to Equal Pay Fight," *New York Times*, September 10, 2021.

She didn't have a clear path forward: Sam Carp, "US Soccer President Cindy Parlow Cone on Equal Pay, the 2026 World Cup and Being a Team Player," *Sports Pro Media*, June 17, 2022.

"As a former player" to *federation and both teams*: Cindy Parlow Cone, "U.S. Soccer Open Letter Invites USWNT and USMNT to Come Together to Resolve FIFA Prize Money Disparity," U.S. Soccer Press Release, September 10, 2021.

"Tomorrow? Yesterday?": Das, "U.S. Soccer Ties."

82 A Challenge to Her Leadership

"I'm actually convinced": Haley Rosen, "UNC Legend Anson Dorrance on the 1991 World Cup and His Complicated Relationship with US Soccer," *Just Women's Sports*, July 29, 2020.

Carlos's platform listed: Staff, "Carlos Cordeiro to Run for U.S. Soccer President 2 Years After Resigning Amid Backlash," *The Athletic*, January 5, 2022.

"After nearly two years" to *"players, coaches, and referees"*: Adnan Ilyas, "Ex-USSF President Carlos Cordeiro to Run for Re-Election," *Stars and Stripes FC*, January 7, 2022. (Note: The platform was taken down after he lost reelection.)

"Imagine if, two years after resigning": Beau Dure, "Will Carlos Cordeiro Return to Rule US Soccer Two Years After Alienating the USWNT?," *The Guardian*, February 16, 2022.

"I frankly think this move represents" to *"no other, less toxic, options?"*: Ilyas, "Ex-USSF President Carlos."

"So much happened under your watch": Dure, "Will Carlos Cordeiro Return."

83 Ticking Clock

Unless otherwise noted, material in this section comes from interviews with Becca Roux, Mark Levinstein, and Cindy Parlow Cone.

"Cindy apologized to us": Sally Jenkins, "In Its USWNT Settlement, U.S. Soccer Essentially Made an Admission: It Was All True," *Washington Post*, February 23, 2022.

84 It Was All True

"landmark win for fairness": Amy Bass, "Women's Soccer Settlement Is Landmark Win for Fairness," CNN, February 23, 2022.

"An unexpected victory": Andrew Das, "U.S. Soccer and Women's Players Agree to Settle Equal Pay Lawsuit," *New York Times*, February 22, 2022.

"a remarkable achievement": Editorial Board, "Opinion: The U.S. Women's Soccer Team's Settlement Is a Huge Victory on Pay Equality," *Washington Post*, February 23, 2022.

"a tacit admission" and *"Nearly two years after"*: Das, "U.S. Soccer and Women's Players Agree."

"The governing body": Sally Jenkins, "In its USWNT settlement, U.S. Soccer essentially made an admission: It was all true," *Washington Post*, February 23, 2022.

"It's honestly": Meg Linehan, "USWNT players reach settlement with U.S. Soccer for total of $24 million in pay discrimination lawsuit," *The Athletic*, February 21, 2022.

"It's a really amazing day" : Robin Roberts, "USWNT Wins Fight for Equal Pay," *Good Morning America*, February 22, 2022.

"one of those incredible moments": Molly Hensley-Clancy, "U.S. Soccer, women's team members settle equal pay lawsuit for $24 million," *Washington Post*, February 22, 2022.

"What we set out to do": Das, "U.S. Soccer and Women's Players."

"proudly stand together" to *"girls who will follow"*: "U.S. Soccer, USWNT Players Reach to Resolve Longstanding Equal Pay Dispute," U.S. Soccer, February 22, 2022.

85 Not a Done Deal

"Yes, I wanted to resolve the litigation": Cone, interview.

"Lost amid this collective back-patting": Steven Bank, "Was USWNT's equal pay settlement celebrated too soon?" ESPN, March 16, 2022.

"monumental not just for us" to *"equal pay locked in"*: Foudy, interview.

This was a huge concern to *member of the class in the suit*: Michael McCann, "Hope Solo Fights U.S. Soccer Alone After Exclusion from USWNT Lawsuit," *Yahoo Sports*, February 25, 2022.

"promise of equal pay" to *"federation in the first place"*: Jenna Lemoncelli, "Hope Solo Attacks USWNT Stars Over Equal Pay Settlement: 'Not a Win,'" *New York Post,* February 24, 2022.

"Are we close": Meredith Cash, "Legendary Goalie Hope Solo Calls the US Women's Soccer Team's Equal-Pay Settlement 'Heartbreaking and Infuriating,'" *Insider,* February 23, 2022.

But Hope Solo continued to *"never going to happen"*: Michael McCann, "USWNT Vet Hope Solo Fights on Against U.S. Soccer—Alone," *Sportico,* March 12, 2022.

86 A Vital Election

"The moment of division is now in the past": Jeff Carlisle, "Cindy Parlow Cone Reelected as U.S. Soccer President, Defeats Carlos Cordeiro," ESPN.com, March 5, 2022.

87 Two Teams, Together

Material on negotiations in this section comes from interviews with Becca Roux, Mark Levinstein, and Cindy Parlow Cone.

Everyone involved: Jeff Carlisle, "USWNT, USMNT CBAs Include Equal Pay: Why U.S. Soccer's New Deals Rewrite the History Books," ESPN, May 18, 2022.

One key player to *best motivated people*: Chris Smith, "Walker Zimmerman Explains the Process Behind US Soccer's Equal Pay Agreement," *90 min,* June 16, 2022.

A leader on the pitch: Laken Litman, "Why Walker Zimmerman Is the Leader the USMNT Needs at World Cup 2022," *Fox Sports,* November 14, 2022.

"to do something no other team had done before": Michael Gallagher, "Zimmerman: Equal Pay for USMNT, USWNT Long Overdue," *Nashville Post,* May 18, 2022.

Let's be on the front foot: Litman, "Why Walker."

Walker knew the most difficult question and *"There was a potential chance"*: Gallagher, "Zimmerman: Equal pay."

And they explored to *riskier potential World Cup earnings* and *Similar but different discussions* to *matches in an equal-pay scenario:* Jeff Carlisle, "USWNT, USMNT CBAs Include Equal Pay: Why U.S. Soccer's New Deals Rewrite the History Books," ESPN, May 18, 2022.

"the weight of the world": Julie Foudy, "Laughter Permitted with Julie Foudy," Episode 91: Cindy Parlow Cone, ESPN podcast, November 9, 2022.

"No one believed": Cone, interview.

Cindy felt daggers to *"something like this?"*: Cone, interview.

"difficult conversations": Andrew Das, "U.S. Soccer and Top Players Agree to Guaranteed Equal Pay," *New York Times,* May 18, 2022.

88 Equal Means Equal

"It's a dawn of a new era": Brian Straus, "U.S. Soccer Announces Historic CBA Agreement, Equal Pay Between USMNT, USWNT," *Sports Illustrated,* May 18, 2022.

"Wow! We're here" to *she handed the mic back*: Cone, interview.

Many of us have to *"let's sign this thing"*: U.S. Soccer, "U.S. Soccer & USWNT Sign Historic Collective Bargaining Agreement—Sept. 6, 2022," YouTube video, September 7, 2022.

"Equal" was another repeating beat: "U.S. Soccer Federation, Women's and Men's National Team Unions Agree to Historic Collective Bargaining Agreements," U.S. Soccer, May 18, 2022.

The linchpin of the contracts to *remaining after U.S. Soccer took its cut* and *The per-game bonuses* to *broadcasting deals and the like*: "U.S. Soccer Federation, Women's and Men's National Team."

"I feel a lot of pride": Associated Press, "U.S. Soccer Makes Pay Equal for Men's and Women's National Teams," *Washington Post*, May 18, 2022.

As the men and women to *The crowd roared*: U.S. Soccer, "U.S. Soccer & USWNT Sign Historic Collective Bargaining Agreement," YouTube video, September 6, 2022.

89 Equality in Action

"literally life changing": Meg Linehan, "The USWNT Make History With CBA signing, But The Players Know There's More To Be Done," *The Athletic*, September 7, 2022.

"That's right": Nancy Armour, "USMNT sharing prize money with USWNT," *USA Today*, December 2, 2022.

90 Women's World Cup

In July 2023 to *ever departed a World Cup*: FOX Soccer, "USWNT vs. Sweden: WILD Penalty Shootout in the 2023 FIFA," YouTube, August 6, 2023.

"We came out and controlled": FOX Sports, "'We Played Beautiful Football Today'—Lindsey Horan Praises USWNT's Performance in Exit from World Cup," YouTube, August 6, 2023.

"World Cup payday" to the graphic: Author calculations based on Emma Hruby, "How Much Will the USMNT Make Off the USWNT World Cup Run?," *Just Women's Sports*, August 7, 2023.

"We're actually all on the same boat": Foudy, interview.

91 The Domino Effect

"How often do we talk": Armour, "USMNT sharing prize."

"It's not easy to look back": Carlisle, "USWNT, USMNT CBAs."

"we hope this will awaken": Das, "U.S. Soccer and Top Players Agree to Guaranteed Equal Pay."

One woman said she could: Amy Woodyatt, "'We Couldn't Lose': Megan Rapinoe Reflects on 'Feeling Desperate' in Fight for Equal Pay," CNN, March 8, 2023.

Inspired by the U.S. team to *sharing with both teams*: Chris Gelardi, "The New Zealand Women's Soccer Team Finally Won Equal Pay," *Global Citizen*, May 8, 2018; Alana Glass, "Brazil Announces Equal Pay for Women's and Men's National Teams," *Forbes*, September 2, 2020; Alexander Netherton, "Football News - Football Association Of Ireland Agree Equal Pay For Both Women's And Men's International Teams," *Euro Sport*, August 8, 2021; Richard Newman, "'An Important Social Signal' – Arsenal Forward Vivianne Miedema Hails Netherlands Equal Pay Deal," *Euro Sport*, June 21, 2022; Sam Marsden and Moises Llorens, "Spain's female footballers to receive equal bonuses in new agreement," ESPN, June 14, 2022; Louise Taylor, "England women's and men's teams receive same pay, FA reveals," *The Guardian*, September 3, 2020.

"How did you do this?": Cone, interview.

"It's been incredible": Krysyan Edler, "How Crystal Dunn Sent Her Soccer Team to the Finals Just 5 Months After Giving Birth," *Deseret News*, October 25, 2022.

"The domino effect": Andrew Das, "U.S. Soccer and Women's Players Agree to Settle Equal Pay Lawsuit," *New York Times*, February 22, 2022.

92 You're Next: The Ongoing Fight for Equal Pay

In the United States today to *participants are female*: Tucker Center for Research on Girls and Women in Sport, "Media Coverage and Female Athletes," November 12, 2013.

women make up less than: GoalFive.com, "7 Causes of Gender Inequality in Sports," February 15, 2022.

U.S. Soccer president Cindy: Zach Koons, "USWNT, U.S. Soccer Agree to $24 Million Settlement in Equal Pay Lawsuit," *Sports Illustrated*, February 22, 2022.

"Our ambition is to have equality": ESPN staff, "USWNT, Equal Pay, and the Women's World Cup Prize Money," ESPN, August 4, 2023.

In 2020, the minimum MSL salary: "Male vs Female Professional Sports Salary Comparison," Adelphi University, May 20, 2021, www.online.adelphi.edu/articles/male-female-sports-salary/.

In basketball, the minimum WNBA salary: Melissa Jacobs, "Summer of Gold: How the 1996 Olympics Inspired a Generation of Female Athletes," *The Guardian*, August 16, 2021.

Women in finance to *hospitality and manufacturing*: "2022 State of Gender Pay Gap Report," Payscale, 2022.

Indeed, unequal pay remains the norm to *barely budged in decades*: Rakesh Kochhar, "The Enduring Grip of the Gender Pay Gap," Pew Research Center, March 1, 2023.

sixty cents on the dollar: "Human Rights Campaign Foundation Releases New Data on the LGBTQ+ Wage Gap," Human Rights Campaign, January 19, 2022; Orion Rummler, "'Those Dollars and Cents Add Up': Full-Time Trans Workers Face a Wage Gap, Poll Finds," *The 19th*, January 28, 2022.

It affects people's well-being to *eighteen and older*: "Women in Poverty, State by State, 2021," National Women's Law Center, October 7, 2022.

"should be seen as much more": Amy Bass, "Women's Soccer Settlement Is Landmark Win for Fairness," CNN, February 23, 2022.

"this lawsuit has put the fight": Ailsa Chang, "The U.S. Women's Soccer Team Struggle for Equal Pay Featured in New 'LFG' Documentary," NPR All Things Considered, June 29, 2021.

"For so long" to *way of viewing the world*: Fine and Fine, *LFG*.

"When you're in it": Foudy, interview.

Part IV: Penalty Kicks

93 Be an Equal Pay Warrior

At the current rate of change to *happen by then*: American Association of University Women, "The Simple Truth About the Gender Pay Gap, 2021 Update," Fall 2022.

In the meantime to *loan payments*: National Women's Law Center, "The Wage Gap: The Who, How, Why, and What to Do," Fact Sheet, September 2021.

Consider Higher-Paying Fields

Part of the wage gap problem to *half of the wage gap*: American Association of University Women, "The Simple Truth."

Learn Key Negotiation Tactics

"You are not powerless": Roux, interview.

It helps to create a vision to *potential employer*: Roux, interview.

Know Your Rights

No employer . . . shall discriminate: The Equal Pay Act of 1963, SEC. 206. [Section 6] (d) Prohibition of sex discrimination.

It shall be an unlawful employment practice: Title VII of the Civil Rights Act of 1964, UNLAWFUL EMPLOYMENT PRACTICES SEC. 2000e-2. [Section 703].

Be An Employer Who Equalizes Pay

Posting salary ranges for jobs: Michelle Singletary, "Pay Transparency Is Catching On," *Washington Post*, January 1, 2023.

"Invite women to the table" to *"coming up behind you"*: Cone, interview.

"The hope is that by fighting". Women's Soccer Innovator Becca Roux on Negotiations," *Clif Bar & Company*, 2022.

INDEX